Books by Laurien Berenson

Melanie Travis Mysteries

A PEDIGREE TO DIE FOR
UNDERDOG
DOG EAT DOG
HAIR OF THE DOG
WATCHDOG
HUSH PUPPY
UNLEASHED
ONCE BITTEN
HOT DOG
BEST IN SHOW
JINGLE BELL BARK
RAINING CATS AND DOGS
CHOW DOWN
HOUNDED TO DEATH
DOGGIE DAY CARE MURDER
GONE WITH THE WOOF
DEATH OF A DOG WHISPERER
THE BARK BEFORE CHRISTMAS
LIVE AND LET GROWL
MURDER AT THE PUPPY FEST
WAGGING THROUGH THE SNOW
RUFF JUSTICE
BITE CLUB
HERE COMES SANTA PAWS
GAME OF DOG BONES
HOWLOWEEN MURDER
PUP FICTION
SHOW ME THE BUNNY
KILLER CUPID

A Senior Sleuths Mystery

PEG AND ROSE SOLVE A MURDER
PEG AND ROSE STIR UP TROUBLE
PEG AND ROSE PLAY THE PONIES

Published by Kensington Publishing Corp.

PEG AND ROSE STIR UP TROUBLE

LAURIEN BERENSON

Kensington Publishing Corp.

www.kensingtonbooks.com

KENSINGTON BOOKS are published by

Kensington Publishing Corp.
900 Third Avenue
New York, NY 10022

ISBN: 978-1-4967-3577-5 (ebook)

ISBN: 978-1-4967-3576-8

First Kensington Hardcover Edition: August 2023

First Kensington Trade Paperback Printing: June 2024

10 9 8 7 6 5 4 3 2 1

Printed in the United States of America

Dedicated to the memory of three wonderful women
who continue to serve as an inspiration:
Helen Sokopp, Ethel Little, and Sister Ann Agnes

Chapter 1

"Must like dogs," Rose Donovan said as she typed the words onto the computer screen in front of her.

"You're crazy," Peg Turnbull replied.

The two women were in Rose's office at the Gallagher House, a women's shelter in Stamford, Connecticut. Rose, an amiable woman in her late sixties, had co-founded the shelter earlier in the year with her husband, Peter. The cramped office had formerly served as a storage room in the repurposed three-story home. It offered only enough space for a desk, a file cabinet, and a somewhat battered rubber plant.

Rose deleted what she'd written and tried again. "Must love dogs?"

"No," Peg said firmly.

Rose was seated behind the desk. She had short gray hair and pleasant features. Her body was as slender as a twig, with skinny arms and skinny legs to match. Her typing paused. Fingers hovering above the keyboard, Rose glanced upward.

Peg, who was four years older, was standing just behind her. As usual, the woman seemed to take up more space than she was entitled to. Tall and broad-shouldered, Peg had a linebacker's build coupled with an equally forceful personality.

Rose frowned at her, exasperated. "Then what do you want me to write? Must adore dogs to the exclusion of all else?"

Peg grinned wolfishly. "That sounds about right. But as you know perfectly well, it's a moot point because I don't want you to write anything."

"Don't be silly." Rose started typing again. "This is a brilliant idea."

"It's the worst idea ever."

An orange and white kitten was observing the interaction from the top of the file cabinet. Marmalade had been in residence at the shelter for little more than a month. In that short amount of time, she'd already witnessed several arguments between the two women, so this was nothing new.

Since both women were ignoring her, the kitten hopped down from her perch and padded across the hardwood floor to the beleaguered rubber plant. One of its shiny leaves drooped down to her level. Marmalade lifted a dainty paw and gave it a swat.

"For starters," Peg said, "why would anyone name a dating site Mature Mingle?"

"Because it's an appropriately descriptive name," Rose retorted. "You're mature, and you're seeking an opportunity to mingle."

"No, *you're* seeking that opportunity for me. Not only that, but at my age, I'm well past mature. In fact, I think I might be entering my second childhood." To illustrate that point, Peg crossed her legs and sat down on the floor. Marmalade blinked her green eyes in Peg's direction, then went back to attacking the plant.

"Hold that thought." Rose pulled up a new screen. "It's perfect. I'm describing your personality as 'playful.' "

"I tried online dating once before," Peg mentioned. "It

was a complete disaster." Maybe that would slow Rose down.

"I've heard." Staring at Peg's nascent dating profile, Rose didn't even bother to turn around. "Melanie told me all about it. One bad experience and you gave up. I thought you had more gumption than that."

Until his death a decade earlier, Peg had been married to Rose's older brother, Max. The two women were sisters-in-law—previously long estranged and now feeling their way toward a tentative rapprochement. Melanie's father had been Rose and Max's sibling, so she was both women's niece.

"I have plenty of gumption," Peg grumbled. "I'm also capable of learning from my mistakes."

Rose was undeterred. "That was years ago. Now you're older and wiser. Plus, you have me to help you sort through your potential dates."

As if that was a plus. Peg snorted under her breath. A decade earlier, Rose had left the Convent of Divine Mercy to marry a former priest. So clearly her talents in that regard were highly suspect.

"It's not as though you have copious experience with men," she said. "If Peter hadn't been posted to your parish, the two of you would never even have met."

That bald statement finally had the desired effect. Rose ceased typing. She turned slowly in her seat. She was only trying to be helpful. And, as usual, Peg wasn't even slightly appreciative of her efforts. Rose was about to give Peg a piece of her mind when she saw the long shiny strands of a shredded leaf littering the floor.

Instead, Rose sighed. "Marmie, cut that out."

The kitten flicked her white-tipped tail. She turned away from the plant and wound herself around Rose's leg.

"Good kitty," Peg murmured.

Rose shot her a look. "How is she a good kitty? She's killing my rubber plant."

"That was then." Peg braced a hand on the floor and levered herself up. "Now she's a good kitten because she stopped when you asked her to. So you should tell her so."

Rose reached down and scratched behind Marmalade's ears. "I thought you didn't know anything about cats."

"I don't. But I know dogs. And also how to modify behavior with positive reinforcement. If you want Marmalade to learn how to behave, you have to teach her the right way to do so."

Rose sighed again. That was another annoying thing about Peg. She was bossy. And she was always sure she knew best. Although this time maybe she did.

"Forget about the kitten," she said. "Will behavior modification work on you?"

"It's doubtful," Peg replied. "I'm pretty set in my ways."

Rose certainly wasn't about to argue with that. "I felt that way once too," she admitted. "As though I knew exactly what the rest of my life would look like because it was already mapped out in front of me."

Peg started to interrupt. Rose held up a hand to shush her. Amazingly, it had the desired effect.

"Then I met Peter and fell in love. I left the convent and got married. And suddenly it felt as though my whole world went from black-and-white to technicolor. It was an utterly amazing feeling—one that I want you to experience too. You deserve to meet a man and be happy again."

"I *am* happy." Peg's reply was firm. "And I already did the whole 'falling madly in love' thing with Max. Our life together was wonderful. But I'm not naïve enough to believe that I could be that lucky twice in a lifetime. Max was one of a kind."

"I get that." Rose nodded. "But you don't have to fall in love again. Maybe you could just enjoy spending time with a stimulating companion."

"I thought you and I were working on being friends

after all these years," Peg said, arching a brow. "Now it sounds as though you're trying to pawn me off."

"One can never have too many friends, especially not at our age." Rose trailed her fingertips down Marmie's back. "You know perfectly well that's true."

Peg really wanted to toss back a snappy retort. Except that all at once she suspected Rose was right. Most of Peg's friends were retired now. Some had moved out of state to be closer to family. A few had passed away. Even the ranks of her fellow dog show exhibitors seemed to be thinning.

Peg definitely wasn't looking to find love. But maybe it wouldn't hurt to broaden her circle of acquaintances.

She leaned down, looking over Rose's shoulder to skim through the information on the screen. It appeared to be mostly complete. Then again, what did she know? She'd never seen a dating profile before.

"Is that everything?" Peg asked.

"Almost." Rose swiveled around to face the desk. "Just a few more questions. Any piercings or tattoos?"

Peg barked out a laugh. "You're kidding, right?"

Rose shrugged. "I already answered all the stuff I knew without asking."

"So you think," Peg replied mysteriously.

Rose refused to rise to that bait. "Date of birth?"

"Absolutely not." Peg reared back. "I have no intention of having my identity stolen from a dating site. Let them look at my photograph and guess how old I am."

"About that," Rose said. "You need a picture for the profile."

"So get out your phone and take one."

Rose stared up at her. "*Now?*"

"Why not?"

"Don't you want to . . ."

Rose flapped her hands like she was trying to communicate something. Peg had no idea what, and considering the subject matter, she had no intention of hazarding a guess.

After a moment, Rose sputtered on. "Comb your hair? Maybe change your shirt and put on some lipstick?"

Peg cast a glance downward. "What's the matter with my shirt?"

"For one thing, it's a T-shirt." *Seriously.* Did Rose even have to point that out? "For another, it says OX RIDGE HUNT CLUB across the front."

"I'm sure the kennel club won't mind. I judge their dog show every fall."

"Now you're being deliberately obtuse."

Yes, Peg supposed she was. "You're saying I should fix myself up."

"Bingo."

"You want me to make myself look like someone I'm not?"

"No," Rose replied with the patience of a saint. Somehow when she'd begun this project she hadn't envisioned Peg tossing quite so many roadblocks in her own path. "I just thought that since first impressions count, you might want to present the best possible version of yourself."

"If I change everything, what will my date think when he sees me in person? Maybe he won't even recognize me. No, I'm sorry. Mystery man will just have to take me as I am."

"Men," Rose said.

"Pardon me?"

"Mystery *men*. There will be more than one. Nobody gets it right on the first attempt."

Peg laughed at that. "I'll be lucky if even one man responds to my profile. You're an outrageous optimist if you're thinking in multiples."

Rose *was* an optimist. She prided herself on looking for the good in everyone. Even Peg, who sometimes required more effort than most.

"Why wouldn't multiple men respond?" she replied stoutly. "You're an interesting and accomplished woman."

"That's very true," Peg acknowledged. "And yet, the thing that will be of most interest to the men on your dating site is what I look like."

"Precisely," Rose agreed. She reached across the desk for her purse. "And that's why we need to be sure to take a good picture."

Ten minutes later, Rose pronounced Peg ready for her close-up. She'd begun the mini-makeover by freeing Peg's shoulder-length hair from its low ponytail at the nape of her neck.

"Your hair is thick and shiny," she said, as she coaxed several gray tendrils forward to curl around Peg's face. "You should wear it loose more often."

"If I do that, it gets in my way."

Rose ignored the comment and dug around in her purse. "Lipstick?"

Peg accepted the tube, opened it, swiveled out the stick, and stared at it.

"Pale peach," Rose said impatiently. "Surely even you can't find fault with that."

Peg dabbed a bit of lipstick on her pinkie finger, then transferred it to her lips. "Better?"

"Getting there." Rose reached up—way up, since Peg towered over her just as she towered over most people their age—and pinched Peg's cheeks with her fingertips.

"Oww!"

"Don't be a ninny. That didn't hurt." Rose took out her phone. "I'll shoot you from the shoulders up so your shirt doesn't show. Now lift your chin and try to look dashing. Perfect. And smile!"

Peg blinked the first time the camera clicked. Then she grimaced for the second take.

"Third time's the charm," Rose informed her. "Otherwise I'm going to have to pinch your cheeks again."

The threat worked. Peg managed to compose herself and smile at the same time.

"Good enough," she said, glancing at the image on Rose's phone. "Now upload the picture and we're finished, right?"

Rose bent down to the computer once more. "Unless you want to look around the site and scroll through some of the men's profiles. It's a two-way street, you know. You don't have to wait for them to come to you."

"Heaven forbid," Peg muttered. "How come you know so much about this stuff anyway? Should Peter be concerned?"

"Hardly." Rose laughed as she straightened. "Online dating is a hot topic here at the shelter. Women who are staying with us often pass the time browsing on dating apps. Some are only window-shopping, but others are hoping to find someone who'll treat them better than the abusive jerk they were with."

"Good for them." Peg sat down in Rose's chair. Without waiting for an invitation, Marmalade hopped up into her lap. Absently, Peg scratched beneath the kitten's chin.

"And then there's Maura," Rose said. "It seems like she's signed up for every single dating site there is."

Peg was acquainted with Maura Nettles, the shelter's live-in housekeeper. She admired the woman's strong work ethic and practical approach to life. Maura wasn't a dog lover, however. Peg intended to keep working on that.

"That sounds exhausting," she said. "How many dates has Maura had?"

"None that I know of. But she keeps trying. She's looking for the perfect man, and she's convinced he's out there somewhere."

Rose reached around Peg, grasped the mouse, and made several adjustments to the page on the screen. Then Peg heard an audible click and Rose grinned at her.

"You're live," she said.

In the moment, Peg couldn't decide whether to feel hopeful or horrified. She picked up the kitten and lowered her to the floor. "So now what happens?"

"Now we wait and see who contacts you." Rose smirked.

Peg wasn't a "wait and see" kind of person. She was more the "everything should happen right now" type. "Unless you've changed your mind about taking the initiative."

Peg shook her head. "I allowed you to sign me up. That's as much initiative as I can stand for one day."

"Your choice," Rose said blithely. Under the circumstances, Peg could only envy her nonchalance. "In that case, it's out of our hands. But I have a good feeling about this, Peg. Brace yourself. Online dating just might turn out to be your next big adventure."

Chapter 2

The Gallagher House was located on an older, moderately run-down street in midtown Stamford. Too close to the busy Connecticut Turnpike to be of interest to affluent millennials or real estate flippers, the area had yet to be gentrified like its more attractive neighbors. A row of tall, narrow houses, each situated on a tiny plot of land, lined both sides of the road. Some had been maintained as family homes during their decades of existence. Others had passed from one set of careless hands to the next and were now plainly showing their age.

The building that housed the women's shelter had belonged to the Gallagher family since the middle of the previous century. Beatrice Gallagher helped Peter and Rose found the shelter, then bequeathed the home to them upon her death earlier in the year. The three-story building had a multitude of windows and a narrow, covered porch. The steps leading up to the front door were newly repaired, but a row of shingles on the porch roof above was beginning to work its way loose.

There was always something that needed to be repaired, replaced, or covered with a fresh coat of paint, Rose thought as she walked back inside after seeing Peg off.

As soon as she and Peter managed to fix one thing, something else broke down. Even with grants, charitable donations, and funding from the city budget, money was always tight. Rose often felt as though she had to pinch every single penny before letting it slip through her fingers.

Then again, having recently spent several years on a mission trip to Honduras, where she and Peter had lived in a tin-roofed hut, cohabiting with more varieties of insects than she'd previously known existed, Rose was well aware of how comfortable her life was now. Clean hot and cold running water? *Check.* Accommodations that weren't toppled by a strong wind? *Also check.* Not to mention the luxury of fresh milk for her coffee each morning.

As Rose shut the front door behind her, Peter came walking down the stairs from the second floor. Nearing seventy, he was a thoughtful and perceptive man who had degrees in counseling and social work. When Peter wasn't making repairs or grimacing over the Gallagher House ledgers, he served as resident counselor for the women who'd sought refuge in the shelter. He had kind eyes, a ready smile, and an innate ability to draw people in and make them feel at ease in his company.

Now, however, her normally affable husband was frowning. Rose stopped in her tracks. "Trouble?" she asked.

Two women sitting in the living room to the left of the front hall immediately lifted their heads. Liz had been at the shelter for nearly a week. Jules had arrived just the night before with a tear-stained face and only the clothes on her back. Under the circumstances, Rose's question had clearly been ill-considered.

She quickly turned to step into the wide doorway. "I'm sorry, I didn't mean to alarm you. Everything's fine. I was merely talking to Peter."

He came over and joined her. "Fine is a relative term. I've just been up on the third floor. Jenny's son, Rocky, flushed his sister's doll's head down the toilet."

Jenny and her two children had currently taken over most of the shelter's top floor. Jenny's three-year-old daughter, Bell, was adorable, but five-year-old Rocky was a menace. Rose knew it wasn't charitable to think such thoughts, but she would definitely be relieved when Jenny's sister arrived in a few days to take the family home with her.

"Just the head?" Liz asked with a grin.

"Yes, although that was bad enough. I managed to retrieve it and unclog the plumbing, but I'm afraid Sissy, the doll, is a lost cause." Peter's statement was punctuated by a loud wail that traveled down the stairwell from the top of the house.

"Maybe not." Jules hopped up. "I grew up with five brothers and sisters, so I'm an old hand at resuscitating dead toys. Come on, Liz, let's see what we can do to help."

Liz rolled her eyes as she walked past them. Apparently she agreed with Peter's assessment of the situation. Nevertheless, she followed Jules up the steps.

"That was nice of them," Rose said. A person who always tried to be helpful herself, it made her happy when other people took the initiative to do the same.

"I wish them luck." Peter didn't sound optimistic. "The doll's hair is tangled in a huge knot and I think she's missing an eye. And that doesn't even address the problem of how to reattach the head to the body."

"Hopefully Jules will surprise you. And if nothing else, working on Sissy will take her mind off her own problems for a while."

It was late August so all the windows in the house were open. When a car backfired on the street outside, the noise was so loud it sounded as though a gun had gone off in the hallway. Rose hurried over to the window to have a look.

The vehicle in question had to be at least twenty years old. A low-slung sedan, it might once have been red but now its color had faded to a sickly shade of dusty rose. One dented and mismatched fender wasn't painted at all. There was a tear in the car's vinyl roof, and judging by the loud rumble coming from the street, its muffler had been removed.

As Rose watched, the car moved past the shelter, leaving a trail of exhaust in its wake. The driver pulled over to the curb in front of a house at the end of the block. Rose pulled her head back inside. She was turning around to say something to Peter when Maura burst into the hallway from the direction of the kitchen.

"What the hell was that?" she asked.

"Backfire," Rose told her.

"Thank God." The housekeeper wore an apron over her faded jeans. She used it to wipe off her flour-covered hands. "I was afraid the porch roof had collapsed."

"Not yet," Peter said cheerfully.

"If you're trying to reassure me, it's not working." Maura was in her late thirties and solidly built. She had short, no-fuss brown hair, five piercings in each ear, and a can-do attitude toward life.

Originally she'd arrived at the shelter in need of protection. Several weeks later, after she'd all but taken over managing the place, it had become clear to Peter and Rose that they needed her help as much as she needed theirs. At that point, Maura had moved into the basement apartment and become the shelter's resident cook and housekeeper.

"I'm trying to be truthful," Peter said.

"Frankly, I'd prefer reassurance." Maura walked over to join Rose at the window.

While they were talking, a second car came down the road from the opposite direction and parked in front of the same house. Three men who looked to be in their twenties, hopped out of the two cars and went inside the home. Rose noted that they hadn't stopped to knock. One of the men had a key. Rose wasn't at all sure she liked the looks of that.

"What's the matter?" Peter asked. He knew Rose well enough that even from across the room he could tell that she was troubled.

"Mrs. Mayberry has visitors."

"Oh?" He came over to have a look. "Anyone we know?"

"No." Rose frowned. "Three rather rough looking young men just let themselves into her house. I hope Mrs. Mayberry was expecting them."

When they'd first moved onto the block, Peter and Rose had introduced themselves to each of the surrounding homeowners. They'd explained the mission of the Gallagher House and emphasized that they intended to be respectful of their neighbors' privacy and mindful of the fact that the shelter was located in a mostly residential area. No one had objected. Indeed, some residents—Mrs. Mayberry among them—considered the shelter to be a welcome upgrade to the slowly deteriorating neighborhood.

Now Peter stared at the two cars at the end of the block. Neither was in good condition, and one had a layer of mud covering its license plate. Peter liked to keep an eye on things, and this looked worrisome.

"I haven't met Mrs. Mayberry," Maura said, considering. "But around here, anything's possible. Maybe she likes hanging out with young men. Could be they're down there playing poker and smoking cigars."

"I highly doubt that," Rose replied. "Mrs. Mayberry's in her eighties. She's healthy enough for her age, but she's also frail and probably not as sharp as she used to be. I think I should take a walk down there and check things out."

"I'll come with you," Peter said.

"No." Rose immediately shook her head. "I don't want to make a big deal of this, especially if it turns out to be nothing. For all we know, Maura's right and Mrs. Mayberry is entertaining guests. But just in case, I think I'll take a stroll past her house and see what there is to see."

Maura and Peter shared a look.

"I feel like taking a stroll too," Maura announced.

Rose glanced down at her apron. "You're in the middle of baking."

"Just muffins. They can wait. And don't you give me that look," she said to Rose as she whipped off the apron and tossed it on a nearby tabletop. "You know you're a scrawny thing. It won't hurt to have someone with a few muscles standing next to you."

"I have an even better idea," Peter offered. "The kitchen is overflowing with tomatoes. Maura, why don't you put some in a basket, and the two of you can take them down to Mrs. Mayberry? Maybe she'd like to share them with her guests."

"Perfect," Rose agreed. "That'll get us inside the house."

Five minutes later, Rose and Maura were out the door and on their way. Maura was in front, carrying a woven basket filled to the brim with ripe red tomatoes. The size of Rose's summer crop ensured that they had plenty to spare. Rose, in sneakers, had to step carefully over the cracked and pitted sidewalk, but she was close behind.

They'd barely gone halfway down the block when the air around them began to pulse with the sound of loud music. It was blasting through the open windows of the house at the end of the street.

"I don't think Mrs. Mayberry is a fan of rap," Rose said.

"Good thing." Maura peered at her over the rim of the basket. "That's hip-hop."

"Really?" Rose sighed. She'd probably never learn to tell the difference.

When they reached the edge of Mrs. Mayberry's property, Maura paused. Rose didn't. Instead she strode across the minuscule, scrubby yard and marched up the steps to the front door. Here the music was even louder than it had been on the sidewalk.

Rose reached over and rang the doorbell. Nothing happened. She couldn't tell whether that was because the bell was broken or because no one—including her—could hear its ring over the sound of the thumping beat. For her second attempt, she rolled her fingers into a fist and pounded on the door itself.

"Geez, gimme a break," someone yelled. "I'm coming!"

Seconds later the door drew open. A slender young man with shaggy black hair and an ill-advised soul patch stood in the doorway. He was dressed in a T-shirt and a pair of jeans that would have needed a good yank upward to reach his boney hips. His feet were dirty. Rose could see that because he was wearing flip-flops.

He stared at Rose. She stared back.

Maura cleared her throat. "These tomatoes are heavy," she said to no one in particular. "I'm just going to put the basket down on the porch."

The man ignored her. "What?" he said to Rose.

She smiled sweetly in return. "We're looking for Mrs. Mayberry. Is she at home?"

He scratched the scraggly stubble on the side of his jaw. "Who wants to know?"

"I'm Rose, and this is Maura." Rose nodded in her companion's direction. "We're neighbors from down the street. We brought Mrs. Mayberry some tomatoes from our garden."

The guy leaned over and looked inside the basket as if he suspected they might be trying to smuggle contraband into the house. His attitude was really beginning to get on Rose's nerves.

She was considering picking up a tomato and tossing it at him when he turned back into the house and yelled, "Hey, Gran! There's someone here to see you."

Gran? Rose and Maura looked at each other. Apparently, this insolent kid was family. Rose supposed that put a new spin on things.

They waited for half a minute, but Mrs. Mayberry didn't appear. Abruptly the man spun around and strode away. *It was no wonder Mrs. Mayberry hadn't heard his call*, Rose decided. This close to the source of the music, she could barely hear herself think.

Left in the open doorway, she peered inside the house. Its floor plan was similar to that of the shelter. From there, she could see into the living room, where the other two men were sprawled across a couch, their gazes fastened on a video game that was playing on a screen in front of them. As Rose watched, one of them blew something up, then pumped his fist in the air.

She turned away and saw Mrs. Mayberry approaching from the other end of the hallway. Rose wasn't tall, but this woman was tiny. Her head, capped by a halo of wispy white hair, barely came to Rose's chin. Mrs. Mayberry's blue eyes were watery, and there was an uncertain smile on her face.

"Hello, dear," she said, holding out a wavering hand for Rose to shake. "It's lovely to meet you."

Rose's heart sank. Then she gathered herself and smiled. "Yes, it's lovely to see you too." She gently clasped the woman's fingers. "I'm Rose, and this is Maura. We run the women's shelter down the block and we've brought you some tomatoes from our garden."

"That's nice," Mrs. Mayberry said as Maura picked up the basket so she could see it.

Rose leaned in closer. "And we wanted to make sure that you're all right. Are you?"

"Yes, dear. I'm fine. My grandson, Donny, came to visit and brought his friends. Are we making too much noise?"

"Maybe a little bit," Maura told her.

The older woman nodded. "I'll ask the boys to turn it down."

Rose tried again. "Do you need anything, Mrs. Mayberry? Is there something we can do to help you?"

The older woman blinked several times, taking a moment to refocus her thoughts. "It's kind of you to offer, but as you can see I have my grandson here. Donny will get me anything I need. Thank you for dropping by."

Donny couldn't have been far away because now he suddenly materialized in the doorway. He grasped his grandmother's arm and drew her back into the house.

"That's enough," he said. He took the basket from Maura, then shut the door in their faces.

Rose and Maura didn't say a word until they were back on the sidewalk, heading home. Then Maura blew out a breath. "That was interesting."

"I agree," Rose replied. She wasn't at all sure what to make of the encounter. "But at least now we know that Donny is family, which means that those three aren't just random delinquents who've helped themselves to her home. I hope that means everything is all right."

"I hope Mrs. Mayberry likes tomatoes," Maura said.

Chapter 3

Wait and see, Peg thought as she drove home to her house in Greenwich. What a terrible idea that was. And how like Rose to blithely assume that something beneficial would result from this silly escapade.

Now that she had time for second thoughts, Peg realized she must have been out of her mind to go along with Rose's scheme. Well, it was too late to back out now. Her profile was *live*—as opposed to her love life, which had been all but moribund for years.

Not that she expected this dubious venture to revive it. In fact, it seemed more than likely that nothing would happen at all. Peg's best plan would probably be to wait until several weeks had passed, then quietly deactivate the profile and put the whole sorry episode behind her. The less said about it, the better.

Peg lived in backcountry Greenwich, where spacious properties abounded and meandering lanes were lined with century-old stone walls. Many years earlier, her house had been the hub of a working farm. Now only five acres of property remained. That was plenty of room for Peg and the three Standard Poodles with whom she currently shared her home.

When her husband, Max, was still alive, there'd been many more Poodles in residence—enough to fill both the house and a kennel building behind it. Peg's life back then was a whirl of constant activity as she and Max exhibited Standard Poodles from their renowned Cedar Crest Kennel at dog shows up and down the East Coast.

Now Max was gone, and Peg was on her own. And although she still attended numerous shows each year, these days she seldom exhibited. Instead, Peg put all her years of experience in the dog world to good use as a popular and highly esteemed dog show judge.

She turned off the main road and let the minivan coast down her secluded road. As soon as the two chimneys that bracketed her peaked roofline came into view, she began to smile. The two adult bitches, Hope and Coral, and younger dog, Joker, would all be waiting for her. Before she even had a chance to park in front of the garage, three black Poodle heads were already popping up in the front windows of the house.

Peg hopped out of the van and went skipping up the steps to the door.

Skipping, she thought happily. *At my age. Imagine that.*

Rose would probably think it was ridiculous, but Poodles always had that effect on Peg. Actually, dogs of any kind would do it. And what Rose wasn't here to see wouldn't hurt either one of them.

When she opened the door, the trio of Poodles came tumbling out in a rush. All three dogs were large in size and similar in shape. Hope, at eleven, wasn't as sprightly as the younger Poodles, but the depth of her emotional connection with Peg was stronger than ever. Coral was a young beauty who'd recently been handled to her championship by Melanie's older son, Davey. Joker had just turned a year old. Still a puppy at heart, he was the clown of the group and more than willing to live up to his name.

"Did anybody miss me?" Peg asked, dropping to her knees.

Immediately she was swarmed by warm, wriggling bodies. Her chest was bumped. Her nose was licked. Joker even managed to slap the pompon on the end of his tail across her face. Peg, with both hands busy trying to caress all three big Poodles at once, was in heaven. Two minutes of general mayhem passed before they all paused to take a deep breath. Peg finally stood up. Dogs dancing around her legs, she led the way through the kitchen to the back door. Having spent the morning cooped up inside, the Poodles were in need of a potty break.

As they raced past her to the enclosed field behind the house, Peg's eye went to her laptop. When she'd departed earlier, she'd left it sitting on the butcher-block table in the middle of the room. Now that she'd noticed it sitting there, she couldn't seem to look away.

It was almost as if the dratted device was calling out to her. *Mockingly.* Like it knew that her profile was on the Mature Mingle website—probably being ignored by scores of older men who'd glanced at her picture, then scrolled by, thinking they could do better.

Peg harrumphed under her breath. She'd never been a beauty, but she was well aware of her own worth. She was smart, hardworking, and endlessly curious about life. Plus, she had a robust sense of humor. Those attributes had always been more than enough for Max. And for her beloved Standard Poodles.

That settled it, Peg decided. Why delay for several futile weeks when she could log into Mature Mingle and delete her profile right now? Rose might mutter and mumble in protest, but at least she wouldn't have the last laugh.

Peg pulled out a chair and sat down. She opened the laptop and frowned at the screen. An icon in the corner told her she had mail waiting.

She sighed, fingers drumming on the table beside the keyboard. Rose had spent nearly an hour that morning working on her profile. Perhaps rather than doing something rash, Peg should pause and consider her options. She could check her mail in the meantime.

When she clicked the icon, a long list of emails appeared. That was nothing new. She'd get around to answering most of them eventually. What was new, however, was the message at the top of the page. It was from the dating site.

Peg stared at the screen for several seconds. Perhaps Mature Mingle merely wanted to congratulate her on joining up. Or maybe they'd written to inform her that she needed to post a better photograph. If that was the case, Peg thought she might replace her picture with a lovely photo of Hope. Let those hypothetical prospective suitors try to figure *that* out.

Oh for Pete's sake, Peg told herself. *Just open the darn thing and see what they want.* Then she did, and her eyes widened.

Mature Mingle had sent a congratulatory message to let her know that there'd been recent activity on her page. The email supplied a link and invited her to come and check it out.

Recent activity? Scarcely an hour had passed since Rose had activated her profile. Surely, they couldn't mean . . .

Peg clicked on the link. There was her own picture staring back at her. The other information she'd furnished was below it. A blinking star at the bottom of the page indicated that she had messages waiting to be read.

Messages? *Plural?* Peg was astounded. How was that even possible? It had to be some kind of mistake. Maybe there was a glitch in the software.

Peg was about to find out when Coral came flying up the steps from the yard and into the kitchen. Joker and Hope followed close behind. Peg had left the back door open, but she hadn't expected the trio of Poodles to return at this rate of speed.

All three dogs went skidding through the kitchen to the hallway that led to the front door. That could only mean one thing. Her canine alarm system was alerting her that someone was here. A moment later as Peg stood up, the doorbell rang.

"Good dogs," she said automatically.

Peg was talking to herself. The Poodles were already at the front door. They adored all visitors. Peg used to feel much the same way, but events earlier in the summer had taught her to be more cautious. She paused to glance out the kitchen window.

A Volvo station wagon was parked in her driveway. Peg recognized the car. Even better, a black Standard Poodle who looked just like Hope was trotting around her front yard, checking out all the interesting smells. That was Faith, Hope's litter sister. Peg's niece, Melanie, had come to visit.

Luckily for Melanie, she was still in the driveway when Peg opened the door. Otherwise she'd have been bowled over by the three big dogs who went racing down the steps. Then it occurred to Peg that Melanie was accustomed to that kind of greeting. She'd probably timed her entrance to avoid the oncoming horde.

Peg smiled at the thought. Despite the many fractured relationships in their family, she and Melanie had been best friends for years—ever since the theft of one of Peg's dogs had brought them together to solve the crime. Peg had rewarded her niece, who'd never previously owned a pet, with the gift of Faith. Now Melanie lived with her husband and two sons in a house that was overflowing with dogs.

Peg considered that a job well done on her part.

"You're lucky you caught me," she said, standing in her doorway. Now there were four black Standard Poodles gamboling around her front yard. Nothing unusual about that. "I just got home a few minutes ago."

"I should have called first." Melanie shaded her eyes against the sun and gazed upward. She'd turned forty on her previous birthday, but she still possessed the slender build of a teenager. Straight, tawny-brown hair hung below her shoulders, and she was dressed casually in a polo shirt and skinny jeans. "Faith and I were out running errands and I decided I was in the mood for cake."

"Cake." Peg's face lit up. Her sweet tooth was legendary. She always had cake. "You've come to the right place."

"I know." Melanie was just as pleased about that as Peg was. She climbed the steps while the dogs were otherwise occupied.

"You lot!" Peg called to the cavorting Poodles. "Come inside before I close the door."

All four dogs quickly came running. When the group reached the kitchen, Peg went to refill the Poodles' bowls with cold water. Melanie was on her way to the refrigerator when she passed by the table and glanced at the computer screen.

Immediately she stopped and turned back. "What's this?"

Water was running in the sink. Peg had a full dog bowl in each hand. Otherwise she might have been able to move faster.

"It's nothing," she said firmly.

Melanie leaned down for a closer look. "It doesn't look like nothing."

Peg placed both bowls on the floor, then strode over to the table. She reached out and snapped the laptop shut. Melanie jumped back just in time.

"Oh my God." Melanie bit her lip like she was trying not to laugh. "That was *you*. On a dating site."

It wasn't as if Peg could refute that. Instead she propped her hands on her hips and went on the offensive. "So?"

Melanie looked dumbfounded. That obviously wasn't

the answer she'd been expecting. She pulled out a chair and sat down at the table. Clearly she'd forgotten all about the cake.

"So this is exciting," she said. "Tell me everything."

"It isn't exciting at all," Peg retorted. "The whole thing was Rose's doing. And you know Rose. She's never had an exciting idea in her life."

Melanie leaned back and crossed her arms over her chest. "What I know about you and Rose is that the two of you were barely speaking to each other earlier in the summer before Sam and I took the boys on vacation. And by the time we got back, you'd somehow become friends." She paused, then added, "I thought that was exciting."

"I think the word you're looking for is unexpected."

"That too."

Peg sat down across from her and affected a nonchalant shrug, as if the development hadn't surprised her too. Her reconciliation with Rose still felt too fragile for Peg to want to discuss it, much less try and explain how it had come about.

"It was simply time for Rose and me to mend our relationship," she said with a finality that pronounced the subject closed. "Now, are we going to eat cake or not? The bakery had a new flavor, hazelnut buttercream. It would be a shame to leave it sitting in the box."

"Of course we're having cake." Melanie jumped up again. "I'll serve."

Several minutes later, Peg and Melanie each had a generous piece of hazelnut cake on a plate in front of them. The Poodles had all had water and were settled on the cool kitchen floor around them.

Peg waited patiently until Melanie had devoured half her slice. Then she said, "Much as I enjoy your visits, I know perfectly well you didn't drop by to eat cake. So I'm assuming something must be wrong. What is it?"

"I'm in need of a second opinion."

Peg relaxed. That sounded easy enough. She was full of opinions. Not only that, but she was always happy to share them.

"Go on."

"As you know, Kevin will be starting first grade next week."

Peg nodded. Melanie's younger son was six. Her older son, Davey, was fifteen and in high school. Kevin attended Howard Academy, the private school where Melanie worked weekday mornings as a special needs tutor.

"He wants his own cell phone."

"*What?*"

"That's what I said." Melanie nodded, pleased at Peg's reaction. "It's a ridiculous idea."

Peg agreed, but she still had questions. "What does Sam think about it?"

Melanie growled something uncomplimentary under her breath.

Peg took that to mean that Melanie and her husband weren't on the same page. She cut off another piece of cake and slid it onto Melanie's plate. In Peg's world, cake, followed by more cake, could cure almost any problem.

"Pardon me?" she said.

Melanie looked up. "Sam's okay with it. He and Davey share the opinion that since Davey has a phone, Kevin should be able to have one too."

"Davey is a teenager," Peg pointed out unnecessarily. "That's totally different."

"Of course it is. But you know what Howard Academy is like. Some of Kevin's classmates had cell phones last year in kindergarten. So he feels left out."

Set on a knoll overlooking downtown Greenwich, Howard Academy had rigorous academic standards and a student body that consisted mostly of offspring of the rich and powerful. Peg could well understand why the school's students would have access to every new and enticing device. But that didn't mean it made sense.

"The problem is, I'm outnumbered," Melanie said, then paused briefly to dig into her second slice of cake. "So I need an ally. Like you. Someone forceful and domineering. Someone who can overrule Davey and make Sam listen to reason."

Peg was sympathetic, but only to a point. And Melanie was not only fast approaching that point, she might have already gone flying past it.

"Besides"—Melanie gestured with her fork for emphasis—"you know you love to argue."

That was true. Even so, Peg knew it was a terrible idea to insert herself in the middle of someone else's family squabble.

"Let me sum up," she said. "You're asking me to do battle with Sam, alienate Davey, and disappoint Kevin—all so that you can avoid doing those things yourself."

Melanie swallowed, then nodded. "That sounds about right."

Of course *she* would think that. The proposal sounded all wrong to Peg. Maybe if she stalled long enough—like until Kevin was a teenager—the problem would solve itself.

"Let me get back to you on that," she said.

Chapter 4

Rose was sitting in the tiny yard behind the Gallagher House filling out a grant application. This summer, she'd grown tomatoes back there. Next year she was planning to add cucumbers. Recently she'd aerated the hard-packed earth around her small garden, and now patches of grass had begun to appear. Maura didn't think that was much of an accomplishment, but Rose was pleased.

Work was boring, so when her phone rang, Rose was just as happy to be distracted. She set her laptop down on the small table beside her wicker lawn chair, picked up the device, and looked to see who was calling.

Most people would have started the conversation with a greeting. Not Peg. "You'll never believe what happened," she said.

"When it comes to you, I'd believe almost anything," Rose replied. "What's happened now?"

"Men have left messages for me on the Mature Mingle website."

"Of course they have." Rose smiled in satisfaction. Thank God Peg couldn't see that.

"You don't sound surprised."

"I'm not."

"Wait a minute." A moment ago, Peg had been enthused.

Now she sounded wary. "Is that because you've already read them?"

Rose sighed. Just when she thought she and Peg had finally reached a place of mutual trust, Peg had to go and ruin things by stomping on Rose's good mood with her size-ten feet.

"Certainly not," Rose retorted. "Just because I set up the account doesn't mean I won't respect your privacy. And now that I'm thinking about it, I'd advise you to change your password. That way we'll never need to revisit this subject again."

There was a long pause on the line. Rose waited Peg out. She'd brought Marmalade outside with her and the kitten was hopping around the yard, batting a small plastic ball between her front feet. That was entertaining.

"I suppose that's your way of saying that an apology is in order?" Peg finally spoke.

"If you have to ask," Rose replied tartly, "then you still don't get it."

Peg sighed audibly. "I apologize. The question was rude. I shouldn't have asked it."

"No, you shouldn't have. I have much better things to do than meddle in your love life."

The magnitude of that fallacy left Peg nearly speechless. Once again, some time passed before she managed to reply. This time, Rose was the one who refused to let the silence linger.

"How many men did you hear from?" she asked.

"Three," Peg said. Then she repeated the number as if she couldn't quite believe it. "*Three!*"

Rose tamped down a laugh. "Did you reply to them?"

"No."

"Why not?"

"Doesn't this seem fast to you?" Peg asked. "I figured

anyone who replied to a new profile that quickly must be desperate."

"Not necessarily." In truth, Rose had no idea of what time frame would be considered normal, but she wanted to sound encouraging. "Maybe they saw your picture and were intrigued."

Peg answered that comment with a derisive snort.

"Okay, here's the important question. Did any of the men look interesting to you?"

"No."

"Why not?" Rose asked again.

"The first one had beady eyes."

Rose wasn't sure why that was a deal breaker, but okay. "Go on."

"The second listed his hobbies as poker and fly-fishing."

"Poker," Rose repeated. The last time she and Peg had gotten themselves mixed up with people who played card games, someone had ended up dead. She supposed she could understand why Peg might be a little gun-shy.

"And number three?" she asked as Marmie's ball bounced off her sandal-clad foot. Rose wiggled her toes and the kitten leaped high in the air, then pounced on them.

"He was fifty years old."

"Wonderful," said Rose. "A younger man."

"Too much younger," Peg replied. "I graduated from college the year he was born. What on earth would we find to talk about?"

Now Rose did laugh. "Not your college years, apparently."

Again Peg paused. Rose could picture the exasperated expression on Peg's face. Lord knew she'd seen it often enough over the last two months.

"This only seems funny because it isn't happening to you," Peg said. "If I'm actually going to do this, I want to approach it seriously. And that means not wasting my valuable time on men who don't seem acceptable right from the start."

"I guess you never heard that old adage about kissing a lot of frogs."

"Quite frankly I don't intend to kiss *any* frogs." Peg huffed. "That's for youngsters. At my age, I know what I want and I have no intention of settling for less."

Rose shifted in her chair, moving her feet away from Marmalade. The kitten's tiny claws were sharp. "Has it occurred to you that maybe your standards are too high? If you insist on being too picky, you might end up not meeting anyone at all."

"If that's how things turn out—"

"Ouch!" Rose exclaimed. Phone in hand, she jumped up from her seat.

"Really?" Peg's tone was dry. "I didn't expect you to be so invested in the process."

"It's not you," Rose managed to say. She was hopping up and down on one foot. "Marmalade bit me."

"Oh?" Peg asked with interest. This sounded vastly more entertaining than their previous topic. "What did you do to her?"

"Nothing." Was that a spot of blood Rose saw on her big toe? She thought it was.

"An unprovoked attack then." Peg sounded disbelieving.

"All I did was wiggle my toes. And now I'm bleeding."

"Does Marmie have all her shots?"

"Of course she does." Rose scooped up the kitten before she could do further damage.

"Do you have all your shots?"

Actually, Rose did. The years in Honduras had necessitated that. "Yes."

"Then I think you'll survive," Peg decided. "Would you like me to bring you a Band-Aid?"

"You're joking, right?" With Peg, it was sometimes hard for Rose to tell.

"Little bit."

"I'm hanging up now," Rose said. "And then I'm going to Google cat scratch fever. If I get it and it's contagious, I'm giving it to you."

"Pish on that," said Peg. She hung up too.

Peter found Rose in the second-story bathroom with her pants leg rolled up and her bare foot in the sink. She'd liberally soaped her foot from toes to heel and she was scrubbing at it vigorously.

"Problem?" he inquired.

Rose glanced at him over her shoulder. "Marmie bit me." She rinsed her foot under a strong stream of water.

Peter stepped over to the sink and had a look. "Where?"

Rose pointed to the knuckle of her big toe. As far as Peter could tell, there was nothing there. Not even a scratch.

"I don't see anything," he said.

Rose was reaching for a towel. She stopped and took a look too. Then she frowned. "Maybe I overreacted."

He took the towel from her hand and gently dried her foot before lifting it out of the sink and placing it back on the floor. "You looked up cat scratch fever, didn't you?"

"Maybe." She reclaimed the towel and hung it back on the rack.

"I remember when you Googled dengue fever," Peter mentioned.

"That's a real thing," Rose said in her own defense.

"It is. But you didn't have it."

"I had most of the symptoms. Plus it was the rainy season."

"You had the flu," Peter said mildly. "Three days later you were fine."

"Lucky for you, I have a good immune system," Rose replied.

"Yes, it is." Peter knew better than to smile. Instead he

changed the subject. "Was that Peg you were talking to outside?"

Rose stepped back and slipped her foot into the sandal on the floor. "Don't tell me you were spying on me."

"Not intentionally. I'd finished my counseling session and I thought I'd come out and see how you were doing with that application. But you were otherwise engaged."

"Yes," she said, "that was Peg."

"I couldn't tell from afar. You didn't appear to be tearing your hair out, so I took that as a good sign."

Together, they walked out onto the landing and down the stairs. Judging by the enticing aromas coming from the kitchen, Maura was already working on dinner. There was laughter coming from the room at the back of the house too. Liz and Jules were probably in there with her. The living room was currently empty. Peter and Rose headed that way.

"Peg and I are mostly getting along better these days," Rose said, as they found seats in a pair of armchairs that faced each other across a low table.

Peter nodded. "I knew the two of you had declared a truce. I was hoping it was still in effect."

"Don't congratulate me on my forbearance just yet," Rose told him. "I may have thrown a spanner into the works."

"Accidently, I hope."

"Not entirely. I had what I thought was a good idea."

This didn't sound too serious. Peter settled back in his seat. "And Peg didn't agree?"

"She did at first. Now she's not so sure," Rose said. "Worse still, I think she may be trying to sabotage the process."

Peter knew from long experience that things always seemed to get complicated when Rose and Peg were together. Apparently this time was no exception.

"Perhaps you'd better tell me about it," he said.

Rose's gaze lifted. She looked over his head, staring out the window in the rear wall of the room. Peter knew there was nothing to be viewed back there but the top of a scraggly tree. He didn't have to be a counselor to recognize avoidance when he saw it.

"I . . . umm . . . convinced Peg to sign up on a dating website called Mature Mingle."

Peter's first impulse was to laugh. His second was to groan. He was quite certain, however, that neither of those responses would please Rose. So instead he merely said, "Are you sure that was wise?"

"It seemed like a good idea at the time," Rose replied.

"And now?"

"I guess you could say I'm having second thoughts."

No surprise there. "And has Peg met any . . . interesting prospects?"

"Three men have responded to her profile so far. She rejected them all out of hand."

"Surely that's not unexpected. Peg is a discriminating woman."

Rose chuckled. "Go ahead and say what you really mean. Peg is critical, demanding, and hard to please."

"I was trying to be nice," Peter said.

"I'd prefer honesty," Rose returned.

"In that case, you shall have it. What in the world made you think it was a good idea to become involved in Peg's life that way?"

Rose threw up her hands. "I wanted her to be happy."

Peter knew he was meant to take his wife's side. But somehow he couldn't quite manage it. "I suspect that if you had asked first, Peg would have told you that she was already happy."

"Well, sure. And she did. But it's one thing for her to be happy with her Poodles, and her dog shows, and Melanie's family, but . . ."

"But what?"

Rose's voice softened. "I wanted her to have what we have."

"Oh? What's that?"

"True love."

Peter exhaled slowly. "Not everyone is as lucky as we are, Rose."

"I know that."

"Do you?" he asked. "If life has taught me anything, it's that I can't remake the world, or society, and even my neighborhood to my own specifications. You have to let people make their own decisions—and, if necessary, their own mistakes."

Rose leveled a glare in his direction. She loved her husband dearly, but he was wrong about that. "Says a man who opened a shelter in a rundown neighborhood for the express purpose of saving people from the consequences of those mistakes."

Peter braced his hands on his knees and rose to his feet. "I hope you're not comparing the Gallagher House to a dating app."

Rose stood up with him. "And I hope Peg is going to take my advice and make a serious effort at finding her Mr. Right."

"Unfortunately it appears we may both be destined for disappointment," Peter replied.

Chapter 5

The following week, Peg went on two dates and came home early from both of them. It wasn't her fault.

Having weeded through several more possible matches—who knew Peg would be such a draw at her age?—she'd sent messages back to two men. Both appeared to have the potential to provide her with an evening of stimulating conversation. She figured that would do for a start.

When the men returned her interest, she'd arranged to meet each of them for a casual date. The first man turned out to be five foot six to Peg's six feet. Peg could have gotten past that—until he opened the conversation by declaring he had a thing for tall women and inquiring about her preferred sexual positions. After that, Peg waited just ten minutes before hustling herself out the coffee shop door.

The second man had lovely manners. He purchased Peg's tea and held out her chair when she sat down. Then he proceeded to spend the remainder of their date talking about himself. Not only did he evidence no curiosity about Peg, he also couldn't seem to discuss current events, the arts, politics, or any other topic she attempted to raise.

After half an hour, Peg was bored stiff. Her Poodles were much better company than this. At least they let her get a word in every now and then.

Peg was a stubborn woman, however. Having started

the process, she was determined to see it through. The third man she replied to was different. Rather than pressuring her to meet up, he'd been content to get to know her through the emails they were now exchanging daily.

Judging by their correspondence, Nolan Abercrombie was witty and urbane. If his profile picture was to be believed, he was also ruggedly handsome for a man his age. There was a twinkle in his eye that Peg found immensely appealing. For the first time, she found she was the one who was impatient to move things along.

Should she extend an invitation, or would Nolan consider her pushy? Peg had no idea. Any experience she'd had in the dating world was many decades out-of-date. Of course things were different now.

For obvious reasons, Rose was the last person Peg would have consulted on that score. But since bullets had come flying through Peg's kitchen window earlier in the summer, Rose had made a habit of turning up periodically to check on Peg's well-being. At least that was the excuse she gave for her pop-in visits.

Peg wasn't buying it. She'd decided that Rose—a woman who'd spent the majority of her life diligently obeying every rule—had finally learned how to play hooky. As far as Peg was concerned, it was about time.

So when Peg's Poodles announced Rose's appearance later that afternoon, she opened the door with a smile on her face. Hope, Coral, and Joker went running down the steps to surround Rose's silver van. The first time that happened, Rose had sat quaking in her seat until Peg went down and rescued her. Now Rose didn't even hesitate before climbing out of her vehicle. That was progress.

"Was I expecting you?" Peg asked from the porch.

"You should have been," Rose replied. "It's been days since I've had an update on your social life. Even Melanie seems to know more than I do. Which, under the circumstances, is entirely unjust."

Rose had a point. Peg watched as her sister-in-law paused in the driveway to greet each of the big black dogs in turn. She even called them by their names. The *right* names. When had she begun to be able to do that?

"Two months ago, you thought my Poodles were going to eat you," Peg commented. "Now you can even tell them apart."

Rose shrugged. Why did Peg always have to make such a big deal out of things when it came to her dogs?

"It's not as though they look alike," she said. "The dog with the gray muzzle has to be Hope, because she's old. And that one looks as if he belongs in a circus, so he must be Joker."

"A circus." Peg harrumphed. "I'll have you know that the continental clip is based on a traditional hunting trim that originated in Germany."

Rose sighed. It wasn't the first time she'd been lectured on Poodle peculiarities. To avoid the remainder of what was sure to be a long lesson, she pointed at the third dog as she headed for the stairs. "And the leftover is Coral."

"Leftover." Peg grimaced. What an ugly thing to say about a lovely bitch.

"You know what I mean. After I've sorted out the other two, she's the one who's left."

Coral flattened her ears against her head.

"Now you've insulted her," Peg said.

Rose was almost sure that wasn't true. "You keep telling me that your dogs understand what people say, but I have yet to see any evidence of it."

"That's your evidence right there." Peg snapped her fingers, and Coral scooted up the steps to join them. "Look at the expression on her face."

Rose hoped Peg was kidding, but apparently not. She actually expected Rose to stare into Coral's dark eyes. Or something equally nonsensical.

Rose didn't see the point, but when Peg continued to glare at her, she leaned down and gave it a try. Nothing happened. Coral looked no different to her than any other black dog. Whatever the Poodle's feelings were, she wasn't about to share them with Rose.

"I liked you better five minutes ago," Peg said when Rose stood up again.

"Don't worry about it," she replied. "I often feel the same way about you."

The women went inside the house, with the three dogs following. Rose closed the door behind them. Peg was already heading toward the kitchen.

"Most people entertain guests in the living room," Rose pointed out.

Peg didn't even break stride. "You're not a guest. Like it or not, you're family."

Rose supposed that was true. She walked into the kitchen and took a seat at the table. Now that they were in Peg's favorite room, she knew what was coming next.

"I don't want any cake," she announced.

"You always say that, but then you eat it anyway."

"Only because you put a plate in front of me and I'm trying not to be rude."

Today's offering was shadow cake, devil's food sponge with vanilla icing. In keeping with Rose's wishes, Peg merely cut her a sliver. "Keep up the good work."

Rose waited until Peg sat down across from her, then said, "So you've been on two dates and neither one was a success. What went wrong?"

"The first guy's opening line was about sex."

"Eww." Rose wrinkled her nose.

"Indeed. And the second one only wanted to talk about himself."

Rose found that approach less off-putting. "You only want to talk about dogs, and yet people still manage to tolerate you."

"That's entirely different," Peg said. "Most of my friends only want to talk about dogs too."

Rose nibbled like a rabbit around the edges of her cake. Peg was right, she'd end up eating it. But only because, after the deprivation she'd seen in Central America, she refused to tolerate waste.

"Who else?" she asked.

Peg glanced up.

"I know there has to be someone who's piqued your interest. It's been more than a week. And according to the Mature Mingle metrics, it's a very active site. So what's his name?"

"Nolan Abercrombie."

Rose chuckled. "He sounds stuffy."

"He's not. At least not in writing. We've been corresponding by email. He's actually quite appealing."

"Good. So when are you going to meet him in person?"

"Soon, I hope." Peg set down her fork.

Rose eyed Peg's plate. There was still cake on it. Peg never stopped eating when she had something sweet in front of her. That was almost a law of nature.

"So what's holding things up?" Rose asked.

"Convention."

"What does that mean?"

"I'm waiting for him to ask."

"Don't be silly. We're not living in the eighteen hundreds, or even the nineteen hundreds. If you think you might be interested in getting to know him further, *ask him*."

Peg frowned. "What if my making the first move scares him away?"

"Then he's not the right man for you. And you're better off knowing that now." Rose stared at Peg across the tabletop. "This isn't like you at all. You're never hesitant about anything. And you're certainly not shy. So what's really going on?"

Peg sat back. "In case you haven't noticed, this idea of

yours yanked me totally out of my comfort zone. So excuse me if I'm still struggling to find my footing. But truthfully . . . ?"

Rose nodded.

"I don't want to be disappointed again. What if Nolan turns out to be deadly dull in person? Or if he's only looking for a hookup?"

"Then I'd imagine you'll deal with him the same way you do with everyone else," Rose replied. "Indomitably."

"Indomitably." Peg let the word roll off her tongue. She liked the sound of it. "Is that how you see me?"

Rose laughed. "Are you kidding? That's how everyone sees you."

"Good to know," said Peg.

Peg's first date with Nolan went swimmingly. They met early in the evening at a small café in Old Greenwich, where they talked and flirted for three hours until they'd closed the place down.

Like Peg, Nolan was in his seventies. He was an inch taller than Peg, in robust health, and still in possession of a full head of iron-gray hair. Over the course of their conversation, Peg discovered that Nolan was intelligent, politically astute, and interested in every aspect of her world. Even his jokes were funny.

Peg didn't believe in miracles. Which made her cynical side wonder if Nolan was too good to be true. Yet there he was, sitting across from her, making her think, making her laugh, and charming the socks off of her. It was almost too much to take in.

Before they parted on the sidewalk outside the café, Nolan had both Peg's phone number and the promise of a second date. When he leaned in and kissed her gently on the cheek, the small caress sent sensation flooding all the way down to her toes. Peg nearly giggled like a schoolgirl.

Their second meeting took place two days later. Peg had

done most of the talking on their first date. This time, she was determined to make Nolan tell her more about himself. She already knew he was a widower with an adult son. Now she learned that he was an Ivy League graduate and that he'd owned a small business that he later sold for enough money to enable him to retire. After his wife's death, he'd spent the next five years globetrotting before ending up in the neighboring town of Darien.

When the evening ended, Peg and Nolan once again went home alone. This time, however, Nolan said goodbye to Peg with a lingering kiss that made her head spin and definitely left her wanting more.

By their third date, Peg felt comfortable enough to accept an invitation to dinner at Nolan's house. They wouldn't be alone; his sister was visiting from out of state. Nolan said she'd asked to meet the woman about whom her brother couldn't stop talking. That admission, shyly delivered, made Peg feel all warm inside.

Hope helped Peg get dressed for the upcoming evening.

"Slacks seem too casual," Peg told the Poodle, who was lying across her bed. "But a dress feels fussy. Like I'm trying too hard to impress."

Hope tipped her head to one side and considered the problem. Four previous outfits had already been tried and discarded.

"Nolan might not even notice what I'm wearing," Peg mused. "But you can bet his sister will."

Hope nosed a midi-length lavender linen skirt that Peg had left draped over the foot of the bed when she'd thumbed through the contents of her closet. Peg took another look at it.

"That could work," she said, rewarding the Poodle with a scratch behind her ears. "I'll wear a silk shell on top, and put a cotton sweater over it in case the evening grows chilly."

It was dark by the time Peg arrived in Darien, but

Nolan's directions were spot-on. His colonial-style home was located in a quiet residential neighborhood. Low hedges flanked both sides of the approach, and a vintage streetlamp marked the end of his driveway. Peg pulled in and parked her minivan in front of a detached, two-car garage.

Nolan must have been watching for her arrival. He was out the front door before she'd even reached the flagstone walkway that crossed the front lawn. He was dressed in khakis, a crisply ironed button-down shirt, and deck shoes with no socks. A cashmere sweater was draped casually over his shoulders.

Nolan held out both hands to her and said, "You look beautiful."

Peg knew that wasn't true. And yet, somehow, when he looked at her like that, she could almost believe him. Nolan accepted the bottle of Cabernet Peg had brought with her. Then he gathered her close for a warm hug.

"I'd been looking forward to introducing you to Barbara," he whispered in her ear. "But now I find myself regretting that we won't have the evening all to ourselves."

Peg was still smiling as she followed him through the door to a wide center hallway whose hardwood floor gleamed with care. A narrow cherrywood table along one wall held a vase filled with fresh flowers. The gilt-framed mirror above it was flanked by a pair of wall sconces that lit the space with a rosy glow.

"Your house is lovely," she said.

"Thank you," a woman's voice replied. On Peg's left, an arched doorway led to a living room furnished in subtle hues of cream and gray. A woman standing just inside the room gave Peg a small wave. "Men are hopeless when it comes to decorating, so I'll take credit where credit is due. Otherwise Nolan will have you believing that he pulled this whole place together by himself."

"You must be Barbara." Peg walked over and extended her hand.

Nolan's sister was tall, svelte, and wearing a garnet-colored sheath dress that showed off her willowy figure to maximum advantage. She appeared to be at least a decade younger than Nolan and Peg. Her blond hair was brushed back from her high forehead and held in place by a wide velvet headband. Barbara grasped Peg's fingers and gave them a hearty shake.

"It's a pleasure to meet you," she said. "I have a feeling you and I are going to become great friends."

"I hope so," Peg replied.

"Not so fast, you two." Nolan chuckled as he stepped in between them. "Let's not forget who has first dibs on Peg's time and attention."

Barbara lifted a sculpted brow. "My brother is feeling possessive already?" She aimed a wink in Peg's direction. "That's unusual. I think you'd better watch yourself with him."

"Don't worry," Peg said meaningfully. "I intend to watch Nolan *very* carefully."

When they sat down to dinner, the conversation remained lively. Over a meal of Caesar salad, grilled salmon, and asparagus—all prepared and served by Nolan—Peg watched the interplay between the two siblings with interest. Considering how many fraught relationships existed in her family, it was a pleasure to see them enjoying each other's company.

"Tell me about your son," she said to Nolan during a short lull.

"Jason's a great kid," he replied, then laughed. "Kid? He's in his thirties. Married once, now divorced. No children, unfortunately, though I remain ever hopeful that he'll find someone new and rectify that situation. He works for a nonprofit in Chicago, which means that I don't get to see him nearly as often as I'd like to."

Barbara turned to Peg. "Nolan tells me that you live with three enormous Poodles. What's that like?"

"Wonderful." Peg smiled. She was always happy to talk about her Poodles' myriad delightful qualities, but now she was more interested in a mutual discussion that would offer additional insight into her host and hostess. "Do you have any pets, Barbara?"

"Unfortunately, no. My life is a bit unsettled at the moment. But once things get back to normal, I'm hoping to look for a puppy. Something small, that would fit into an apartment. Nolan says you know a great deal about dogs. Maybe you could recommend a breed?"

"Of course." Peg nodded. That would be easy. "I'd be happy to. I'll also help you locate a reputable breeder."

Since Nolan had cooked, Peg and Barbara took over cleanup duty. After that, the three of them sat down in the living room with snifters of brandy. The evening seemed to fly by. Before Peg knew it, it was nearly eleven o'clock. She never stayed out this late. Her Poodles would be wondering where she was.

Nolan walked Peg out to her car. The night air was cool, and the sky above them was filled with stars. They paused in the driveway, neither one wanting their time together to end just yet.

"Thank you for a wonderful evening," Peg said. "I really enjoyed meeting Barbara. And discovering that you're such a good cook."

"Don't get your hopes up." Nolan chuckled. "Tonight's dinner exhausted nearly my entire culinary repertoire." He leaned down and kissed her. "I had a wonderful time too, Peg. Here's hoping this evening was the first of many more to come."

Peg sincerely hoped he was right about that.

Chapter 6

"I'm worried," Rose said.

"So what? You're always worried," Maura replied. "In case you haven't realized it yet, it's what you do."

The two women were sitting at the dining room table in the Gallagher House. They were supposed to be discussing the upcoming week's menus, but as usual, their conversation had gotten sidetracked. For practical reasons, many of the shelter's recent meals had featured tomatoes. Once they started talking about that, the conversation had veered off in an entirely new direction.

Now Rose was frowning as though she had something on her mind. When she and Peter had opened the shelter, the dining room had been a rather noxious shade of mauve, courtesy of the home's previous residents. Three coats of paint later, the walls were now a soft cream. But even that cheerful color couldn't brighten Rose's mood.

"No, it's not," she said firmly. In the convent, she'd been known for her composure and serenity. Surely she'd brought those admirable traits with her to the outside world. Hadn't she?

Apparently Maura didn't think so. "Take it from me, I know a worrier when I see one. My mother was like that too. She'd see a speck of dirt on the floor and know for sure it was a spider. And she hated spiders." She smirked at Rose across the table. "By the way, I heard you had dengue fever."

Rose's frown deepened. "Where did you hear that?"

"This place doesn't have the thickest walls. I'd think you would have figured that out by now. So . . . this dengue thing, is it contagious? Do I have anything to worry about?"

"That's not funny."

"It is to me," Maura said.

"Perhaps you'll find unemployment amusing too."

Maura snorted. "That's an idle threat if ever I've heard one."

"You're right," Rose admitted. "Peter and I would be utterly lost without you."

Maura cooked and cleaned. She played with children who were staying at the shelter. Best of all, she answered the door in the middle of the night when a woman fleeing from an abusive situation needed a warm bed and a kind smile. Abruptly it occurred to Rose that in the time Maura had been at the shelter, she'd probably made herself more indispensable than Rose was herself.

That was a sobering thought.

"I'm not worrying about dengue fever," Rose said. "And neither should you."

"That's a relief."

"But I am a bit concerned about Peg."

"Peg?" Maura was surprised. "Now there's a woman who's capable of taking care of herself. I'd want her on my side in a bar brawl. Not only is she just about the most frightening woman I've ever met, she also has those big black dogs to back her up."

"Peg's Poodles don't bite." Peg had told Rose that often enough that she felt safe in repeating it with reasonable certainty.

"You're sure about that?"

"They wouldn't dare. Think about it. Would you do something if Peg told you not to?"

"Heck no." Maura laughed.

"There you have it."

"Have what? You still haven't told me why Peg's in a pickle."

Rose gathered up the pad, pen, and coupons they'd been using to make their list and stacked them in a neat pile. She told herself that she was organizing her thoughts, but really she was just stalling.

"You might have heard that I helped Peg sign up on the Mature Mingle dating site," she said after a minute.

"Might have heard?" Maura laughed again. "Everybody knows about that, even Clyde, the delivery guy. As I heard it, you didn't just *help* Peg sign up, you pushed her into it."

Rose winced slightly. Then nodded.

"And now there's a problem? I can understand why you might be worried. I'd be worried too, if Peg was mad at me."

"She isn't mad," Rose said quickly. "In fact, she seems rather pleased with the way things are progressing. But that's the problem. I think she's letting herself move too fast."

"At her age, she'd better move fast," Maura mumbled under her breath.

Rose pretended not to hear that. "It's been years since Peg was seriously involved with a man. It's—I don't know—like she's out of practice."

Maura shuddered to think what Peg might be out of practice doing. She turned her thoughts in a different direction. "You're talking as though falling in love is like doing algebra. It's not. It's instinctive. Nobody forgets how to do it. I take it she met a nice man through the dating site?"

Rose nodded.

"And they've met up how many times?"

Rose counted back. "Three."

"Is the sex hot and heavy?"

Rose reared back in her seat. With a jolt, Maura remembered that her employer was an ex-nun. "Sorry about that."

Rose flapped a hand in the air. She was either dismissing the question or fanning her red face. Maura couldn't tell which.

"No, that's all right," Rose replied primly after several seconds had passed. "It's a valid question. I believe, although I am not certain, that Peg and Nolan have not yet attained that level of intimacy."

Maura wondered whether Rose realized that when something upset her, she became all prissy and began to embellish her vocabulary. It seemed like a funny thing to have as a tell, but there it was.

"A guy with a name like Nolan doesn't sound like he'd be fast on his feet, if you know what I mean." Maura figured that euphemism sounded tame enough both for Rose and for any other former clergy members who might come wandering by. In this house, you never knew.

"I hope you're right," Rose said as she considered that comment. "But from listening to Peg, I still get the feeling that she's allowing herself to get involved too quickly. It's barely been two weeks. How well could she possibly know him?"

"Peg's an adult. And a fast study," Maura said. "I moved in with my ex after less than a month."

The conversation paused as both women pondered the ramifications of that decision.

"Okay," Maura conceded. "So maybe I'm not the best example."

"I'm going to tell Peg that I want to meet Nolan," Rose decided. "I should check him out and make sure he's on the up-and-up."

"You think that'll help?" Maura was dubious. Rose meant well, but she was a cream puff. A minnow oblivious to sharks in the shadows. And there were plenty of sharks out there in the real world. Maura knew that for a fact.

"Of course."

Maura nodded then. What choice did she have? The gesture was one of acknowledgment rather than agreement, but Rose didn't have to know that.

"Good, I'm glad that's settled. Anything else?" Maura wasn't expecting an answer. She got one anyway.

"Mrs. Mayberry," Rose said.

"I've been keeping an eye out. As far as I can tell, the grandson and his friends haven't been back."

"I think you're right." Rose had been keeping watch too. As had Peter. Their street had been mostly quiet lately. "And while it seems like that might be a good thing, I'm not sure it is."

"Why not?"

"When we dropped off the tomatoes that day, how did Mrs. Mayberry seem to you?"

"Old," Maura replied with the casual disregard of someone who had yet to hit forty.

"Mrs. Mayberry *is* old," Rose said. "That's my point. I wonder if she's competent to be on her own. She and I had met before, and yet she didn't appear to recognize me. It could be that she's in the early stages of dementia."

Maura considered that and decided it was a possibility.

"I wonder how often she leaves her house?" Rose mused. "And how she gets around when she does."

"I don't think she has a car. I know she has her groceries

delivered because I've seen the van come by. But other than that, I've never given her much thought."

"I haven't either." Rose frowned. "And now I feel bad about that because maybe it's past time we did. The nearest bus stop is more than a mile from here. What if Mrs. Mayberry had an emergency of some kind or needed medical care?"

"She could call over here for help," Maura said.

"Yes, of course. But does she know that?"

"Maybe not," Maura agreed. "She might not even have our phone number."

"That's what I was thinking." Rose braced her hands on the table, pushed back her chair, and stood up. "Let's go do something about that, shall we?"

"Now?"

"Why not? We've just concluded that Mrs. Mayberry rarely leaves her home. She'd probably welcome a visit from two friendly neighbors."

"You mean pushy neighbors," Maura grumbled. Nevertheless, she rose too. When her employer set her mind on a charitable mission, she knew better than to try to dissuade her. "The kitchen is still full of tomatoes. Maybe we should take her a few more."

"Next time," Rose said brightly. She led the way out of the room.

The walk down the street took just a few minutes. Nearly all the houses Rose and Maura passed had their doors and windows closed and locked. Few cars were parked along the curb. This time of day, many of the residents would be at work.

Even on weekends, Digby Avenue wasn't a particularly sociable neighborhood. People who lived there had often gone through some kind of adversity in their lives. Now they tended to keep their heads down and their thoughts to themselves. Rose and Peter had been hoping to be able to change that, but their friendly and outgoing approach had yet to make much of an impact.

When they reached Mrs. Mayberry's house, Rose noticed several details that had escaped her attention on their previous visit. There was a rotten board on the woman's front steps, and her porch hadn't been swept in a long time. Paint was peeling on her front door, and part of the doorframe was warped.

While Rose was considering those problems, Maura reached around her and knocked. A minute passed. The door remained closed. Maura and Rose looked at each other, unsure what to do next.

"Maybe Mrs. Mayberry takes a nap in the middle of the day," Rose said.

"Then we shouldn't disturb her." Maura was ready to go.

Before they could move away, the door opened slightly. Mrs. Mayberry peered out through the slender crack. She was dressed in a housecoat and slippers, and a pair of glasses with thick lenses was perched on her nose. The gnarled hand that grasped the door's edge was laced with blue veins.

"Can I help you?" Her voice quavered briefly, then her expression cleared. "Oh, you're the ladies who brought me the tomatoes. Thank you, they were delicious."

"I'm glad you enjoyed them," Rose said. "I'm Rose, and this is Maura. We live just down the block."

"Yes, of course. You told me that last time. I bet you've come to retrieve your basket. I asked Donny to return it, but I'm sure it's still here somewhere. Why don't you come inside while I take a look around?"

Rose and Maura stepped into the dimly lit hallway. When Maura closed the door behind them, it grew darker still. Like the shelter, this house's first floor featured an abundance of tall windows. Unfortunately they were all closed, and most were covered by heavy drapes. The air inside the house was stuffy and warm.

Mrs. Mayberry shuffled down the hall toward the kitchen, her fingers trailing lightly along the wall beside her. Rose and Maura followed. The house was cluttered and in need of a cleaning, but otherwise it appeared to be in decent shape. Rose was glad to see that. Perhaps her fears about Mrs. Mayberry's circumstances had been unfounded.

Then they reached the kitchen.

"Whoa," said Maura. She stopped abruptly in the doorway.

Rose, who was behind, nearly ran into her. She peered over Maura's shoulder and stifled a gasp.

Every available surface in the room was littered with something. Dirty pots and pans, a laundry basket, moldy fruit, a tall pile of yellowing newspapers, and an open loaf of bread all vied for space on the counter. The sink overflowed with dishes, and the refrigerator door had been left partially open. A garbage can in the corner was stuffed with fast-food containers that looked as though they might have been there since Donny and his friends had last been by.

"There it is," Mrs. Mayberry said happily.

Rose's basket, thankfully empty, was sitting beside the back door. Seemingly oblivious to the mess around her, the older woman walked across the room to retrieve it. Rose tiptoed gingerly after her. Maura had planted herself in the middle of the floor. She was already rolling up her sleeves.

"Since we're here," Rose said gently, "do you mind if Maura and I do a little straightening up?"

Mrs. Mayberry turned and slowly looked around. She blinked several times, as if she was observing the chaos in her kitchen for the first time.

"Perhaps that would be a good idea," she said. "Living alone, I sometimes let things slide for a day or two. And then it seems like they just get away from me."

"I understand, Mrs. Mayberry." Rose took the woman's arm and guided her to a chair beside a small table. She quickly cleared away the stack of empty cartons that was piled on the seat. "You just sit down, and Maura and I will have everything put back together in no time."

"Thank you, that's very kind." The older woman gave them both a smile. "And please, do call me Mabel."

Chapter 7

Peg was up early on Saturday morning. It was going to be a beautiful late summer day, warm and clear with barely a cloud in the sky. That meant perfect weather for a dog show—and Peg should know. She'd been to hundreds over the course of her life, as both a competitor and a judge.

Today, however, Peg was going to do something she hadn't done in a long time. She'd be attending the show as a spectator. Both Rose and Nolan were going with her. That should prove to be interesting.

Peg's original plan had been to spend the day at the event with Nolan. With their relationship progressing nicely, she'd felt it was time to introduce him to her world. The Mohegan Lake show always drew a good entry, and it was conveniently located in nearby Fairfield.

Then Rose had gotten involved, and Peg's lovely, uncomplicated plan became something else entirely. Having prodded Peg to start dating, Rose apparently felt she was entitled to an opinion about Peg's romantic decisions. When she heard that Peg had scheduled an outing with Nolan for the weekend, Rose had invited herself along.

Peg began her morning by taking the Poodles on a lengthy walk along the bridle paths behind her property. Since she'd be away for most of the day, it made sense to give the dogs a good run first. They would miss her less if they were asleep.

After that, Peg went to pick up Rose at the small, ranch-style house in Springdale she and Peter were currently leasing. When she pulled her minivan into the driveway, Rose was ready for her. She came striding out of the house dressed in a multicolored T-shirt, white cropped pants, and sensible flat-soled shoes. She was carrying a sunhat in her hands.

"This will be fun," Rose said as she opened the passenger side door and slid onto the seat.

"Really?" Peg glanced over her shoulder as she backed out onto the road. "Last I heard, you thought dog shows were silly."

"That was just my first impression." Rose clipped her seat belt into place. This would only be the second dog show she'd ever attended, so she was trying to keep an open mind.

"I believe you said something about fluffy dogs prancing around in circles."

"Perhaps I did," Rose allowed. "But this time I won't be looking at the dogs. I'll be watching Nolan."

"I'm sure he'll appreciate that," Peg said drily.

It was much too early in the day for arguments. Nevertheless, she'd already decided that while Rose was watching Nolan, Peg would be keeping an eye on Rose. She wasn't about to let her sister-in-law ruin things by inserting herself into Peg's budding relationship.

The dog show was taking place in a large park. Two parallel rows of rings had been set up in the middle of a freshly mowed field. A green and white striped tent covered the aisleway between the two rows. A second tent nearby provided a shaded space where exhibitors could prepare their entries for the ring. Ample parking was available in an adjoining lot.

Nolan was already at the show site when they arrived.

He and Peg had arranged to meet at the catalog table near the show's entrance. Wearing blue jeans, loafers, and a pale-yellow shirt with the cuffs rolled back, Nolan was standing beside the table. He'd purchased a catalog and was flipping through the pages.

"I hope we haven't kept you waiting long," Peg said when he looked up as they approached.

"Not at all. You're right on time." Nolan's gaze went to Rose. He smiled and held out his hand. "You must be Rose Donovan. It's a pleasure to meet you. I'm glad you could join us today."

Rose's eyes widened. Peg had said Nolan was handsome, but that was an understatement. No wonder Peg was infatuated. The man looked like George Clooney's father.

"It's lovely to meet you too," she said as they shook hands.

"Peg tells me I'm in the hot seat today. Apparently I require your approval."

Rose shot Peg a surprised look. She hadn't expected Peg to divulge that.

"I'm not worried," Nolan added jovially. "I'll just make sure to be on my best behavior."

Peg looped her arm through his. "Let's go look at some dogs, shall we?"

The three of them strolled across the lawn in the direction of the rings. Judging had started at eight o'clock, so the show was already two hours old. Peg saw a class of Bichon Frises—one of the non-sporting breeds she was approved to judge—gaiting around their ring. She steered Nolan and Rose that way.

"I know a bit about dog shows," Nolan said to Peg. He gestured toward the row of Bichons. "For example, the purpose of this class is for the judge to pick which dog is Best in Breed. Later, all the breeds will compete against each other for Best of Show."

Best *of* Breed, Peg corrected automatically in her head. And Best *in* Show.

Not only that, but Nolan had gotten lucky. The Winners Bitch class had just ended and the specials—already finished champions—were now filing into the ring to compete for Best of Breed. Upon their approach, Nolan had been pointing toward a different class entirely. Plus, his explanation had somehow managed to skip over the group competition.

'How interesting," Peg murmured. "Tell me more."

Rose gave her a sidelong glance. What was Peg up to now?

"I'll tell you something more," she said. "Those are very fluffy dogs."

Peg snorted a small laugh, but Nolan addressed the comment seriously.

"They are indeed," he told them. "The hair is specially groomed to look that way. Some of these dogs are clipped before they go in the show ring, and others get blowouts from a hair dryer."

"Imagine that." Peg couldn't quite decide whether to be amused or annoyed by the fact that Nolan was mansplaining dog shows to her. Either way, it was a novel experience.

Something in Peg's tone must have alerted Nolan because he suddenly began to backpedal. "What am I thinking? Of course, you already know these things. From what you've told me, you have lots of experience with dogs."

"Peg doesn't just have experience," Rose said. "She's an acknowledged expert. She's a dog show judge who's approved for all the breeds in the Toy and Non-Sporting Groups. And that's a lot of dogs."

Peg swung around to face Rose. "How do you know that?"

"What? I listen when you talk."

"Not about dogs." Peg was sure about that. She'd

watched Rose's eyes glaze over when she was rhapsodizing about Poodles.

"Maybe not always," Rose admitted. "But at least sometimes."

"Obviously I need to defer to your greater judgment," Nolan said to Peg. "Why don't you give us a tour around the showground? After that, maybe you can help me make some sense of this catalog."

"I'd be delighted," Peg said with a smile. "Step right this way."

They spent a highly entertaining morning—at least in Peg's estimation—browsing from one show ring to the next. Nolan continued to offer half-baked explanations for things he knew nothing about. Meanwhile, Rose attempted to grill him for personal information in what she seemed to think was a subtle manner. Neither Nolan nor Peg was fooled.

Eventually Peg showed Nolan how to decipher his catalog, which didn't help him much since he didn't know any of the dogs or exhibitors. Rose unwisely purchased a corn dog from a concession stand and nearly threw up. And Peg developed a sunburn on her nose.

None of that mattered to her. She was in her element and having a wonderful time.

"You certainly know a lot of people," Nolan commented when they'd watched the completion of the Papillon judging. Afterward, the judge had come over to ringside to greet Peg and shake her hand.

"These are my friends and colleagues," she said. "I've been a member of the dog world forever."

"They're all dog fanatics." Rose poked Peg's side.

"We are, indeed." She refused to take offense. "All the exhibitors you see here today are working for the preservation and betterment of their breeds. What a worthy goal that is."

"I just thought they were all just here to win ribbons," Rose teased.

"And points toward their championships," Nolan added. Clearly he'd been paying attention to what Peg had to say. "I know I must seem like a bit of a dunce today—hopefully you will chalk that up to overenthusiasm on my part—but I actually have a connection in your dog show world. A man my company used to do business with was a dog breeder. He took his prize pooches to all the important events."

"Who would that be?" Peg asked with interest.

"His name is Charlie Vargas. I seem to recall he had some rare breed that came from Hungary."

"Vizslas," Peg said. The breed wasn't actually rare, but she was beginning to feel like she'd already corrected Nolan enough times today.

Nolan snapped his fingers. "That's the one. Do you know him?"

"I do. Like me, Mr. Vargas is a judge now."

"Great guy," Nolan said. "One of the best. I haven't seen him in years. He probably wouldn't even remember me."

"Speaking of the best." Peg nodded toward the row of rings where workers were dismantling the smaller rings and merging them into one big one. "It looks as though Best in Show is about to begin. Let's go watch and pick our favorites."

"Right," Nolan enthused. "Maybe we'll get lucky and pick the winner."

Luck had nothing to do with that, Peg knew. She'd chosen plenty of winners in her day. Not only that, but she was reasonably sure she already knew which dog would win BIS today. But why ruin Nolan's fun?

"I already know my favorite," Rose said, striking out ahead of them. "It will be the fluffy one."

* * *

"So?" Peg said to Rose on the way home. "What did you think?"

It wasn't an idle question. Peg realized she actually wanted to hear Rose's thoughts. It was beginning to occur to Peg that maybe she needed to clarify her own thinking as well.

She wasn't entirely pleased by the way she and Nolan had parted at the showground. Having made himself agreeable all day, Nolan was obviously disappointed that he and Peg wouldn't be getting together after the show. Instead she'd demurred, insisting that she had to take Rose home. It had been a relief to have the excuse to fall back on.

That wasn't at all how she'd been expecting their outing to end. But at some point during the day, Peg had begun to notice the tiny cracks in Nolan's near-perfect façade. It was a real shame because he'd been doing so well up until then. Once she'd plucked him out of his comfort zone and deposited him in hers, however, Nolan wasn't nearly as appealing as he'd previously appeared. The fact that he'd been determined to continue explaining—incorrectly—how dog shows worked had really gotten on her nerves.

Peg was also confused by the way Nolan had casually dropped Charlie Vargas's name. Charlie was a prominent figure in the dog show world. Of course Peg knew him. Now she couldn't help but wonder why Nolan had bragged about his connection, then dismissed it a moment later. Was he worried that Peg might ask Charlie about him? If so, perhaps she should do just that.

Abruptly Peg realized that Rose still hadn't answered her question. She took her eyes off the road and glanced across the front of the minivan. Rose was sitting upright on her seat, hands clasped in her lap, staring straight out the windshield. Peg thought Rose looked like she'd been sucking on a lemon.

"Well?" she prodded.

"Nolan's certainly handsome."

"But?"

Rose turned to face her. "Why does there have to be a 'but'?"

"Because with you, there always is. You wanted to meet Nolan, and now you've spent almost an entire day with him. You must have formed an opinion. What is it?"

"You're a complex woman, Peg."

Peg nodded. She'd concede that.

"Compared to you, Nolan seemed a little shallow." Rose paused. "No, maybe superficial is a better word."

"Explain," Peg said.

Rose swiveled in her seat to face the driver's side of the van. "Today might have been different than your other dates because you were in your milieu and Nolan was clearly out of his—but have you ever noticed that he agrees with everything you say?"

Peg thought back. Then frowned. Rose was right—and Peg should have realized that earlier. It wasn't just today. Nolan almost always deferred to her opinions, had done so even during their previous interactions. No wonder she'd thought he was such a scintillating conversationist. Nolan had been parroting her own ideas back to her.

"Dammit," Peg said. Now she was annoyed. And Rose still wasn't finished.

"It's as if Nolan tells you what he thinks you want to hear, rather than expressing how he really feels," Rose said. "Have you and he ever had an argument?"

"No."

"Even a mild disagreement?"

"No, but that doesn't mean anything. I've only known him for a short amount of time. Which actually goes back to your previous point. What you're saying about Nolan is how most people act when they meet someone new—

everyone tries to project a better, more engaging, version of themselves."

"You don't," Rose pointed out.

"No, but I probably would if I could figure out how to make it credible."

Rose doubted that. She heard Peg sigh unhappily.

"Nolan told me I was beautiful. I probably should have known something was up when he said that."

"Oh, Peg," Rose said gently. "That's not what I meant at all."

"No, you meant to be honest, and I appreciate that." Rose nodded.

"Usually I'm a pragmatist. Now it appears that I've been acting rather silly. I was dazzled by the notion that someone like Nolan could actually be interested in me. He made it easy for me to let my guard down. So you're perfectly correct to question our connection."

"I'm glad you agree."

Peg smiled. "I'm glad you came with me to the dog show."

That made Rose laugh. "Those are words you probably never imagined yourself saying."

"Indeed." Their exit was approaching. Peg switched on her blinker and prepared to turn off the highway. "Your presence saved me from making what was probably a poor decision. Nolan was disappointed he wouldn't be coming home with me tonight. I used you as my excuse."

Rose felt her heart clench. "I hope you're not just saying that. Because I'd feel terrible if you're unhappy about the way things turned out. I never meant to get in your way."

"You didn't," Peg replied. "After today, it's clear that Nolan and I are going to have to reevaluate our relationship. Maybe we'll even need to start over. I want a connection that's based on honesty. With someone I can trust. I plan to call him tomorrow and tell him exactly that."

"Good idea," Rose agreed.

Chapter 8

"Oh no," Rose said.

"What's the matter?" Two days later, Peter was sitting at their kitchen table in Springdale. He gazed up at her from behind the morning paper. Peter was old-fashioned. He liked news he could hold in his hands.

A small TV was sitting on the counter, its volume on low. Rose was watching her version of the news while she scrambled eggs for their breakfast. She gestured toward the screen wordlessly. Peter turned in his seat and had a look.

A headline scrolled across the bottom of the screen: FATAL HIT AND RUN ACCIDENT KILLS PEDESTRIAN.

Peter grimaced. "In Stamford?"

Rose nodded. She'd removed the frying pan from the burner and was wiping her hands on a nearby towel.

"Drivers around here are getting worse all the time," Peter commented. Then he looked at his wife closely. "Are you all right?"

"No. I have to go."

"Go?" Now she had his attention.

"I'm taking the minivan. Can you take the bus to work?"

"Yes, of course." Peter turned back for another look at the television. The morning show had moved on to another story. Clearly he had missed something.

"Where are you going?" he asked. Maybe that would help.

"I need to see Peg. Right away. She's probably already heard the news."

"What news?"

Rose was halfway to the door. She paused and glanced back. "The person that was killed last night? That was Nolan Abercrombie, the man from Mature Mingle whom Peg's been seeing."

Usually when Rose arrived at Peg's house, the front door opened before she even had a chance to get out of her van. Rose knew she had Peg's Poodles to thank for that. Once, she'd considered Peg silly for allowing dogs to dictate her behavior. Now Peg's response to their high jinks had begun to seem almost normal.

This time, however, even after Rose had coasted the length of Peg's driveway and parked in front of her garage, nothing happened. The door to the house remained firmly closed. No big black dogs came galloping down the stairs to greet her. For a moment, Rose was almost disappointed. Then she gave herself a mental kick and got over it.

Surely Peg must be home, she thought as she climbed the steps. It was barely eight o'clock on a Tuesday morning. Where else would she be? Probably not at a dog show. Rose was no expert but from what she'd surmised after spending time with Peg, those usually took place on weekends.

When she rang the doorbell, Rose heard the Poodles begin to bark inside the house. That was something. Something *better* would have been the door opening. Unfortunately that didn't happen.

Rose rang the bell again. Then she tried the doorknob. To her surprise, it turned in her hand. Maybe people who lived with big scary dogs didn't have to worry about keeping their doors locked.

Rose pushed the door open slightly and stuck her head inside. "Peg? Are you here?"

"I'm in the living room," Peg said. "You might as well come in."

It was hardly an enthusiastic invitation. Nevertheless Rose opened the door and stepped inside. There she found three Poodles arrayed across the hallway, blocking her path. Three sets of dark eyes gazed up at her expectantly. Rose had no clue what that meant she was supposed to do.

"Hi, guys," she said.

Three pomponned tails lifted and wagged back and forth. Like maybe the Poodles thought they were all going to have a conversation.

"I'm here to see Peg," Rose told them.

Three heads turned and looked toward the living room.

"Yes, I know where she is," Rose said. "I'm waiting for you to get out of the way."

"Good luck with that." Peg appeared in the doorway. "Those three will talk your ear off if you let them." She snapped her fingers. The Poodles immediately dispersed.

Rose followed Peg into the living room. They took seats across from each other on chintz-covered love seats that flanked a natural brick fireplace. The room was spacious and its windows usually let in plenty of light. The day was overcast, however, and Peg hadn't turned on any lamps. The gloomy ambience seemed to suit both their moods.

"I guess you heard the news," Peg said.

Rose nodded. "I came right away to see what I could do to help. I'm so sorry."

"Sorry?" Peg lifted a brow. "I appreciate the sentiment, but there's really no need to offer me condolences."

"There's every need—" Rose began, but Peg wasn't having it.

"Nolan and I were just getting to know one another. We were friends. Perhaps, in time, our relationship might have progressed—"

"Oh pish," said Rose.

Peg stopped speaking. Her eyes widened. That was *her* word. No one else used it. Hope, who had turned in a circle and lay down at Peg's feet, lifted her head and stared at Rose too.

"Pish," Rose said again for good measure. "I know you hadn't known Nolan long, but your feelings were involved. How could they not be? The man was a veritable Prince Charming. At least that was what he wanted you to think."

"Yes," Peg conceded unhappily. "And he was rather convincing too. But as you know, we were both beginning to suspect that might merely be a façade. Now I can't help but wonder if I ever really knew Nolan at all."

Abruptly Rose stood up. "Have you had breakfast yet?"

"No. But the Poodles have eaten."

Of course they had. Peg would never neglect their needs.

"Let me make you something. You'll feel better on a full stomach."

"Thank you, but I'm not hungry."

"How about a cup of tea?"

Peg stared up at her. "How will that help?"

"I don't know. I'm just trying everything I can think of."

"Maybe you could try letting me sulk in peace," Peg said.

Rose sat back down. "You're not sulking. You're grieving."

"I'm not," Peg insisted. "Not really. Nolan and I got along beautifully—at least in the beginning. But he was only in my life for a few short weeks. Our acquaintance was far too brief to have that kind of impact."

"Perhaps," Rose said softly. "But Nolan himself is just

part of what you've lost. Recently you'd allowed yourself to be open to possibilities you hadn't considered in a long time. Experiencing those feelings—and the potential they had to impact your life—had to be exciting. Now you've suddenly been yanked back to reality. It's inevitable that you'd also be mourning the loss of what a relationship like that could have meant, if only things had gone differently."

Peg frowned. "I thought Peter was the counselor in your family."

Rose shrugged.

Peg patted her thigh with her hand. Hope knew what that meant. She hopped to her feet, then jumped up to join Peg on the love seat. Peg wound her arms around the Poodle's neck. She always felt better with a dog in her lap. She sat for several minutes and thought about what Rose had said.

"You may be smarter than I give you credit for," Peg said finally.

"I do hope that someday you'll pay me a compliment that doesn't sound like an insult."

"If we both live enough, it may yet happen," Peg replied mildly. "Didn't you offer me tea a few minutes ago?"

"I did. But I was waiting for you to come to your senses first."

Peg nudged Hope off her lap and stood up. "Consider it done."

The Poodles ran on ahead as Peg and Rose walked to the kitchen. Peg handed out peanut-butter dog biscuits all around, then brewed herself a cup of tea. Rose made use of the coffee maker Peg kept around for guests but had never learned to operate.

Five minutes later, the two women were sitting across from each other once again, this time at the kitchen table.

"Don't you dare offer me cake," Rose warned.

"I had no intention of it," Peg said. "This doesn't seem like a cake kind of day."

Rose took a cautious sip from her cup. The coffee was scalding hot. "The report I saw on this morning's news called Nolan's death an accident."

Peg gazed at Rose across the table. She could guess what her sister-in-law was thinking. Rose had a suspicious mind. For that matter, so did Peg.

"Go on," she said.

"I'm just wondering why—if the collision was truly an accident—the driver of the car didn't stay around to try and help. Or call nine-one-one. Like a normal person would do."

"Maybe he or she panicked."

"Maybe he or she had an ulterior motive."

"Such as?"

"They wanted Nolan dead."

There, she'd said it. Rose had blurted out what Peg had to be thinking too. When Peg didn't respond, she added, "What do you suppose Nolan was doing in Stamford at that time of night? Didn't you tell me he lived in Darien?"

"I did," Peg said. "The report I saw didn't specify where the accident happened. What part of Stamford are we talking about? Business or residential?"

Rose didn't know either. She got out her phone and took a look.

"It's both. One of those mixed-use areas. But listen to this. The article says the deceased was identified as Nolan Abercrombie, age seventy-four, of 498 Bleecker Street, Stamford." Rose lifted her gaze and looked at Peg.

She looked surprised too. "That's not correct."

"Maybe it was his work address?" Rose guessed.

"Nolan was retired."

They pondered the ramifications of that incongruity.

"It's probably an error," Rose said. She tucked her

phone away. What was the point of being able to check on things quickly and easily if the answers she got only raised more questions? "It's not as if reporters always get their facts straight. Especially now, when people think it's more important to flood the internet with content than to worry about its veracity."

"Maybe," Peg mused.

Rose reached for her coffee. It was finally cool enough to drink. "When was the last time you spoke with Nolan? On the way back from the dog show, you told me you were planning to call him."

"I did. I called the next morning, but he didn't pick up."

"I'm sure you left a message." Peg tended to get snorty when people weren't available to talk to her on demand. She always left messages. "Did he call you back?"

"No. So I tried again that afternoon. And left another message."

Rose could well imagine what that one might have sounded like.

"Frankly I thought it was a little odd. Before that day at the show, Nolan always answered my calls or returned them immediately. In fact, he was the one who usually initiated contact. So when he went a whole day without speaking to me, I wondered if he was giving me the silent treatment."

"Whatever for?" Rose asked.

"For ditching him on Saturday night."

"You didn't ditch him, you drove me home."

"Yes, but Nolan made it clear when we parted at the show that he'd anticipated a different end to the evening." Peg frowned now, thinking back.

"In other words, you thought he was pouting like a child, simply because you'd politely put him off?"

"Yes. Which is why I refrained from calling him again. I'd already begun to have doubts about our suitability—

and that juvenile behavior on his part only confirmed my suspicions."

"So you didn't talk to Nolan for a whole two days and somehow he managed to get himself killed," Rose said. Then she clapped her hand over her mouth. "I'm sorry, that was insensitive."

"Insensitive," Peg allowed. "But essentially correct. Although I don't see how my talking to him would have made a difference."

"Unless that led to him being at your house at eleven o'clock last night, rather than in downtown Stamford."

Peg gave Rose a scornful look. She was quite certain they'd already dismissed that possibility.

"Okay, strike that." Rose refused to be cowed. Considering how often Peg managed to get on her last nerve, she didn't mind returning the favor once in a while. "So now what?"

"I'd imagine there will be a funeral for Nolan," Peg said. "We should attend."

"And maybe you should call Rodney."

Peg had started to get up. Now she settled back in her seat.

Rodney was Detective Rodney Sturgill of the Stamford Police Department. Initially Peg had become acquainted with him due to Melanie's crime-solving escapades. Over time, she and Rodney had become friends—and occasional allies who were respectful of each other's abilities. Peg had the good sense to nurture their relationship whenever the opportunity arose.

"Rodney," she said. It was half-question, half-statement.

"He might know something," Rose pressed. "Like whether Nolan's death was really an accident, or if the police are investigating it as suspicious?"

"Rodney always knows many things. He's usually not inclined to share them with me."

"Depending on the answer to my question, he will be this time."

"Oh?" Peg said. "Why is that?"

Clearly she hadn't thought things through. Rose enjoyed being the one with insight for a change. "You and Nolan have spoken frequently over the past few weeks. Your number will be all over his phone. Actually I'm surprised Detective Sturgill hasn't contacted you already."

Chapter 9

Rose's prediction proved to be correct. Right after she left, Peg received a call from the Stamford PD. She was rinsing out their mugs and placing them in the dishwasher when the phone rang.

"Peg? This is Detective Sturgill."

If he was going to call her by her first name, she would do the same. "Hello, Rodney."

He sighed. Peg had known he would. When the detective was on official business, he liked to observe the formalities. Apparently just for himself, however.

"I'm calling about a matter you appear to have a tangential connection to," he began.

"Nolan Abercrombie's death." Peg sat back down at the table. "I heard about it on the morning news. And Rose was just here."

"Rose Donovan?"

He didn't sound entirely happy about that development. Sturgill and Rose had history. That wasn't Peg's problem. If she'd been in Rose's shoes, she would have long since forgiven the man. When he'd investigated Rose as a suspect in the death of the Gallagher House's benefactor, he'd only been doing his job.

"She's the only Rose I know," Peg told him.

"Perhaps you should cultivate a broader range of friends."

"Rose is a relative. I'm afraid there's no getting rid of her."

Lord knew that was true. Peg herself had tried for years.

Sturgill cleared his throat. "Back to the matter at hand. It seems you were acquainted with Mr. Abercrombie. Could you tell me how that came about?"

"Certainly," Peg replied. "I signed up on a dating site where Nolan was a member. He and I formed a match."

Peg heard a strangled sound, quickly muffled. She wondered whether Rodney was choking or laughing. Neither option seemed complimentary.

"Do you have a problem with that?" she asked crisply.

"Of course not. Please continue."

"There isn't much more to tell you. He and I exchanged messages, and then we arranged to meet in person. Including our outing to a dog show on Saturday, we'd only gone on a handful of dates."

There was thirty seconds of silence as Rodney pondered that. Or maybe he was writing something down. The fact that he'd called her had to mean there was something questionable about Nolan's vehicular accident. Peg wondered if that meant she was being considered as a suspect. That would certainly liven up her life.

"When was the last time you saw Mr. Abercrombie?" Rodney asked.

"Saturday evening, when we parted in Fairfield."

"What took the two of you to Fairfield?"

"The Mohegan Lake Kennel Club."

"Right," he said, as if that meant something to him. He hated to be caught out.

If it had been important, Peg would have explained further. But it wasn't, so she didn't bother.

"And when was the last time you spoke with him?"

"That same evening, in Fairfield."

"You left several messages on his phone," Sturgill pressed.

"Two messages," Peg corrected. "I did. Yes."

"And did he call you back?"

Peg was quite certain that question had already been asked and answered, at least through inference. Being a suspect suddenly didn't feel like as much fun as she thought it would.

"He did not."

"Do you have any idea why Mr. Abercrombie would have been walking along Grove Street last night?"

"None whatsoever," Peg replied.

"When the two of you parted on Saturday, had you and Mr. Abercrombie made plans to get together again?"

"We had not."

"Why not?"

"Why is that any of your business?" Peg asked.

The detective paused again. Peg wondered whether he was reluctant to answer her question or if he was simply trying to come up with a suitable way to frame his reply.

"This isn't public knowledge yet," he said after several seconds had passed, "but I'm investigating the probable murder of your sometime date."

"I'll keep that under my hat," Peg replied. She was certain Rose didn't count when it came to promises to law enforcement. "The notion of murder I understand. What does the probable part mean?"

"At the moment, we're keeping all avenues of investigation open. Judging by what we can tell from the scene, it appears that Mr. Abercrombie was on the sidewalk and not in the road when he was struck. Also there are no skid marks. Whoever hit him seemed to make no attempt to avoid him. In fact, just the opposite. Still, there may be other factors that we have yet to take into consideration."

"Such as?" Peg prompted.

"You know I'm not going to answer that, Peg." Rodney sounded like a schoolmarm scolding a recalcitrant student.

"But you answered my previous question so nicely."

"Only because the press was at the scene. As soon as

they update their stories, the word will be out anyway. Much as I like you, Peg, you know I can't offer you special treatment, especially under these circumstances."

"The circumstances being that Nolan and I were acquainted?"

"I think the two of you were more than acquainted. A handful of dates sounds like a relationship to me. And since we have yet to track down anyone who saw or engaged with Mr. Abercrombie yesterday, right now it's possible you were the last person to spend time with him before he died."

"I'm sure that's not the case," Peg replied.

"For your sake, I hope not. Let's not forget that the last time you got involved in something you shouldn't have, someone shot up your house. I'd hate to see you put yourself in jeopardy again."

"The shooting part was hardly my fault."

"I'm not worried about whose fault it was." Rodney's tone softened. "I'm worried about keeping you safe. Is there anything else you think I should know about Mr. Abercrombie? Any ideas about why someone might have wanted to harm him?"

"None. But then, he and I were just getting to know one another. I'm hardly an expert on his life."

"Judging by what happened to him, that's probably a good thing," Rodney said.

Peg wanted to call Nolan's sister, Barbara, to offer her condolences, but she didn't have the woman's phone number. Nor was she able to locate it online. Surely the police would have been in touch with Barbara, since she was staying at Nolan's house—but it wasn't as if Peg could call Rodney back and ask for that information.

Belatedly it occurred to her that, despite the numerous topics they'd discussed that evening, Peg had never found out where Barbara was visiting from or how long she would be in town. Now those both seemed like curious omissions.

Looking back, she found herself wondering if Nolan had managed that conversation the same way he'd apparently directed their other interactions. He'd prompted Peg to offer opinions and supply information while both he and his sister divulged little in return. What did it say for Peg's manners that she'd allowed herself to be flattered into dominating the conversation? Worse still, she hadn't even noticed it happening at the time.

After the initial story left the news cycle, Peg heard nothing more about Nolan's death until a midweek article about traffic fatalities in Fairfield County mentioned that he would be buried at a local cemetery the following day. There was to be a small graveside service with his friends and loved ones in attendance. Peg was about to call Rose when her phone rang.

"Did you see it?" Rose asked. "Are you going?"

"Of course I'm going. I want to pay my respects and offer my condolences to Barbara and Nolan's son."

"You need to find closure," Rose said.

Peg exhaled loudly. Why did Rose insist on making everything so difficult? "What I *don't* need is your attempt to soothe me with psychobabble that's intended to tell me how I ought to feel."

"Fine," Rose replied after a pause. "Far be it from me to want to help. But I'm going with you."

"I assumed you would," Peg said. "I'll pick you up, and we'll go together."

At one-thirty the following afternoon, Peg was waiting outside the Gallagher House in her minivan. The sun was shining in a sky that was studded with fluffy white clouds. A light breeze ruffled the leaves on the trees.

Funerals should only take place in gloomy weather, Peg decided, as she drummed her fingers on the steering wheel. Saying goodbye to a loved one—or even someone who'd merely been a new friend—on such a lovely day made the burden seem like even more of an affront.

Rose came hurrying down the front steps, only a minute or two late. She was dressed in a cobalt-blue suit with low heels and a small hat that reminded Peg of Jackie Kennedy. Peg herself was wearing black from head to toe. She cast a look at Rose as the woman climbed into the minivan beside her.

"Blue is the best I could do on short notice," Rose said, although Peg had carefully not commented.

Peg turned the key and pulled away from the curb.

"My habit was black," Rose said.

As though Peg had asked a question, which she most definitely had not.

"I wore black every single day for more than thirty years," Rose continued. "A nun's habit is meant to be both drab and functional. It's designed both to quell vanity and to make you feel that, in God's eyes, you are all the same."

Peg kept her eyes on the road. Truthfully, she had no idea what to say. Which didn't seem to matter because Rose was still talking.

"I don't own any black clothing. Not a single piece. My closet is a riot of colors and textures. Every morning I take pleasure in deciding what to wear—because now it's *my* choice. And frankly, I've decided that God can keep an eye on me more easily when I'm wearing pink or yellow. Because bright colors make me stand out."

Peg glanced over at her. "You look fine."

"You're lucky I managed to find something this dark," Rose retorted.

Peg nearly smiled. To her surprise, she found her mood beginning to brighten. She had the most astonishing conversations with Rose. The woman's point of view was almost always unexpected. Peg would never admit it aloud, but she enjoyed that. It kept her on her toes.

Twenty minutes later, Peg drove between the tall stone gateposts that marked the cemetery entrance. Discreet signs directed her to Nolan's gravesite. She came to a line of cars parked by the edge of the tree-lined road. The article had mentioned a small service, so Peg hadn't expected there to be many mourners. Now she had to drive a good distance past the site of the ceremony before she could find a place to park.

"I didn't anticipate such a large turnout," Rose said as they walked back the way they'd come.

"Nor did I," Peg agreed. "There must be at least forty people here. Though we probably shouldn't be surprised that someone as charismatic as Nolan would have many friends."

The wooden casket was already in place, suspended on a bracket above the freshly dug grave. A spray of lilies, their stems circled by a white ribbon, was displayed on top of it. There was a small canopy nearby and chairs had been set up around the gravesite, though no one was sitting down. A pastor stood ready to officiate the service.

At first glance, Peg didn't see Barbara. Nor anyone who looked as though he might be Nolan's son, Jason. Nearly all the mourners were decades older than she imagined he would be. Some people were gathered in small groups, conversing in low tones. Others were standing by themselves, seemingly lost in their own thoughts.

Rose stepped close to Peg's side and whispered, "Are you noticing the same thing I am?"

"What's that?"

"Nearly all the people here are women. Aside from the pastor, I barely see a single man. Or even any couples. Doesn't that strike you as odd?"

"At our age, I suppose that's not entirely surprising," Peg said. "Men don't live as long as we do."

She paused and took another look around. It quickly became clear that Rose was right. Now that Peg had been made aware of it, the imbalance between the genders really was notable.

The women surrounding Nolan's gravesite were a diverse group. By Peg's estimation, they ranged in age from fifties to eighties. Their hair came in every shade and style; their figures varied from slender to positively zaftig. All the women appeared to have had one thing in common, however. Each possessed an air of unmistakable affluence. Peg was more oblivious to the whims of fashion than most women, but even she could spot designer handbags and important jewelry.

Rose was shaking her head. She wasn't buying Peg's explanation. And, suddenly, Peg wasn't either. As her gaze moved from one group to the next, a suspicion began to form in her mind. One she didn't like at all.

"Surely you don't think . . ." Rose began.

"That Nolan met all these women on Mature Mingle?" Peg sounded as horrified as she felt. "Is that even possible?"

"I don't know," Rose mumbled. "Maybe . . . if he'd been on there a while. But surely that's an absurd idea—"

The pastor stepped out from beneath the canopy, then moved to stand beside the casket. When he cleared his throat, the mourners stopped talking among themselves. Everyone turned to face him.

It was time for the service to begin.

Chapter 10

Peg had hoped she might feel uplifted by Nolan's service. Instead the ceremony felt interminable. Though it lasted no longer than twenty minutes, she spent most of that time squirming in place. Even Rose's none-too-subtle nudge wasn't enough to quiet the furious thoughts rocketing around inside Peg's brain.

First, the pastor read two passages from the Bible. Then Barbara stepped forward to deliver a short eulogy. As she praised Nolan's strength of character, Peg was sorely tempted to offer a rebuttal. Rose must have read her mind because she lifted her foot at a crucial moment and stamped down hard on Peg's toe. That shut her up.

Peg glanced around the assembled group as a woman came forward to recite a poem. Many of the mourners had their heads bowed and their hands clasped. A few were sniffling into their handkerchiefs. A woman wearing a hat with a short veil and a slash of red lipstick across her mouth was sobbing theatrically.

Peg's gaze slid away, then abruptly stopped when another woman caught her eye. This one was brunette and medium-tall. Probably in her fifties, she looked like an athlete. Her well-muscled frame made Peg think of mini-marathons and killer forehands. Judging by the glare the woman was directing at Nolan's casket, she and the deceased hadn't parted company on good terms.

"Stop gawking," Rose whispered. "It's rude."

"I can't help it," Peg replied. "I feel as though every woman here has a story to tell—and I'm beginning to think that I'd be eager to hear all of them."

Improbably, another woman walked over to the casket and began to warble a song. *Oh good grief*, Peg thought. *That was just adding insult to injury.*

Apparently she wasn't the only one who felt that way. Several women looked surprised. Others were amused. Even Rose was biting her lip to hold back a smile.

Thankfully, the song appeared to bring the audience participation segment of the service to an end. The pastor read a psalm, offered a blessing, then asked the mourners to keep Nolan in their prayers and to go in peace.

The man barely finished speaking before Peg was already on the move.

"Where are you going?" Rose hurried to catch up.

"I want to talk to Barbara."

That terse explanation didn't help Rose at all. "Who's Barbara?"

"Nolan's sister." Peg nodded toward an attractive blonde who was standing beneath the canopy, receiving condolences. "I met her when I had dinner at Nolan's house."

Barbara was already surrounded by more than a dozen mourners who'd all had the same idea as Peg. Rose was about to join the back of the group when she realized that Peg had changed her mind and veered off in another direction. *It figured.*

Once again, Rose hurried after her. Now Peg was approaching one of the women she'd been eyeing earlier. This one was at least a decade younger than Rose, with a toned physique that made her feel soft and flabby by comparison. She had no idea why Peg had singled her out.

When Rose came up beside the pair, they were already shaking hands and taking each other's measure.

"This is my sister-in-law, Rose Donovan," Peg said.

"Gina Malone." The woman nodded in Rose's direction. Apparently Rose didn't rate a handshake.

"I saw you glaring at Nolan's casket earlier," Peg said. Rose winced slightly. Peg wasn't one for subtlety.

"So what?" Gina said coolly. "Was Nolan a particular friend of yours?"

"Actually, he and I had only known each other a few weeks."

Gina smirked. "You were still in the honeymoon stage then."

"Pardon me?"

"Nolan was still on his best behavior, wasn't he?"

"Perhaps." Peg wasn't about to admit anything more personal to someone she'd just met. "He and I were just getting to know each other. It seemed as though we had quite a few things in common."

Gina laughed. "Look around," she invited. "See how diverse this group of women is?"

Rose and Peg both nodded.

"Every woman here would probably say the same thing you just did. That Nolan, he was a charmer all right. He had plenty in common with lots of women."

"It sounds as though you must have known him better than I did," Peg said.

"Better than most, not as well as some." Gina shrugged. "At least I caught on before I lost my shirt. That's figuratively speaking," she added with a wink, "because all my clothes came off on our first date."

"I think that's more than we needed to know." Rose was pretty sure she was blushing.

Gina's eyes swung her way. "What about you? Were you another one of Nolan's *friends*?"

"No," Rose replied quickly. "Of course not."

Gina appeared to find the double-denial amusing. "There's no 'of course not' about it. Nolan got around. And why wouldn't he? He was a handsome, virile man. You get to be a certain age and you realize that guys like that are pretty thin on the ground. It's no wonder he was popular."

"And yet it appears that your relationship with him didn't end well," Peg said.

"Not even close." Gina looked at Peg sharply. "Did yours?"

Peg gestured wordlessly toward the casket.

"Oh, right." Gina frowned. "Sorry."

"Clearly you were angry with Nolan," Rose said. "And you're implying that's true for other women as well. But most of the women here seem to be genuinely upset by his passing."

"Maybe they're delusional." Gina snorted. "Actually, I know some of them are. They think they're still in love with Nolan—and that given the chance, he'd have come back to them eventually. Now that's never going to happen. Women cry when you destroy their fantasies."

"That's pretty harsh," Rose said with a frown.

"That's me being realistic." Gina turned to Peg. "Trust me, you had a narrow escape."

"Excuse me," Peg said. She was looking at someone over Gina's shoulder. Apparently this conversation wasn't scintillating enough to hold her interest.

Peg was like a magpie, Rose thought. *Always flitting off in search of the next shiny object.*

Abruptly Peg walked away. Rose and Gina watched her leave, then turned back to each other.

"Sorry about that," Rose said. "Peg has a short attention span."

"Or maybe she just didn't want to hear the truth."

"No, I don't think that's it." Rose glanced in the direction Peg had gone. Now the contrary woman was striding toward a tree. What the heck was that about?

"Trust me, no woman who thinks she's in love wants to hear the truth."

"In love?" Rose gulped. "No, Peg and Nolan certainly weren't there yet."

"Then Nolan must have been off his game. Most women fell at his feet after the first couple dates. Ask anyone here. They'll all tell you the same story."

"How do you know so much about Nolan's life?" Rose asked curiously. "It doesn't seem as though the two of you were on good terms."

"We weren't," Gina replied. "At least, not recently. I run a summer camp for underprivileged kids in Norwalk—"

"You do?" Rose's face lit up. "How wonderful. My husband and I run a women's shelter in Stamford."

"Is that the Gallagher House?" Gina asked eagerly. "On Digby Avenue? I've heard about it. Actually I've been meaning to stop by. You and I should get together sometime and compare notes. I think there are aspects of our two programs that might complement each other nicely."

"I agree." Rose took out a business card and handed it over. "And please do come by. Whenever you want. I know Peter would be delighted to meet you."

Gina tucked the card away and gave Rose one of her own. "This has turned out to be a more productive afternoon than I anticipated."

"For me too," Rose said. "I'm glad we met, and I hope we have a chance to get together soon."

The crowd around the gravesite was thinning as mourners began to slip away. Nolan's sister still appeared to be busy, however, so Rose decided to go in search of Peg. As she drew near the mature tree where she'd last seen her, Peg stepped out from behind its broad trunk. A moment later, a man appeared on the other side. Dressed in jeans and a black sweatshirt, he had short dark hair and a stocky build. He aimed an irate glance at Peg, then went storming off.

Rose looked after him briefly, then turned back to Peg. "What did you do now?"

"Why do you always assume everything is my fault?"

"Because it usually is." Surely Rose didn't need to point that out. "Who was that man, and why were you talking to him?"

"I believe he was Nolan's son, Jason."

"Don't you *know*?"

"Not exactly."

"You were just having a conversation with him," Rose said. "How did that come about if you didn't know who he was?"

"Nolan told me about Jason. He lives in Chicago, but naturally I expected him to be here. I thought he might deliver the eulogy. Or at least accept condolences with his aunt, Barbara. But as you pointed out earlier, there were almost no men at the service—and none that were young enough to be Nolan's son."

Rose sighed. "You're telling me that you marched over here and accosted that man because he was young?"

"That's right," Peg said stubbornly. "I asked him if he was Jason, and he said yes. So who else could he be but Nolan's son?"

"You didn't think it was odd that he was hiding out over here, looking like someone who'd been hired to trim the trees?"

"Well, yes," Peg admitted. "And I intended to ask him about that. Except then we got off on the wrong foot."

Of course they had. No doubt it hadn't occurred to Peg that Jason had kept to the fringes of the ceremony precisely because he didn't want to talk to anybody.

"I invited him to come and join the rest of us," Peg said. "And he told me to go away and mind my own business."

That wouldn't have gone over well. Of all the people

Rose knew, the one least likely to mind her own business was Peg.

"Which you didn't do."

"Certainly not. He'd piqued my curiosity."

"Heaven forbid," Rose muttered.

Peg ignored that. "I told him I was a friend of his father and that Nolan had been very proud of him and his life in Chicago."

"Okay." That didn't sound like something that was likely to cause offense.

"Jason didn't say a thing." Peg sounded annoyed. And also baffled. "He just stared at me as though I was talking gibberish."

"Funerals are hard on everyone," Rose said. "And perhaps especially hard for him since his father had passed away under suspicious circumstances. For whatever reason, he'd decided to remove himself from the principal gathering and observe the service from afar. You might have taken that as a sign that he didn't want to be disturbed."

"I suppose you may be right," Peg conceded.

Rose reached over to loop her arm around Peg's. "I think we've done our bit. Are you ready to leave?"

"Not quite yet. I still haven't had a chance to speak to Barbara. Let's go do that now. It looks like just about everyone else has had their chance."

Rose's first impression of Barbara was that she didn't look anything like her brother. Barbara's complexion was milky white, while Nolan's skin had had an olive cast. Barbara's eyes were a striking shade of blue; Nolan's had been brown. Nolan had possessed a strong physique. Barbara looked like a china doll.

Maybe it was the tragic circumstance that gave Nolan's sister such an air of fragility, Rose reflected. She hoped Peg would treat the poor woman gently rather than blundering her way through this conversation too.

As the person currently speaking to Barbara moved away, Peg approached the woman with both arms outstretched. She clasped Barbara's hands in her own and said, "I am so very sorry for your loss."

"Thank you. That means a lot." The reply sounded automatic, as if it had been delivered numerous times before, which it probably had.

"I know we only met once, but Nolan always spoke very highly of you."

"Indeed?" Barbara pulled back, her hands slipping free from Peg's.

"I'm sure this must be hard for you . . ." Peg paused as if she thought Barbara might want to consider that she wasn't the only one who'd lost someone. Nolan's death had affected Peg too.

When Barbara didn't reply, Rose stepped in instead. "If there's anything we can do to help—"

"No, but thank you." Barbara barely glanced at Rose. "I'm fine. Now, if you don't mind . . . ?"

Barbara turned and walked away. She exited the other side of the small canopy and strode toward a dark car that was waiting by the edge of the road. As they watched, Barbara climbed in the back seat and shut the door.

"Is it just me," Peg said, "or was that awkward?"

"It was definitely awkward," Rose agreed. "But you know . . . funerals. Living in the convent all those years, I've probably been to more than my share. One thing I learned is that there's no right way or wrong way to do them. Everyone deals with grief differently. All you can do is try to be understanding."

Peg could see the truth in that. Maybe Barbara had fled because Peg's appearance had reminded her of happier times spent together with Nolan.

As for Peg, her fling with Nolan had been so very brief that it now seemed like little more than a wonderful fantasy—or an enticing dream that vanished when she awoke. Rose had called Nolan Prince Charming, but Peg knew she was no fairy-tale princess. Clearly there'd been problems with their relationship—and a dark side to Nolan that Peg had never even suspected.

Now he was dead, the victim of a highly suspicious "accident." Detective Sturgill would say that wasn't Peg's problem, but she didn't agree. Nolan had inserted himself into her life for purposes of his own—purposes she still didn't entirely understand.

Several days had passed since Peg had been floored by the shock of Nolan's death. In that time, she'd regained her equilibrium. Peg no longer thought of Nolan Abercrombie as a man for whom she'd briefly had feelings.

Now he'd become an enigma that needed to be solved.

Chapter 11

Saturday's dog show was in northern New Jersey. The drive would take ninety minutes, first across the Tappan Zee Bridge, then south on the Palisades Parkway. Peg had to get up at the crack of dawn to get her Poodles fed and exercised before she needed to leave. She was due in her ring to judge her first breed at eight a.m. sharp.

Peg was a stickler for punctuality. Hired to judge numerous breeds and planning to spend most of the day on her feet, she intended to adhere to her judging schedule with precision that a Swiss watch would envy. Many of the exhibitors showing under her today would have also done so previously. It was no secret she kept a speedy ring; everyone would adjust their pace to keep up.

The grass was still wet when Peg walked across the showground to the row of rings just across the field. It was a good thing she'd worn sturdy sneakers. Damp now, they'd be dry within the hour. By that time, Peg would have taken off her light sweater and hung it over the back of her chair. An hour after that, she would don her sun hat. Peg was an old hand at this. She knew what to expect and how to prepare for most contingencies.

Dog shows were her passion and her life's work. They were the reason she'd been able to carry on in the terrible months after Max's death. Thankfully, that time in her life was well past. Now, the prospect of spending a late summer day enjoying the privilege of being able to put her hands on beautifully trained and turned out dogs produced only a heady sense of anticipation. After the tumultuous week she'd had, it would be a relief to simply settle down and go back to work.

Peg's ring was empty when she arrived. That was unusual. On most show days, the ring steward would already be in place, setting up the judge's table, checking in early exhibitors, and making sure the ring was ready for use. Once the show started, Peg would be busy judging dogs, and her ring steward would be the person tasked with ensuring that everything else ran smoothly.

Stewards were assigned to each ring by the kennel club sponsoring the show. Peg had been a fixture in the dog world for so many years that it wasn't unusual for her steward to be a friend or acquaintance. Often the person was a fellow breeder. It had been years, perhaps decades, since she'd been paired with a steward who wasn't skilled at the job. Until, perhaps, today.

No matter. Peg went to work setting things up herself. There wasn't much to be done, especially since the bag containing the judge's book, the colored class ribbons, and the exhibitors' armbands had yet to arrive. Presumably it was in the hands of the missing ring steward.

Peg glanced at her watch. It was seven forty-five. She sat down on the chair beside her empty table and scanned the surrounding rings. All appeared to be in order everywhere else.

A steward in the neighboring ring, busy setting up his table, cast a nervous glance in Peg's direction. Peg raised a brow. The man stopped what he was doing and walked over to the low, slatted barrier that separated their rings.

"I believe Ruth Bixby was supposed to be stewarding for you today," he said.

"Ruth?" Peg smiled. "That will be lovely. As soon as she arrives, we'll have things put to rights in no time."

"Except . . . she's not coming," the man continued. He swallowed heavily. "She called in sick."

"Nothing serious, I hope."

He shrugged. "It was very last-minute. She said she'd send a replacement so we didn't have to scramble to find someone else on such short notice."

"I see," Peg said. "Another club member?"

"Maybe." Now he bit his lip. The poor man looked as though he'd rather be anywhere else other than standing there explaining to Peg why her ring wasn't ready and her steward was AWOL.

"I see," Peg said again. She didn't really, but a comment seemed to be called for. She gave her schedule a mental toss out the window. It was beginning to look as though today was going to be one of those days.

"Mrs. Trumbull?" an eager voice asked.

Peg turned toward the in-gate, where her first breed's exhibitors were already beginning to assemble.

A young lady who barely looked past high school age was standing outside the ring. Smiling tentatively, she clutched the missing bag of supplies to her chest. A long pink ponytail was slung forward over her shoulder and her eyes were wide as saucers.

"*Turn*bull," Peg corrected, standing up. "Peg Turnbull. But you can call me Peg. And you are?"

"Maddy Bixby. I'm Ruth Bixby's niece."

Peg pondered that for a moment, then she pushed up the sleeves of her sweater. "Well, Maddy, it looks as though you and I are going to be working together today. Have you ever served as a ring steward before?"

"No, ma'am." Maddy hurried over to the table and dropped the heavy bag on top of it. The bag landed with a thud. "Aunt Ruth told me you'd be able to show me everything I need to know."

Of course Peg could do that. She was quite proficient at stewarding herself. If only Maddy had arrived half an hour earlier, Peg would have gladly taken her in hand. Now, however, Peg was supposed to be judging dogs, starting in approximately five minutes and continuing throughout the remainder of the day.

Oh well. There was nothing she could do about that now.

Peg upended the bag and began to sort through its contents. Maddy spied the steward's badge. She snatched it up and pinned it to the front of her shirt. At least that was one less thing for Peg to do.

"We're already running late," she said as she stuffed the colored ribbons into their slots. "Let's get started, shall we?"

It wasn't the most auspicious beginning to the day. But by midmorning, Peg and Maddy had settled into a rhythm that was, if not precisely steady, at least workable. The steward next door showed Maddy how to decipher the breed schedules and distribute the numbered armbands for each upcoming class. Fortunately Maddy was able to recognize most of the non-sporting breeds Peg would be judging.

Peg supposed that was something.

Just before the lunch break, the Standard Poodle entry was called to the ring. Peg flexed her fingers happily as the first class, Puppy Dogs, filed through the in-gate. Peg had drawn a large entry, and there were majors available in both sexes. That meant Peg would have the opportunity to put her hands on numerous delightful Standard Poodles, starting immediately with the three black puppies in front of her.

Peg awarded Winner Dog and the coveted championship points that came with it to a handsome Poodle presented in the ring by a professional handler whom she'd known for years. In strict adherence to the rules, neither of them acknowledged the other during the judging, despite the fact that their friendship was well known to all.

There was always the possibility that a disgruntled exhibitor would cry foul when Peg put up a friend for the win. But what else was she to do? At this point in her life, she knew *everyone* in the Poodle world. Plus, Crawford Langley not only understood exactly what she wanted to see in a Poodle, he had the good sense to consistently bring it to her. That was the reason he often won under Peg—and other judges as well. Preferential treatment had nothing to do with it.

Next it was the Standard Poodle bitches' turn. Peg whipped through her Puppy and Bred-by-Exhibitor classes handily. The bitches she'd seen thus far were slightly underwhelming. Hopefully her Open class would provide her with an entry worthy of the day's major points.

There were five bitches in the class. Peg's eye immediately went to a dainty, typey silver Poodle standing in the middle of the line. On the first circuit around the ring, Peg was delighted to see that the bitch moved as well as she looked. Now she was itching to get her hands on her. Perhaps, after Peg had awarded her the points, she would take the silver bitch all the way to Best of Variety. That would be satisfying.

When the silver was brought forward for her individual examination, Peg paused to appreciate the bitch's square outline and gorgeous head. Then she stepped in front of the Poodle and said to her handler, "Show me her bite, please."

Dog show judges have a choice when it comes to checking out a dog's teeth and bite. They can either open the dog's mouth themselves or they can request that the handler do it for them. Peg generally preferred the latter method. Putting the responsibility on the handler, however, meant that she might not be shown what she wanted to see.

The silver bitch's handler reached forward with both hands. He used his right hand to cup the Poodle's jaw and his left one to quickly lift her lips. They'd barely risen before he dropped them back into place. He also managed to make sure that his fingers blocked much of Peg's view.

Peg frowned. She'd only been given a momentary glimpse of the Poodle's mouth. No doubt that was the handler's intention—which definitely didn't bode well. Even with that brief look, Peg thought she'd seen at least one missing tooth, and perhaps a level bite.

Now she was faced with a dilemma. She loved everything else about this silver bitch—and her handler clearly knew that. Peg wanted this Standard Poodle to win today, and so did he. So by performing his task badly, he was merely helping the process along. After all, Peg could hardly penalize what she couldn't see. The bitch's handler was offering her a choice. She could ask again to see the bite. Or she could step back and continue with the rest of her examination. No one would be the wiser.

Except that Peg would know. Dammit.

Peg lifted her gaze. She stared at the young handler, who was waiting to see what she was going to do. He was relatively new on the dog show circuit. He'd only shown to Peg a handful of times. Otherwise, he'd have already known how this was going to go.

Peg lifted a brow. She nodded toward the very pretty Poodle's mouth. "Once again, please. Maybe a little more slowly this time?"

The handler had no choice but to comply. He showed Peg what she needed to see and none of it was good news. On an otherwise lovely specimen she could forgive one missing incisor, or perhaps make a special exception for two. But the silver bitch's bite was off as well. It wasn't just level, it was slightly undershot.

Peg sighed. She knew what she had to do, but she wouldn't enjoy doing it. The pretty bitch placed third in her class of five. Despite her faults, her overall quality still managed to trump the merits of the two Poodles who placed below her.

Her handler accepted his yellow ribbon with good grace. "You know I'll be able to finish her championship anyway," he told her.

"I'm sure you will," Peg agreed. The silver was a truly lovely Poodle. "But not under me."

The next twenty minutes were spent in a flurry of activity. Peg wrapped up the Standard Poodle judging by awarding Best of Variety to the current top-winning special. Then the morning's win pictures were taken by the show photographer. After that, it was finally time for lunch.

Peg reminded Maddy twice that the young woman was due back at their ring at twelve forty-five *sharp*. Then she struck out for the hospitality tent where the judges' lunch was being served. It had been an unexpectedly taxing morning, and she was happy for the respite.

Even after the decision was already made, Peg couldn't help but wonder whether it would have been better to close her eyes and put the silver bitch at the head of the line. It would have meant setting aside a scruple or two. But was that the worst thing?

At her age, Peg sometimes felt she was one of few remaining judges who believed that a breed standard was the bible for its breed—a blueprint for perfection that was meant to be adhered to. She couldn't help but notice that many of the newer, younger judges were more lenient than she was, often bypassing tough black-and-white decisions in favor of the gray areas around them.

The pretty silver Poodle was a conundrum. Peg knew her handler had been correct. She would finish her championship handily under other, easier judges. So had Peg gained anything by turning her away? More importantly, would she feel better or worse right now if she had given the bitch major points? It was a question she didn't feel inclined to answer.

Peg set those thoughts aside as she slipped beneath the overhang and entered the tent. A lunch display offered prepackaged sandwiches and salads, along with a selection of drinks. Two long tables, lined with chairs, were set up in the center of the tent. More than half the seats were already occupied. Peg made her selections quickly: a turkey sandwich, a bag of chips, and a bottle of cold water. Then she made her way to the end of the nearest table and sat down.

She'd just finished unwrapping her sandwich when another judge came over, plopped her food down on the table, and sat down across from her. Peg had known Izzy Hicks for an elephant's age. At one time, she and Izzy had competed with each other in the groups: Izzy's Bulldogs against Peg's Poodles. Now they judged at many of the same shows. Izzy was a few years older than Peg. Having slipped and fallen the previous winter, Izzy currently walked with a cane. But her eye for a good dog was just as sharp as ever, and the speed with which she could sort out and correctly place a class rivaled Peg's.

Izzy leaned her cane against the table, then lowered herself slowly into her chair. "These old bones will be the death of me," she grumbled.

"You've been saying that for years," Peg replied around a mouthful of turkey. "Nobody takes you seriously anymore. Wait and see. You'll probably come and dance on my grave."

"I doubt that." Izzy grinned. "Unless the handler of that silver bitch you dumped in your Open class comes after you with a cleaver."

"You heard about that?"

Izzy nodded.

"That was fast. It only happened half an hour ago."

"It's a dog show, Peg." Izzy popped the plastic top off her salad. "Everybody knows everyone else's business. Otherwise, what's the point of being here?"

"Fair competition between conscientious breeders, all of whom are aiming to produce the best representative of their breed?"

"In your dreams." Izzy laughed.

"Why, Izzy," Peg said, "it sounds as though you're becoming a cynic."

"Damn straight." She poked around the plastic bowl and came up with a soggy tomato wedge. "And it's probably about time. So what was the matter with that oh-so-pretty bitch? It had to be something."

"Two missing incisors and undershot." Peg polished off her sandwich and reached for her chips.

"Sheesh. Back in our day, no one would have dared to take a Standard Poodle with those problems into the ring."

"At least not until after a trip to the dentist," Peg muttered.

Izzy put down her fork and looked at Peg across the tabletop. "I need to ask you something."

"Shoot."

"I saw you last week at the Lake Mohegan show. I had the whole Herding Group. You must have walked past my ring three or four times, so of course I wondered why you were wandering around like that. Then I saw who was with you."

"That was my sister-in-law, Rose," Peg said.

"Not her. The other one. Nolan Abercrombie."

Peg had been lifting a potato chip to her mouth. Now her hand stilled. Then she put the chip back down. "You know him?"

"In a manner of speaking. Though I haven't seen him in

years. At least four or five. Did you meet Nolan through Charlie Vargas?"

"Umm . . . no." Peg wasn't being cagey. At dog shows, even the tent posts had ears. She had no intention of bringing up her connection with Mature Mingle here, where the word would inevitably get out.

"I'm only asking because that's how I met him. Charlie had brought Nolan to a show. I have no idea why because the guy didn't look particularly interested in the proceedings. But when I won Best in Show with Bullet—you remember him?"

"Of course," Peg replied. "He was the top winning Bulldog of his day."

"Right. After Nolan saw that, apparently he asked for an introduction and Charlie obliged. I have to say I was flattered."

"I can imagine. Nolan was a very handsome man."

"Handsome? He was damn near magnetic."

"Were the two of you . . . involved?" Peg went back to eating her chips.

"For a short time." Izzy rolled her eyes. "That was about how long it took Nolan to figure out that people who show dogs don't make a lot of money doing so—even when they win Best in Show."

"Oh," said Peg.

"Oh, indeed." Izzy finished her salad. She began to gather up her trash. Other judges around them were checking their watches and pushing back their chairs. "Anyway, I was surprised to see him last week. And especially surprised that he was there with you, whom I've always credited with impeccable taste." She cackled out a laugh at that. "So I just thought I'd issue a small warning. I know you're no fool, Peg, but just be careful. Nolan isn't necessarily what he appears to be."

"Thank you for that." Peg rose from her seat. She

picked up both her garbage and Izzy's, leaving her friend's hands free to deal with her cane. "But I'm afraid you're a little late."

"Really? That's too bad."

"Nolan won't be charming any more women," Peg told her. "Someone ran over him with a car."

Izzy didn't appear unduly upset by the news. "Probably a woman," she said.

Chapter 12

On Sunday afternoon, Rose and Peg met up at a Starbucks in Greenwich. Peg ordered a chai tea latte and a piece of cinnamon coffee cake. Rose spent ten minutes reading the entire menu, then asked for black coffee.

Judging by the long-suffering look on Peg's face, she was embarrassed to be seen with Rose. Or at least with Rose's order. Not that Rose could help that. Memories of the impoverished village in Honduras where she and Peter had spent time were still fresh in her mind. Even months later, she sometimes felt overwhelmed by the abundance that Americans took for granted.

Peg was still looking peeved when they sat down at a quiet table near the rear of the room. Once, Rose would have ignored that. Or felt that she was the one in the wrong. Not anymore.

"What?" she asked, sliding into a chair across from Peg.

"You know this place is famous for their coffee, right?"

"That's why I ordered it. Look, I even got the big size."

"Tall," Peg corrected.

"Whatever it's called, I'll probably be up all night." Rose was ready to change the subject. "How was your dog show?"

"Interesting."

Rose doubted that. She couldn't imagine devoting a

whole day to sorting through a bunch of dogs, most of whom looked exactly alike. And yet, Peg managed to make a living doing just that. It boggled the mind.

"Nolan's name came up."

"Oh?" Now *that* was interesting. "In what context?"

"I don't believe you've met my friend Izzy Hicks."

Rose shook her head. For obvious reasons, she'd barely met any of Peg's dog show friends.

"Apparently, she was another one of Nolan's *particular* friends, to borrow a term from that disgruntled woman at the funeral."

"Gina Malone," Rose supplied her name in case Peg had forgotten. "She gave me her card. She runs a summer camp for underprivileged children. Isn't that great?"

"Sure." Peg sounded as though her thoughts were somewhere else entirely. She broke off a piece of coffee cake with her fingers, then popped it in her mouth. "Izzy saw us with Nolan at the dog show last week. She warned me against getting involved with him."

"As did Gina," Rose said.

She eyed Peg's cake with a twinge of envy. Was it possible that repeated exposure to Peg's eating habits was causing her to develop a sweet tooth? Rose certainly hoped not.

"Which is a moot point, because now nobody is getting involved with him," Peg said.

She gave her plate a small nudge in Rose's direction. Rose was pretty sure that was an invitation to help herself, so she did. There wasn't any cutlery, so Rose used her fingers too.

The nuns would have been horrified. Peg didn't even seem to notice.

Instead she said, "So what are we going to do about that?"

Rose assumed "that" referred to Nolan's murder. "I was wondering how long it would take you to get around to asking. Because it seems to me that we ought to do *something*. I didn't particularly like the man, but he didn't deserve what happened to him."

"No, he didn't," Peg agreed. "Despite what people are saying about him now."

"Do you think Gina was right? Was Nolan only courting you to earn your trust so he could take advantage of you?"

"It's beginning to look that way. Izzy told me he was only interested in her for her money."

Rose nodded unhappily. "Gina wasn't quite that blunt, but she implied the same thing."

"I'm not rich," Peg said.

Rose considered that as she helped herself to another small piece of the coffee cake. Considering some of the things she'd seen, rich was a relative term. Still, she understood what Peg meant.

"Nevertheless, you might appear rich to someone who checked you out online."

"Why would someone do that?" Peg sounded outraged. "I'm a private person, living a private life. And besides, I doubt there'd be anything to see."

"No website for Cedar Crest Kennel?"

"No. I've never needed one. Everyone who's interested in my Poodles knows where to reach me."

"You must be listed somewhere as a dog show judge."

"Yes, but—"

"And since you own your house, you pay Greenwich real estate taxes."

Peg nodded grudgingly.

"College alumnae association?"

She nodded again.

"You see where I'm going with this?" Rose asked.

"I suppose I do." Peg picked up the remaining piece of coffee cake and shoved it in her mouth.

"Plus," Rose added, "now there's your profile on Mature Mingle. Someone who knows their way around the internet could easily discover your age, your marital status, your hobbies, your address, and much, much more. You're a woman in your seventies with a penchant for Poodles, living by yourself on a piece of property that's no doubt worth a bundle. That's probably enough to make you seem vulnerable."

Peg was growing more uncomfortable by the moment. "Anyone who knows me could tell you that's not true," she snapped.

"But that's the whole point, isn't it? Nolan didn't know you, at least not when he initially chose to target you."

Peg sighed. "There's something I haven't told you."

Rose stared across the table. "Please don't tell me you gave that man money. Or worse, access to any of your accounts."

"I'm not that stupid," Peg retorted.

"No," Rose allowed, "but you were infatuated . . . at least for a little while."

"Longer than I should have been apparently," Peg grumbled. "But the subject of my finances did come up. It was the night I had dinner at Nolan's house. Barbara talked about a tech start-up that Nolan had recently invested in. She implied that he was already seeing significant returns. I got the definite impression that I was meant to praise Nolan's financial acumen and inquire about the possibility of investing too."

"Which you didn't do."

"Certainly not. I merely nodded and kept eating. When they'd finished their discussion, I changed the subject, and Barbara and Nolan seemed happy enough to follow my lead. To be honest, I hadn't given the conversation another thought until just now."

"Nolan was probably just trying to plant the seed in your mind," Rose mused. "He must have thought there'd be plenty of other opportunities to reel you in."

"That's a terribly mixed metaphor," Peg pointed out. "But I get the gist of what you're trying to say."

"So Nolan was most likely a con artist. And if you hadn't had your wits about you, you might have become another of his victims. What Gina said at the funeral is true. You probably had a narrow escape."

"When did she say that?"

"Just before you rushed off to corner Nolan's son." Rose stood up. "I'll be right back."

She returned to the table five minutes later and set a small plate down in the middle between them. Peg peered at it. "What's that?"

"A lemon bar." Rose handed Peg a fork. "And this time I want my fair share."

"It's not very big." Peg sectioned off a wedge. "So you'd better eat fast." She chewed, then swallowed. "You're the only person I know who gets something tart when they want something sweet."

"Be glad I didn't buy a granola bar," Rose said. "Let's get back to your earlier question. What are we going to do about Nolan?"

"I thought we'd already settled that. Nolan's murder feels personal to me. How can it not? I intend to get to the bottom of it." Peg looked up from the plate. "I assume you'll join me?"

"Of course." Rose thought they'd already settled that too. "Since you haven't brought it up, I feel obliged to point out that Detective Sturgill won't be happy about our involvement."

Peg shrugged. "What Rodney doesn't know can hardly bother him."

"He was at Nolan's funeral service, skulking around in the background and observing everything that went on. Did you notice?"

"I did not." Peg was annoyed. She hated missing out on anything.

"Probably because you were too busy running around bothering everyone else."

"Of course I was trying to talk to people. You were the one who pointed out the attendees' demographic. It occurred to me that we might be in the midst of a gathering of potential suspects."

"Gina said something about every woman at the funeral having essentially the same story to tell about Nolan," Rose mused. "Do you suppose she knew many of the women that were there? And if so, how?"

"Good questions." Peg eyed the last bite of the lemon bar. "You should ask her. You should also find out more details about her relationship with Nolan. Because clearly she's still holding a grudge."

Rose reached over and used her fork to divide the last small piece in half. Then she snagged hers before Peg could grab them both. "While I'm doing that, what will you be up to?"

"I'm curious about who Nolan Abercrombie actually was," Peg replied. "I find myself wondering if he was putting on an act the entire time he and I were together. It's possible that I never got to know—or even catch a glimpse of—the real man behind the façade."

Rose nodded thoughtfully.

"I'll start by visiting Nolan's house to see if Barbara is still in town. Maybe Jason will be staying there too and I can kill two birds with one stone."

Peg had finished her tea. Rose's coffee cup was still half-full, even though it felt as though she'd already drunk more than enough. Now that they'd mapped out the beginnings of a plan, Peg would probably want to go rushing off somewhere else. She never seemed to sit still for long. Rose hated the idea of wasting the rest of her coffee, but she didn't want to chug it down either.

Instead of standing up to leave, however, Peg said, "Do you think it's a good idea for Kevin to have a cell phone?"

"Excuse me?" Rose blinked.

"Kevin, Melanie's son, wants his own phone. She asked me about it last week, and I've been so busy that I never managed to get back to her. Melanie wanted me to convince Sam it was a bad idea."

"*You?*" Rose snorted.

"I know. As if I need to be in the middle of that."

"And Sam was in favor of Kevin having one?"

"Mostly," Peg said. "Or at least he wasn't opposed."

"Kevin will be starting first grade, so he's what . . . six?"

"I guess so."

"Who do you suppose a child that age would call?"

"Another six-year-old?" Peg ventured. She had no idea. "Maybe he wants it to play games. Apparently, his classmates all have phones, and he feels left out."

"Peer pressure can be very persuasive," Rose said. "Nevertheless, I think Melanie should hold firm. Six is too young. No matter how many of his overprivileged friends have parents who feel differently."

"Good answer," Peg replied. "Then you'll talk to Sam?"

"No way. That's your job."

"Yes, but you and I are going to be working together. So it only makes sense to divide our responsibilities."

"I see." Rose most certainly did. "So your idea of working together is you off-loading your problems onto me?"

"Not all of them." Peg looked affronted. She pushed back her chair and started to rise. "Certainly none that have anything to do with Poodles, or even dogs in general."

Rose considered that. Then she brightened. "Since we're sharing responsibilities, there's a woman I'd like you to meet. Her name is Mabel Mayberry, and she lives near the shelter. She's in her eighties and is a little vague about life in general. She's let things slide around her house, and there's also a possibility of elder abuse."

Abruptly, Peg sat back down. "I'm sure you and Peter have put a stop to *that*."

"Not just yet. For now, we're mostly keeping an eye on things. We want to be sure about what's going on before we act."

"Precisely what do you expect me to do?" Peg asked.

This time, it was Rose who stood up. "I expect you to deal with your own problems," she said. "Just as I intend to deal with mine."

Rose smiled as she exited the coffee shop. It was nice for Peg to be the one who was left with her mouth hanging open for a change.

Chapter 13

Nolan's house was part of a small neighborhood sandwiched between the Ox Ridge Hunt Club and Wee Burn Country Club. Now that she was arriving in daylight, Peg saw there were fewer than a dozen homes on the narrow lane. All were colonial in style and painted in muted colors with contrasting trim. Each was surrounded by at least an acre of beautifully tended lawn.

As she'd done on her previous visit, Peg parked her minivan in front of the detached garage. Both garage doors were closed. The house was quiet as well. Peg couldn't help but contrast that silence with the boisterous greeting received by visitors to her home.

Even though there were no dogs in residence, it was still a charming property, Peg decided. She wondered who had inherited the house upon Nolan's death. Since Barbara and Jason both lived elsewhere, she supposed it might be put up for sale.

Peg walked around to the front door and rang the bell. Muffled chimes sounded within the home, but no one answered the door. After a minute, she rang again. Still nothing happened. Peg was regretting that she hadn't asked for Barbara's phone number at the funeral when a voice came from behind her.

"Nobody's home," a man said. "I saw Ms. Weatherly leave about an hour ago, and she hasn't come back."

A low stone wall separated Nolan's property from the one next door. The man was standing beside a small shed on the neighboring lawn, holding a rake. He was in his early forties, dressed in work clothes, and about a week past his last shave. The grass at the man's feet looked pristine. Peg couldn't imagine what he needed the rake for.

"Excuse me?" she said.

"You're looking for Barbara Weatherly?"

"I am," Peg confirmed, delighted to discover Barbara's last name. "I was hoping to catch her before she left town."

"I wasn't aware she was going away." The man set down the rake and stepped over to the other side of the wall. "I'm Ben Larson. My wife and I have lived here two years, and I haven't seen you before. Are you a friend of Barbara's?"

Good for Barbara, Peg thought. She had a suspicious neighbor. When it came to home security, that was almost as useful as a houseful of dogs.

"My name is Peg Turnbull," she said. "Barbara and I met recently through her brother, Nolan."

Ben Larson shook his head. "I haven't met Nolan. Actually, I didn't even know she had a brother." His gaze narrowed. "It's interesting you should say that she's planning to leave town because when Barbara takes a trip she usually asks me to keep an eye on things for her."

For one of very few times in her life, Peg found herself at a loss for words.

"So now I find myself wondering why you're really here." Ben looked her over carefully as if he thought he might have to give her description to the police later. "Are you selling something?"

"No, of course not—"

"You don't look like a Jehovah's Witness."

Peg nearly laughed at that—except there was nothing funny about the fact that the conversation suddenly seemed to be spiraling out of her control.

"You should be aware that every house on this road is hooked up to an alarm system. It may feel like we're in the country, but the response time from the police station is under six minutes."

"Wait. Please." Peg held up a hand to stem the flow of words. "Clearly there's been a misunderstanding. Can we start over?"

Ben nodded grudgingly.

"What did you mean a minute ago when you said you watched the house for Barbara when she left town?"

"I think my meaning was clear." Ben crossed his arms over his chest. "She does the same for my wife and me when we're gone. Do you have a problem with that?"

"No," Peg replied. "Except that I thought this house belonged to Nolan Abercrombie."

"Who's he?"

Peg felt a sinking feeling in the pit of her stomach. "Barbara's brother."

"Never heard of him."

"And you say you've lived next door to this house for some time?"

"That's right."

"I was just here last week." Peg was sadly aware that she was beginning to sound desperate. "I had dinner with Nolan and Barbara. Nolan said this was his house and that his sister was visiting him from out of town."

Ben peered at her closely. After a pause, he said, "Are you sure you have the right address? Lots of these small lanes around here look alike. Maybe you should be somewhere else entirely."

Peg was beginning to agree with that sentiment. Still, she had no choice but to press on.

"I may be an older woman," she said sternly, "but I am not confused about where I am. Or where I visited last week. I was here." She turned and pointed. "In that house."

Ben lifted his hands, a gesture of capitulation. He began to back away. "If you say so."

"Before you go, please do one last thing," Peg said. "Describe Barbara Weatherly for me."

Ben didn't have to stop and think. "Nope. That's not happening."

"Then let's do this. I'll describe her for you. Will you at least tell me if we're talking about the same person?"

"I guess I can do that," he allowed.

"Tall, blond, attractive . . . mature." Peg paused, then added, "Sultry voice."

Unexpectedly that last part made Ben smile. "Yeah, that's her. What did you say your connection was again?"

"I was dating her brother."

"Oh, right. The guy I never heard of."

Peg sighed. "Nolan told me this was his house and that Barbara was a visitor." She wondered if she was beginning to sound like a broken record.

"That can't be right," Ben said. "It's Barbara's house, and she lives there. That's how it's been since we moved in. It sounds like that Nolan guy was feeding you a line."

"It does, doesn't it," Peg said flatly. She felt like sighing again, not that it would help. "I don't understand, though. Why would Barbara go along with the ruse?"

Ben shrugged. Obviously, the situation made no more sense to him than it did to Peg.

Behind him, the door to his house opened. The sound of a crying baby could be heard from within. A woman stuck her head out and called, "Ben! Your turn."

"Sorry, gotta go," he said. "I'm supposed to be working

from home, but our newborn's colicky and I couldn't get anything done, so I came outside. Now my break's over. I hope you get things figured out."

"Thank you," Peg said. "Have you tried taking the baby for a ride in the car? I've heard that helps."

Already on his way to the house, Ben paused and glanced back. "In the car? Sure, why not? At this point, I'm willing to try anything."

Melanie lived in North Stamford, a location that suited Peg's purposes perfectly at the moment, since it only required a small detour to stop there on her way home. With her husband, two children, and six dogs in residence, things were often chaotic at Melanie's house. Peg didn't mind that in the slightest. Especially since she often showed up unannounced and added to the chaos herself.

As Peg got out of her minivan in the driveway, she could hear screams of laughter coming from the backyard. She bypassed the house and walked directly to the gate leading to the spacious yard. Since the last time she'd visited, someone—presumably, Sam—had hung a tire swing from a branch of the large oak tree that also held Davey's treehouse. Kevin was sitting on top of the tire, with his legs dangling through the opening and his small hands wrapped around the sturdy rope that attached the tire to the branch above it.

Fifteen-year-old Davey was standing behind his brother, shoving the swing higher and higher. To add to the excitement, the family's two male Standard Poodles, Tar and Augie, were running around the tree, barking like a pair of nitwits. Kevin's dog, a small, spotted mutt named Bud, was on the ground beneath the swing. Each time the bottom of the tire passed above his head, Bud leaped up and tried to grab it with his teeth.

Watching the small dog bounce off the rubber tire, flip

to one side, and still somehow manage to land on his feet, Peg could only marvel that Bud hadn't yet knocked himself silly. None of what was happening looked safe to her. Then again, she'd never had children of her own, so what did she know?

When Peg let herself into the yard, the two big black Poodles came running over to say hello. Tar and Augie were father and son; both were finished champions. Tar was also a group and Best in Show winner. It was a good thing he was handsome, because Tar was the only dumb Poodle Peg had ever met. She ruffled her hands through both their topknots, then allowed the dogs to escort her to the back door of the house, which was standing open.

Three more black Standard Poodles were asleep on the kitchen floor. Lying side by side were Melanie's older bitch, Faith, and her daughter, Eve. Plum, litter sister to Peg's Joker, was reclining on the other side of the table. All three heads popped up when Peg let herself inside. Immediately their tails began to wag. Peg stooped down low to gather the trio into her arms for a hug.

Sam came walking into the kitchen as Peg rose to her feet. The man was just as good-looking now as he'd been when they'd first met many years earlier. His light blond hair had darkened to a shade of molten gold, and there were new creases bracketing his smile, but Sam's appeal was still undeniable. Peg had needed to throw Sam and Melanie together several times before they'd finally figured out that they were meant for each other. Now they'd been happily married for eight years.

"Hello, Peg." Sam leaned down and kissed her cheek. "I didn't know you'd be stopping by today."

"I didn't know either," she said. "But I was in the vicinity and it seemed like a good idea. Are you aware that your children appear to be risking life and limb in the backyard?"

"Kev's on the swing, isn't he?" Melanie frowned as she entered the kitchen. "I was afraid that might be a problem."

"I showed them how to use it carefully," Sam said.

Peg slanted him a look. "Perhaps they weren't listening during your tutorial."

Sam headed for the door. "I'll go have a look."

Peg thought Melanie might go too, but she remained behind. A small smile played around her lips as she watched Sam hop off the deck and approach the boys. Then she realized Peg was staring at her.

"What?" Melanie pulled out a chair at the table and sat down. "I'm not going out there. I'm always the one who has to be the bad guy and spoil everybody's fun. Let Sam take the blame for once."

Peg sat down opposite her. There was a bowl of fruit in the center of the table. "Apple?" Melanie offered.

Peg glanced dismissively at the assortment of fruit. "I always give you cake."

"Cake doesn't last ten minutes in this house," Melanie said with a laugh. "Why do you think I eat so much of it at your place? There are Oreos in the pantry. Will they do?"

"I suppose."

The three Poodles followed Melanie to the pantry. She handed out dog biscuits before returning to the table with the bag of cookies. Melanie pushed the fruit bowl to one side and set the Oreos down between them. They both helped themselves.

Melanie twisted her sandwich cookie apart and ate the cream in the middle first. Peg was too impatient for that. She popped the whole Oreo in her mouth at once. She was already eating her second cookie by the time Melanie had finished with her first.

"If you've come to talk to Sam about Kevin's cell phone, you're too late," Melanie said.

"Oh?" Peg asked with interest. "What happened?"

"I lost the battle." She grinned. "And then I won the war."

"It sounds as though I should congratulate you," Peg mused. "But I think I need more details first."

"Sam got Kevin a phone, but he'd only had it a day before he managed to lose it."

"A not entirely unexpected outcome."

Melanie nodded. "When Kevin left his phone somewhere accessible, Bud picked it up, took it outside, and buried it under a rock. By the time Sam found the phone, its screen was cracked in two places, and there were teeth marks all over the case."

Peg was quite certain there were holes in that story large enough to drive a truck through. "Considering how badly Kevin wanted a phone, it's surprising he'd have been so careless with it," she mentioned. "Especially so soon after he'd gotten it."

She paused for Melanie to comment. That didn't happen. Melanie merely arranged her features into a bland expression and ate another Oreo.

"Did he actually leave his phone where Bud could reach it, or did your little pack rat have some help?"

"Aunt Peg, you have a devious mind."

"Of course I do. Unless I'm mistaken, it's one of the things you like best about me."

"Let me put it this way," said Melanie. "I might have noticed the phone was on the floor next to Kevin's train set, and decided not to pick it up and put it somewhere safer. But Sam and I had previously had a conversation about whether or not Kev was old enough to be able to take responsibility for something that valuable. I said he wasn't. Sam said it would be a good learning experience."

Melanie tipped her head to one side. "And it was. Just not in the way that Sam expected."

Peg reached for another Oreo. "I thought parents were

supposed to display a united front in front of their children."

"Not when one of them is wrong," Melanie said firmly.

On that note, Peg decided it was time for a change of subject. "Remember when you saw my profile on the dating site?"

"How could I forget?" Melanie chuckled. "Mature Mingle. I looked it up. How's it working out for you?"

Of course she'd looked it up, Peg thought. Melanie was every bit as nosy as Peg was herself. "Not perfectly. There's been a small wrinkle."

The back door was still open so the Poodles could come and go. Melanie glanced outside. Sam and the boys were in the middle of the yard near the oak tree. Well beyond earshot.

"Tell me all about it," she said.

"I met someone—"

Melanie squealed out loud. "I want to hear everything!"

"You'll have to let me speak for that to happen."

Melanie stuffed another cookie in her mouth, then mimed zipping her lips.

"His name was Nolan Abercrombie. And in the beginning, he and I got along beautifully."

Melanie began to hum the wedding march. Peg kicked her under the table. Melanie jumped in her seat and Faith hopped up to see what was wrong. Now Peg had two pairs of eyes staring at her. That didn't help.

"Perhaps I should just skip ahead to the end," she said. "Nolan's dead."

Melanie gasped. Too late, it occurred to Peg that she probably should have softened the delivery of that news.

"How awful for you," Melanie said. "I'm so sorry."

"Don't be," Peg replied. "I'm over it."

"That was quick." Melanie didn't sound convinced.

She pushed the bag of Oreos over to Peg's side of the table. Never one to refuse an invitation to something sweet, Peg helped herself to two cookies, one for each hand.

"It turns out that Nolan wasn't who he appeared to be. Apparently he was a con man who scammed vulnerable women whom he'd met online."

"Son of a bitch," said Melanie.

Since she and Peg were both dog people, the retort wasn't the pejorative it might have been. Nevertheless Peg appreciated the sentiment.

"Indeed," she agreed.

"How did he die?"

"In a hit-and-run accident that wasn't really an accident."

Melanie considered that. "You're looking into what happened, aren't you?"

Peg nodded.

"And you want my help?"

"Not exactly. Rose and I—"

"Are working together," Melanie finished for her. "I guess that makes sense since she's the one who signed you up for Mature Mingle in the first place. I assume she'd met Nolan?"

"Yes."

"Then that works out perfectly."

For a moment, Peg almost thought Melanie sounded disappointed. Then they both heard the clatter of approaching footsteps on the deck and Melanie's face lit up. Peg's problems were forgotten.

"Oreos!" Kevin cried gleefully as he came hurtling through the doorway.

He snatched up the bag and shook it. Only a single cookie fell out. Before he could pick it up, Davey reached around him and grabbed it.

"Hey, that's mine!"

"Come and get it." Davey held the cookie above his brother's reach as they headed toward the living room.

"There's another bag in the pantry," Melanie said. Nobody appeared to be listening to her. She looked back at Peg and shrugged.

"Have fun with Rose," she said.

Chapter 14

Rose called the phone number on Gina's card and set up a meeting for Monday afternoon. As Gina lived in the nearby town of New Canaan, she recommended that they meet at Waveny Park. Rose hadn't been to the park before, but she was happy to agree. She pictured a grassy field, a few trees, and maybe a children's playground. There would probably be a bench where she and Gina could sit and talk.

Rose's first inkling that the image she'd formed in her mind was all wrong came when she turned in the half-mile driveway and drove through acres of wooded land before finally reaching Waveny House, a Tudor-style mansion on a hill overlooking what had formerly been a vast estate. Rose pulled her van into the nearest parking lot. From there, she could see soccer fields, platform tennis courts, and a swimming facility. Picturing the athletic woman she'd met at Nolan's funeral, Rose could only hope that Gina didn't have anything too strenuous in mind.

Rose was frowning down at her phone, tapping out a text to say she'd arrived, when there was a knock on her window. She looked up to see Gina standing outside the minivan. She was casually dressed in cargo shorts, a scoop-neck T-shirt, and a pair of running shoes that looked like they might be capable of tackling a marathon on their own. Gina smiled and gave Rose a small wave.

"I thought we could walk while we talk," she said when Rose got out and locked the van behind her. "Waveny has great trails. You don't mind, do you?"

"Umm . . . I guess not," Rose replied.

At least the sun was shining and she was wearing sneakers. Hopefully she'd be able to keep up. Otherwise how could she ask Gina about her relationship with Nolan? It really wasn't fair the way Peg managed to make questioning people look so easy. She was always ferreting out all sorts of interesting information. Meanwhile it seemed like Rose was always just getting run off her feet.

Gina had been heading for a trailhead. Now she stopped walking. "I'm getting the impression that exercise isn't your thing?"

"Not usually," Rose admitted.

"It's good for you." Gina thumped a hand on her chest. "Gets your heart pumping and your blood flowing."

"I'm pretty sure my blood is already flowing. Otherwise, I think I'd know."

"At our age, your mantra should be 'Use it or lose it.' "

"I appreciate your enthusiasm. But in my case I think I've already lost it."

"Okay, not a walk then." Gina reconsidered. "How about a stroll? Nice and easy. This place really does have wonderful trails, and we'll be in the shade nearly the whole time."

"That sounds perfect," Rose said with a smile. "And much more my speed."

The two women walked in a companionable silence until they'd crossed the parking lot and entered the woods. The trail was wide and well maintained. The ground yielded easily beneath Rose's feet. Leaves on the branches above them were still green, with just the merest hint of the vibrant colors to come.

"I'm guessing you didn't ask me here to talk about my summer camp," Gina said.

Rose turned and looked at her. "Why do you say that?"

"Because we probably could have covered that on the phone. You want to ask about Nolan Abercrombie, don't you?"

"Actually, yes," Rose said. "Am I that transparent?"

Gina shrugged. "Your friend wasn't taking any pains to hide her curiosity at his funeral. Why was that?"

"Peg's inquisitive about everything. Plus, she was just beginning to realize there were things Nolan had told her about himself that probably weren't true. It was a pretty rude awakening for her."

"She isn't the only one," Gina said.

"Did you meet Nolan through Mature Mingle too?"

Gina looked surprised. "Mature Mingle? You mean the dating site?"

Rose nodded.

"I had no idea he was trolling there too," she said thoughtfully. "No, Nolan and I met at the gym. We used to work out around the same time every week. The guy looked damn hot in gym shorts. It didn't take me long to realize that I wanted to rip them off him."

Rose hated that once again Gina had made her blush. Surely she wasn't that much of an innocent.

"Looking back, I think that's why Nolan's MO was so successful for him," Gina continued. "He wasn't obvious about pursuing women that interested him. Instead he kept us at arm's length until we were the ones panting after him. We felt like we were the ones in control. I suppose that made it easier for us to drop our guard, and that's when Nolan moved in for the kill."

"The kill?" Rose repeated.

"Yeah, Peg said she never got that far, right?"

"She and Nolan had just started dating a few weeks before he died."

"Then she was probably the last woman in his long, sorry line. I first met Nolan three years ago. He told me he was new to the area at the time. Who knows? Maybe it was true, maybe it wasn't. He also said he was a financial planner. We'd been together about a month when he asked if he could take a look at my retirement funds. He assured me he was making the offer for my sake. Since he was a professional in the field, he wanted to be certain that my money was invested properly."

"And you let him?" Rose tried not to sound too incredulous.

"Yeah, I know. It was stupid of me," Gina said with a frown. "But, at the time, I thought we were a solid couple. I was falling in love with him, and he told me he felt the same way. Under the circumstances, it seemed to make sense."

"Then what happened?"

"I'm sure you can guess the answer to that. Nolan was smart the way he went about critiquing my portfolio. He didn't say it was all wrong, just that it needed a few tweaks. There were areas where I was playing it safe and not getting much of a return. Nolan told me he had access to investments that were similarly low risk, but with much higher earnings. So I sold some bonds and put the money in his account."

"You never saw that money again, did you?" Rose asked.

"Nope, it was gone for good. Even worse, right around the same time, I found out that Nolan was cheating on me." Gina paused for a laugh that didn't sound the slightest bit amused. "It turned out that while I was thinking he and I were in a serious relationship, he was seeing two other women. Talk about a blow to my self-esteem. I felt like the biggest idiot in the world."

"Ouch," Rose said. Having led a sheltered life, she couldn't imagine being involved in a situation like that. But at least she could easily understand why Gina was still nursing a grudge.

"It's like I said at the funeral"—Gina glanced Rose's way—"Peg was lucky to have parted from Nolan when she did. Tell her she should put him firmly in her rearview mirror and move on."

"Yes . . . well." Rose grimaced slightly. "That's not going to happen."

Gina abruptly stopped walking. "Why not?"

"Peg thinks of herself as an amateur sleuth."

Rose had no qualms about throwing Peg under the bus. Someone had to take the blame for this interrogation, and there was no reason why it had to be her. She braced herself for Gina's reply.

What she hadn't expected was for Gina to laugh with delight. "For real?"

"I'm afraid so."

"Like Miss Marple?"

"More or less." Rose didn't think it would enhance Gina's opinion to explain that most of Peg's cases seemed to revolve around dogs.

"Has she solved any actual mysteries?"

"Quite a few. You might be surprised."

"I'm already surprised," Gina said. "Are we talking mysteries like 'where's my missing scarf?' Or serious stuff, like murders?"

"The latter. I've even helped once or twice," Rose added modestly.

She thought they might start walking again, but now Gina seemed rooted to the spot. She stared at Rose, her eyes widening.

"Is that what this is? Some sort of cross-examination?

We're not going to talk about the camp at all, are we?" Before Rose could reply, Gina had already rushed on. "Nolan is dead, and you and Peg are investigating. What a hoot! Am I a suspect?"

Gina paused for several seconds, then shook her head. "No, I think I'm more of a witness. Right? That would be my role. Although I wouldn't mind being a suspect . . . I think that sounds more interesting. Well? So? Which is it?"

Rose winced slightly. It was a shame Peg wasn't there to answer that question with her customary aplomb. Caught off guard, Rose realized she had no idea what would be the right thing to say.

"You tell me," she managed finally. "*Should* you be a suspect in Nolan's murder?"

"Let me think for a minute." Gina started to walk again. Rose fell into step beside her. "I hated the guy after what he did to me, so there's that. It wasn't just the money, it was the way he went about it. I just felt so *used*, you know?"

Rose nodded sympathetically.

"But if I was going to kill him, I would have done it years ago. There'd be no reason for me to wait until now to exact my revenge. So that's a point in my favor."

That earned Gina another nod. It was fascinating to listen to her lay out the facts and plead her case. Abruptly it occurred to Rose that Gina might make a better mystery-solving partner for Peg than she was.

That was a depressing thought.

"Here's another thing." Gina was still talking. "If I was going to kill that bastard, I wouldn't have run over him with a car. First, because who wants a big dent in their bumper that you'd then need to get fixed? And second, because if I was mad enough to kill him, I'd want my face to be the last thing he saw before he died."

"That's rather dramatic," Rose said.

"Yeah, well, you asked."

Rose was quite certain she hadn't—at least not for details like that. It was a good thing she and Gina were on the same side. Otherwise Rose probably should have thought twice before accompanying her on a solitary walk through the dense woods.

"I'm thinking I would have shot him," Gina mused.

Again, not a reassuring fact.

"Do you own a gun?" Rose felt compelled to ask, even though she wasn't entirely sure she wanted to hear the answer.

"No, but I could get one. It's not hard these days."

Depressingly true, Rose thought. "Okay, so what's your conclusion?"

Gina looked over at her. "I didn't do it."

"Are you sure?"

"Pretty sure. Which doesn't mean I'm not happy that someone else had the guts to step up and do it."

Pretty sure. Rose heard that equivocal reply loud and clear. She had no idea what it meant, however. Maybe Peg would know.

"So if it wasn't you," Rose said, "who did kill Nolan?"

"I can think of plenty of possibilities."

"You can?" Rose hadn't expected that.

"Yeah, sure. You saw most of them at Nolan's funeral."

"You mean all his women."

"I mean all of Nolan's dupes." Gina smirked, then softened the comment by adding, "Just like me."

"It sounds as though you must know some of them."

"I do. A group of us get together every month or so. We call ourselves a support group because that's what we do—we support each other. Mostly, we just sit around, drink wine, and talk about what's going on in our lives. The good and the bad, which would be where Nolan fits.

Although he's the reason we initially met, so I guess we should give him credit for that."

"How did that come about?" Rose asked curiously.

"One of the women tried to sue Nolan. She hired a lawyer who did some digging around to see if there were other victims who'd either be willing to join the suit or testify on her behalf. Then the case never went to court. Heddy had given the assets to Nolan willingly, and her lawyer didn't think he could prove undue influence, so it fell apart. But the upshot was that a group of women, all of whom were connected to Nolan in some way, ended up knowing each other. After that, we decided to keep in touch, and our get-togethers grew out of that."

Rose wondered what her counselor husband would think about that. Most likely, Peter would think it was terrific that Nolan's victims had decided to wrest back control of their own narratives. Unless one of them turned out to be Nolan's killer, of course.

"Would it be possible for me to attend one of your meetings?" she asked.

"I'd imagine that'd be all right. I'll have to check with the other women and see how they feel about it. But we just got together last week, so we probably won't be meeting again for a while."

That didn't sound like it would be much help. Rose and Peg needed to talk to those women now.

Gina must have been reading Rose's mind, because she said, "In the meantime, I could give you a list of their names and phone numbers. That way, each woman can decide for herself whether or not she wants to talk to you."

"That would be great," Rose said. "Thank you."

"Don't thank me yet. They may tell you to get lost."

Rose doubted that. "Or maybe they'll welcome the chance to tell their stories to a sympathetic audience."

"You mean a suspicious one," Gina retorted.

The trail had taken them on a looping circle through the woods. As they turned a corner, Rose could see the path was coming to an end. The lot where they'd left their cars was up ahead. She didn't have much time left.

"Are there any women in the group whom you think Peg and I should talk to first?" she asked.

"What do you mean?" Gina said, then frowned. "Oh, wait, I get it. Likely suspects, right?"

"Precisely."

"That's not up to me. You and Peg will have to figure that part out for yourselves."

She'd picked a fine time to become circumspect, Rose thought. "What about Heddy, the woman you mentioned a minute ago?"

"She's long gone."

Rose gulped. "Dead?"

"My word, you have a vivid imagination. It was nothing as dramatic as that. Heddy moved to Anchorage to be closer to her son and his family. I doubt even your friend, Peg, could conjure up a suspect from Alaska."

Too bad, Rose thought, but she couldn't complain. Even without a solid lead from Gina, she'd still gotten nearly everything she wanted.

"I'll email you that list," Gina said when they'd reached their vehicles. "And I guess I should say good luck."

"Thanks."

"You'll need it. From the way those women talk about Nolan, any one of them could have been behind the wheel of that car."

Rose arrived back at the Gallagher House to find that Maura was hosting a tea party. That came as a surprise. Peter, Mabel Mayberry, and Marmalade were her guests.

The event was taking place in the dining room. Maura had covered the somewhat battered tabletop with a white damask tablecloth. A flower-sprigged teapot sat on a trivet, and there were matching cups and saucers nearby. A tray in the center of the table held a selection of finger sandwiches with the crusts cut off. A second plate was filled with sugar cookies.

Mabel was seated on one side of the table. Peter was sitting across from her. Maura was at the head of the table. Marmalade sat on the windowsill, watching everything from a safe distance.

All four turned to look at Rose as she walked through the front door, glanced toward the dining room, then stopped in her tracks. Mabel was wearing a floral summer dress. Maura had affixed a large floppy bow to the top of her head. Peter had even put on a tie for the occasion.

Rose, by contrast, looked as though she'd recently been tramping through the woods. Which she had. They invited her to join them anyway.

"Rose, dear, please come and sit down." Mabel patted the chair next to her. "We're having tea. Isn't that lovely?"

"It certainly is." Rose was delighted that Mabel had remembered her name. She entered the room and took the proffered seat, and looked around the table. "What brought this about?"

"Peter and I were talking about Mabel earlier, and it occurred to me that it would be a good idea for them to renew their acquaintance," Maura said. "And now you've arrived just in time."

She poured tea into the china cups and handed them around. Mabel helped herself to several small sandwiches. Rose passed Peter a cookie, then took a sandwich for herself. It turned out to be peanut butter and jelly.

"Mabel was just telling us that she's lived on this street for more than forty years," Peter told her. "She and her husband were friends with Beatrice and Howard Gallagher."

"That must have been quite a while ago," Rose said.

The house that was now a shelter had once been a starter home for their benefactor, Beatrice, and her late husband, Howard. When Howard made his fortune, the family had moved to a fancier neighborhood.

"Indeed it was." Mabel had a dreamy expression on her face. "My William was still alive then, and things were very different. Most of the homes around here belonged to families with children."

"William was your husband?" Rose took a bite of her sandwich. The peanut butter stuck to the roof of her mouth.

Mabel nodded. "He and I fell in love, married young, and raised our family here. Those were wonderful times."

"I'm sure they were," Peter said gently. "Rose told me that she and Maura had the opportunity to meet your grandson. I believe his name is Donny?"

Mabel slowly sipped her tea before replying. "Donny is a good boy. He looks after me."

The three other people at the table shared a look. They weren't convinced of that.

"I'd imagine it isn't easy for you, living on your own," Peter said. "Sometimes you must get lonely."

Mabel looked uncertain. "Donny is a good boy." she said again. "He looks after me."

"Peter and I would like to help look after you too," Rose said.

"I do the grocery shopping for the shelter," Maura told Mabel. "I could stop by your house once a week, pick up your list, and add it to ours."

"Peter's good at fixing things, and I could help with scheduling doctor's appointments and such," Rose said. "Would that be all right with you?"

Mabel gazed around the table. Her expression was both bewildered and hopeful. "Why would you do all that just for me?"

Peter reached across the table and laid his hand on top of her much smaller one. "Because that's what neighbors do. They help each other."

Mabel sat very still as she took that in. "And maybe we could have tea again sometime?"

"Absolutely," Maura replied. "I'll put it on the schedule."

"Do those ideas meet with your approval?" Peter asked.

"They do indeed," Mabel replied with a smile. "That would be lovely."

Chapter 15

Peg arrived home in a serious snit.

Not at Melanie, of course. If anything, Melanie had cause to be annoyed with her. Perhaps Peg might have broken the news that she and Rose were working on another mystery—one for which Melanie's services weren't needed—more diplomatically. Diplomacy had never been Peg's strong suit, however, and Melanie had to be well aware of that by now. So Peg was going to assume that she and her niece were fine.

No, the person who was the target of Peg's ire was Nolan's sister, who maybe wasn't his sister after all. Nor was the woman visiting from out of town. Instead she appeared to be living in Nolan's house, which now didn't even seem to belong to him. No wonder Barbara hadn't wanted to talk to Peg at the funeral. She probably didn't want to give Peg a chance to raise any awkward topics or uncomfortable questions.

At least her name was actually Barbara, Peg thought with a frown. And now that she had a last name, she could find a phone number. Then Peg would give the woman a serious piece of her mind.

But when Peg entered the house, her Poodles had a different idea. And being Poodles, they were skilled at making their preferences known. Hope, Coral, and Joker were all waiting for her on the other side of the door. Tails wagging, bodies undulating in delight, the trio of big black dogs surged forward to surround her legs. Coral nudged her head into one of Peg's hands and demanded a pat. Joker jumped up, placed his front paws on her shoulders, and licked her chin.

Hope, who'd reached the age when such boisterous displays of affection were behind her, merely stood and stared up at Peg reproachfully. That response hit Peg the hardest. She and Hope had been together for eleven years. Sometimes it felt as though the two of them had grown old together. Hope knew and understood every one of Peg's moods. She was also effortlessly able to tug on Peg's heart strings.

Peg set Joker down on the floor, ran her hand the length of Coral's back, then stooped down so that she and Hope were face-to-face. "I'm sorry, I know you hate being left behind." Peg looked into the bitch's dark eyes. Her hands framed the Poodle's cheeks, and her fingers stroked the sides of her graying muzzle. "I'll try to do better."

While Hope and Peg were sharing a conciliatory hug, Coral and Joker started racing in circles around the small hallway. Another minute and they'd both be bouncing off the walls. Peg levered herself to her feet. Joker and Coral were sending her a message she understood as clearly as if it had been spoken aloud.

Wasn't she aware that they'd been cooped up inside for hours? Surely, she knew that Poodles needed regular exercise. Not only that, but they'd been deprived of human companionship for what felt like forever. Now it was most certainly time for a very long walk.

Peg couldn't fault her dogs' logic. Nor could she disagree. She strode through the house and went straight to the back door. The three Poodles followed happily. All was forgiven. Life was good.

Quick, Mom! Open the door. Race you to the back gate!

The gate was at the far end of the fenced field. The Poodles were halfway there before Peg had even reached the bottom of the steps. The opening led to a network of riding trails that crisscrossed numerous private properties in backcountry Greenwich. At one time, it had been a common occurrence to see horses trotting along the wide paths. Unfortunately, the trails were mostly quiet now.

Once they'd all passed through the gate, Peg let the Poodles run on ahead of her. As the dogs zoomed back and forth across the shady lane, she pulled out her phone and went to work. It hardly took any time at all to locate Barbara Weatherly's phone number. Peg immediately called it. When Barbara picked up, she sounded wary.

"Hello, Barbara. This is Peg Turnbull."

There was a long pause. Afraid the other woman might disconnect the call, Peg said in a stern voice, "We need to talk."

"About what?"

As if there could possibly be any question about that.

"Nolan. You. And the shenanigans the two of you have been up to."

"I have no idea what you're talking about." Barbara sniffled. "Please leave me alone."

"That's not going to happen." Peg was just getting warmed up. "If you don't want to talk to me, I'll take my questions to the police."

A small sound came through the line. Barbara might have gasped. Or maybe growled. When she spoke again, her voice had hardened. "Go ahead. I've already spoken to the detective who's in charge of the case. He knows I had nothing to do with Nolan's death."

Barbara added another sniffle for good measure. Peg wasn't fooled.

"That's interesting," she said. "Who did you tell Detective Sturgill you were? Nolan's sister? An old friend? Or maybe the person who owns the house he's been passing off as his own?"

"How dare you!" Barbara snapped.

"I might say the same to you," Peg replied mildly.

Since her bluster hadn't worked, now Barbara tried moderating her tone. "I don't know what you mean. Whatever you've heard, whoever you've been talking to, they must have been telling you lies. People are saying horrible things about Nolan now that he's no longer here to defend himself."

"But you're here," Peg said. "You can defend him. All I want is to hear the truth."

"The truth." Barbara sighed.

Peg wondered if that was a foreign concept for the woman. At this point, she wouldn't trust Barbara to make change for a dollar without keeping a nickel back for herself.

"Tomorrow morning," Peg said. "I'll drop by your house so we can finish this conversation in person. If you're not there, my next stop will be the Stamford PD. I'm sure Detective Sturgill will be interested in what I have to say."

"Don't show up before eleven. I'm not an early riser."

"You'll get up tomorrow morning," Peg said pleasantly. "Or you can talk to me in your pajamas."

Peg picked up Rose outside the Gallagher House the following morning. She'd sent Rose a text after she'd gotten off the phone, and they'd agreed to go and see Barbara together.

Rose had dressed for the warm day in a yellow seersucker blouse and a denim skirt that tied at the waist. She had espadrilles on her feet and a big smile on her face. During the drive there, Peg had been rehearsing what she intended to say to Barbara. Now she found herself putting that thought aside and smiling in return.

"You look happy," she said as Rose climbed in and carefully fastened her seat belt.

"Of course I'm happy." Rose settled into her seat. "The sun is shining, birds are singing, and I'm embarking on an adventure."

"You are?" Peg cast her a skeptical glance before pulling away from the curb. "When?"

"Right now. With you."

"I don't know what you have in mind. I merely intend to have a conversation with Barbara."

"A known suspect," Rose pointed out. "And based on the way she behaved at the funeral, a cagey one at that. Now I get to watch you give her the third degree. Who knows what kinds of clues she might unwittingly reveal?"

"The third degree?" Peg repeated. She reached the end of the block and turned left, heading toward the turnpike on-ramp. "You sound like Hollywood's idea of a low-level gangster."

"Don't make fun," Rose replied. "I'm trying to learn things. I need to catch up to you."

"You were meant to have learned something last time."

"I did. I learned that the best policy was to let you take the lead, then blame you later for everything that went wrong."

Peg made a rude noise, which Rose politely ignored.

"You spoke with Barbara yesterday," she said. "Why are we visiting her now? Why didn't you just ask her your questions over the phone?"

"Because it's easier for someone to lie when you can't see their expression and demeanor."

"So you're not expecting Barbara to tell us the truth?"

"Sadly, no. I'm beginning to suspect that she and Nolan were two of a kind. For starters, she doesn't appear to actually be Nolan's sister."

Rose swiveled around in her seat. "Then who is she?"

"That's one of the things I intend to find out."

As Peg sped up the on-ramp onto the turnpike, Rose gripped her armrest and uttered a small prayer. Highway traffic tended to stoke Peg's competitive urges. She drove with scant regard for speed limits or the needs of other vehicles.

"What else?" Rose asked to distract herself from the cars whizzing past her window.

"It seems that Barbara wasn't in Connecticut visiting Nolan. According to a neighbor I met yesterday, she's the owner and full-time resident of the house Nolan told me was his."

Rose frowned. That didn't make sense. "Why were you talking to Nolan's neighbors?"

"*Barbara's* neighbor," Peg corrected. "And there was only one. He told me that he'd lived next door to Barbara for two years. During that time he'd never met, nor even heard of Nolan. Which is why we're on our way there now. Let's see how much of this mess she'll be willing to clear up for us."

When Peg took her eyes off the road to glance her way, Rose's breath caught in her throat. Peg didn't seem at all troubled by the fact that they were hurtling along at warp speed—and that the person with her foot on the gas pedal wasn't looking where they were going.

"So that's what I've been doing," she said. "What did you accomplish yesterday?"

Rose was eyeing the van's steering wheel, in case she might have to reach over and grab it. She blurted out the first thing that came to mind. "I went to a tea party."

There was a long pause as Peg thought about that. Thankfully, she managed to watch the road at the same time. "That sounds useful."

"It was, actually. Maura invited our elderly neighbor, Mabel Mayberry, to the shelter. Remember I told you about her?"

Peg nodded.

"The tea party was a way for all of us to get to know one another better. And for Peter, Maura, and I to try to discover how much help Mabel needs with day-to-day life."

"Did it work?"

"It did." Rose sounded pleased. "Now Mabel knows that if she has a problem or needs help with something, we're there for her."

"Well done, you," Peg said.

"I also took quite an informative walk with Gina Malone."

"The testy woman from the funeral?"

Peg's gaze swung Rose's way again. Rose really wished she would cut that out. At least, until they'd turned off the highway.

"Yes, that one."

"And you didn't think to *start* with that?"

Rose supposed Peg did have a point. Water under the bridge, however.

"We're talking about her now, aren't we? Gina told me all about her relationship with Nolan and how he offered to invest money for her—which promptly disappeared. But get this. Gina wasn't the only woman that happened to."

"I think we're already aware of that," Peg said. "Aren't we?"

"Yes, but what we didn't know was that one of Nolan's women initiated a lawsuit against him." Rose was on a roll now. "The suit didn't go anywhere, but what it did accomplish was to bring together more than a dozen women whom Nolan had scammed. And those women got together and formed a group."

"A group," Peg repeated dubiously. "Are we talking about a book club? Or maybe a knitting circle?"

"No, it's a support group of sorts. Where wine gets drunk and the women let off steam by griping about their experiences with Nolan and whatever else is going on in their lives."

"In other words," Peg said with interest, "women with motives."

"Exactly."

"We need to find out who those women are."

"Already done," Rose announced.

"*What?*"

Rose smiled in satisfaction. It felt good to be a step ahead of Peg for once. "Gina emailed me a list of their names and phone numbers last night. After we talk to Barbara, we can get to work on that."

"Well, look at you." Peg sounded pleased. "Sitting over there pretending that you don't know what you're doing. This is quite a coup. You're turning into a bit of an overachiever."

Rose laughed. "Praise from you, Peg? I hardly knew such a thing was possible."

Peg had slowed the van so she could read the street signs. Ben had been correct to say that these small roads all looked alike. "Yes, well, don't get used to it."

That prompted another laugh. "Believe me," Rose said, "I don't intend to."

Chapter 16

Peg stopped the minivan in front of Barbara's house and parked by the edge of the road. She didn't get out right away, and neither did Rose. Instead the two of them gazed at the large, dove-gray house.

"That's a pretty place," Rose commented. She didn't say what she was really thinking—that in this picturesque neighborhood, the two-story home with its wide lawn and meticulous landscaping, must be worth a great deal of money. Which likely meant that its owner was well-off financially, whether by fair means or foul. "Are you sure it doesn't belong to Nolan?"

"At this point, I'm not sure of anything," Peg said. "By the way, I forgot to mention that Barbara told me not to show up before eleven."

Rose glanced at her watch. It was just past ten-thirty. How like Peg to assume that everyone would acquiesce to her agenda.

"We're early," Rose said, stepping out of the minivan. "I hope Barbara's at home."

Peg hopped out too. She slammed her door behind her. "Don't worry. She'll be there. She might still be in bed, however."

Rose opened her mouth. Then closed it again. *Nope.* She wasn't even going to ask.

Peg led the way across the lawn, marching toward the front door like a woman on a mission. When she was intent on something, Peg was like a tornado, sweeping all opposition from her path. Left to follow behind, Rose could only envy Peg's unwavering belief in the righteousness of her causes.

Sometimes it felt to Rose as though she spent half her time second-guessing the decisions she'd made. In the convent, the right to make her own choices had been taken out of her hands and delegated to a Higher Authority. So when it came to knowing how to demonstrate initiative, she was definitely playing catchup. Maybe this was an opportunity to practice asserting herself.

Rose squared her shoulders and lengthened her stride. She caught up with Peg, and the two of them reached the front of the house together.

The home's front door was painted hunter green to match the shutters. Low urns on either side of the stoop were tightly packed with late-summer blooms. Rose recognized marigolds in shades that varied from yellow to bronze. The brass knocker on the door was shaped like a seahorse.

Rose started to reach for it, but Peg stepped around her and rang the doorbell instead. *It figured.* Rose should have known better than to try to take the lead when Peg was around. She pulled her hand back, pretending she'd only meant to scratch her head. Peg gave her a quizzical look. She was probably wondering if Rose had fleas.

Then the door opened, and Rose released a breath she hadn't realized she'd been holding. At least their arrival hadn't gotten Barbara out of bed. That should count for something.

Barbara was not only upright; she was also fully dressed. A filmy lavender tunic topped matching slacks and a pair of sexy, strappy sandals that Rose immediately coveted even though she would never have a place to wear them.

Barbara's eyes were red and swollen, as if she'd recently been crying. Other than that, her appearance was flawless.

Rose had barely had a chance to speak to Barbara at the funeral, so despite what Peg said, she'd intended to reserve judgment. Now, however, gazing at Barbara's puffy face, Rose found herself feeling skeptical instead. She didn't need to possess Peg's acumen to suspect that here was someone skilled at portraying whatever role a situation might call for.

"Hello, Barbara." Peg didn't wait to be invited inside. She merely stepped past Barbara and entered the house.

Rose wasn't that brave. Instead, she held out her hand. "I'm Rose Donovan. We met at Nolan's funeral."

Barbara glanced at her briefly, then turned to address Peg. "I thought you were coming alone."

That left Rose to hop inside the house to join them before the door was closed in her face. Nobody was paying any attention to her. Considering the way Peg and Barbara were glaring at each other, maybe that was a good thing.

"You were wrong," Peg said. She glanced around the beautifully appointed hallway. "I remember when you told me you were the one who'd decorated this house. I probably should have had my suspicions then."

"Suspicions about what?" Barbara asked.

"Everything that transpired between me and Nolan," Peg replied. "All of which subsequently appears to have been a lie."

Barbara walked into the living room and took a seat beneath a large oil painting of Venice's Grand Canal, portrayed in hues of blues and pinks. Rose and Peg sat down on a low couch opposite her. Though the day outside was bright, the lighting in this room was dim.

Rose assumed that was a purposeful choice. And another subliminal indication that Barbara had something to hide.

"Tell me something," Peg said, leaning forward in her

seat. "Did Nolan ever really care for me? Or was acting as though he did just part of his game plan?"

"How would you expect me to know that?" Barbara's shoulders lifted in a dainty shrug. Rose noted that she hadn't denied the second part of Peg's query. "Nolan was a private person. He didn't wear his emotions on his sleeve."

"Or more likely his emotions were never involved at all," Peg replied. "I know there were other women. Lots of them. And that once Nolan had gained their trust, his next step was to talk about his investments and offer help with theirs. Maybe that sounds familiar to you?"

Barbara looked as though she wanted to say no. But, of course, she couldn't. Not only had she been present when Nolan touted his financial prowess to Peg, she'd been the one to initiate the conversation.

"Maybe something about a tech start-up?" Peg prodded. "One offering significant returns?"

Barbara remained stubbornly silent.

"What Nolan did was despicable," Peg continued. "But you can't sit here and pretend to be innocent either. You were part of his schemes all along. Women—especially older women who know better—are justifiably suspicious of men who appear too good to be true. But your position as Nolan's sister lent him credibility. You made women feel that it was all right to relax and enjoy themselves with him. Meanwhile, you were just as guilty of scamming them as he was."

"You don't understand," Barbara said. "You've got it all wrong."

"Which part?" asked Rose. She was trying to sit up straight like Peg, but the deep couch cushions kept swallowing her.

"None of it was my fault. Nolan was using me too."

Peg looked disgusted by the evasive tactic. Rose wasn't so sure. She supposed it was possible that Barbara had been another of Nolan's victims. Then again, it was also possible that her desire to see the good in people meant that she was just being gullible.

"Explain," Peg said sharply.

"Nolan isn't actually my brother."

"That's not news." Peg stifled a pretend yawn.

"But we'd been friends for a long time. Dating is ridiculously difficult for mature women." Barbara looked back and forth between them. "You know that yourselves."

Rose recognized that ploy. Barbara wanted them to agree with her so she and Peg would feel as though they were all on the same side. Nevertheless, she nodded anyway.

"Nolan used to introduce me to acquaintances of his whom he thought I might be interested in getting to know. I did the same for him. It was all very innocent, let me assure you."

Rose didn't feel assured. She assumed Peg didn't either.

"Go on," she said.

"He really was a financial adviser. He was good at it, too." Barbara sounded as though she might be trying to convince herself as well as them. "But he bet wrong on a real estate deal and lost a lot of money. Mine as well as his."

Barbara paused in case Rose and Peg wanted to express sympathy for her plight. They did not.

"So there we were, both approaching retirement age without the funds we needed to support our lifestyles," she continued. "Then Nolan came up with an idea."

"A scam, you mean," Peg said. "A plan to bilk unsuspecting women out of their retirement funds in order to enhance your own."

"We were only going to do it once," Barbara said earnestly. "One score to set us both up for life. Nolan chose the woman carefully. She was immensely wealthy, with a portfolio of investments so large she wouldn't even miss the paltry sum we needed."

"It isn't just about the money," Rose said. "It's also

about how a woman feels when she's allowed herself to become vulnerable with a man, only to find out that he was just using her."

"I know that," Barbara retorted.

"And it wasn't just one time," Peg added. "We know that Nolan took advantage of multiple women."

"Yes, but that wasn't my fault. Or my decision. Nolan was the one in charge, and he was thrilled by how easily we succeeded that first time. He got a real rush from taking the risk and then reaping the reward."

Peg nodded, encouraging her to continue.

"After that, he immediately wanted to try again. And he got cocky. He decided that the world was filled with older women who were just looking for a chance to fall in love with a catch like him."

"Yuck," Rose said.

"I felt the same way," Barbara told them. "I told Nolan that we'd gotten what we needed and I was finished."

"Except you weren't," Peg pointed out. "Otherwise you wouldn't have been letting him use your house to entertain."

Rose noted that Barbara didn't bother to tell Peg she was wrong about whose house they were in. Or to ask how she'd found out. At the moment, that was probably the least of her worries.

"For his plan to work, Nolan needed to keep up appearances," Barbara said. "He had to look successful, like a man with money to spare. It was obvious that my house in Darien was more impressive than his bachelor digs in Stamford."

"So you were helping him score with women," Rose said.

"That's not true," Barbara snapped.

Peg poked Rose in the side. "I think you meant to say she was helping him score *points* with women."

"Oh." Rose frowned. She hadn't realized there was a difference.

"You still haven't told us why you continued to go along with Nolan's schemes after telling him you were finished," Peg said.

"Because I had no choice. Nolan was blackmailing me. He told me that if I didn't cooperate, he'd turn me over to the police and tell them I'd been the mastermind behind our first scheme. In hindsight I know I behaved foolishly, but I knew that Nolan was skilled at handling money. So I made the mistake of trusting him."

Rose and Peg shared a look. That sounded like a familiar refrain.

"What I didn't know at the time was that Nolan had used my name and Social Security number to open the account where he stashed the money we'd already made. It turned out he was more cunning than I'd given him credit for. Because if the police had gone looking for those illicit funds, they would have been traced straight back to me."

"Blackmail makes a good motive for murder," Rose said. "Maybe you were the one who wanted Nolan dead."

"Don't be ridiculous," Barbara said sharply. "Of course I was annoyed with him. But Nolan and I were friends. Good friends. I tolerated his flaws, just as he did mine. Neither of us would ever have harmed the other."

Rose wasn't convinced by that answer. However, she was impressed by the sincerity with which Barbara delivered it. The woman was obviously skilled at deception. In her line of work, she'd need to be.

"If you weren't angry enough to want to kill Nolan," Peg said, "then who was?"

Barbara didn't even hesitate. "Jason."

"You mean Nolan's son?"

"Yes. I saw you talking to him at the funeral."

"It wasn't much of a conversation," Peg said. "Jason

didn't want to talk to me. He told me to mind my own business."

"I'm not surprised. He and Nolan were estranged. They barely had a relationship at all. I hadn't even expected him to show up."

"Estranged?" Peg stiffened. "That's not what Nolan told me about his son. It's not even close. Was *everything* he said to me a calculated lie?"

Barbara just shrugged. She wasn't about to defend the man.

"So Jason doesn't live in Chicago and work for a non-profit?"

"No." She smirked. "I have no idea where Nolan got that line from. He probably pulled it out of thin air. The truth is Jason is illegitimate. Nolan never married his mother, nor acknowledged Jason as his son."

Peg growled a crude word under her breath. If Rose knew any crude words, she might have done the same.

"Jason's mother forced Nolan to take a paternity test at some point, so he knew Jason was his. But as far as I know, he never paid support or played a part in Jason's life. The kid tried to connect with him when he turned eighteen, but Nolan refused to see him. He tried again five years ago when his mother died, but Nolan dodged him that time too."

"Nolan was a schmuck," Peg said with feeling.

Rose nodded in agreement. "Jason deserved better."

"He's not the only one," Barbara muttered.

"I'd like to talk to Jason," Peg said. "Do you know how we can get in touch with him?"

Barbara stood up and walked over to an ornate, spindle-leg desk in a corner of the room. She opened a drawer, pulled out a leather-bound address book, and thumbed through it before writing something down on a slip of paper.

"The phone number I have is old, but it's probably still

good. Jason uses Abercrombie as his last name. The last time Nolan mentioned him, I believe he was living in Norwalk."

Barbara gave the piece of paper to Peg, then walked them to the door. They were barely on the other side before she shut it behind them.

"Did you notice how eager Barbara was to point you in Jason's direction?" Rose asked when they were back in the minivan.

Peg nodded as she turned the key. "After we'd backed her into a corner, I suspect she'd have done just about anything to turn the spotlight away from herself."

Rose laughed. "Why, Peg, are you saying you didn't believe everything Barbara told us?"

"Not by a long shot," Peg replied.

Chapter 17

Before they'd reached the end of the road, Peg and Rose had an argument over what to do next.

Rose wanted to contact the first few names on the list Gina had given her and see if anyone was available to chat. Peg wanted to track down Jason. Rose recommended they split up and each go their own way. Peg vetoed that. She never wanted to miss out on any of the action.

That left them at an impasse.

"I'm the driver," Peg said. "That means I get to choose."

Rose narrowed her eyes. "Fine." She crossed her arms over her chest mutinously. "Then take me back to the Gallagher House and I'll pick up my own van."

Peg knew that wasn't going to happen. "The Gallagher House is in Stamford. Jason is presumably in Norwalk. From Darien, they're in two opposite directions. The best idea is to take this new information we got from Barbara and run with it."

The minivan coasted to a stop. Neither woman appeared to notice. Thankfully there were no cars behind them.

"Even assuming you can get in touch with Jason, what makes you think he'll talk to you?" Rose asked. "He wanted nothing to do with you at the funeral."

"The same could be said for the women on your list," Peg retorted. "Maybe none of them will agree to see you either."

"Don't be ridiculous. Of course, they'll see me. Everybody likes me."

Peg's brow rose. "Are you implying that people don't like me?"

Rose bit her lip and remained mum. It occurred to her that if Peg booted her out of the minivan, she'd be stranded in Darien, and then Peter would have to come and get her. Of course he'd do it, but he'd probably also enjoy a chuckle at her expense. Sometimes he treated Rose's alliance with Peg as a partnership they'd cobbled together over tea and cake for his own private amusement.

Meanwhile, the minivan still wasn't moving.

Peg decided she could sit there all day. She'd given up on getting an answer to her question, but since Rose was wrong, it didn't matter. Peg wasn't about to give in. It was the principle of the thing.

"Your problem," Rose said suddenly, "is that you believe that you're an eminently reasonable person."

"Which I am."

"No, you're not. You are only reasonable when things are going exactly the way you want them to. As soon as someone voices an opinion that's contrary to yours, you dig in your heels."

"That's because my opinion is usually the right one," Peg replied. "Just because other people don't recognize that immediately doesn't mean they don't come around in the end."

"They come around"—Rose gritted her teeth—"because *they* are trying to be reasonable."

"As am I."

"Oh really?"

"Yes," Peg said. "Really."

"Good. Let's put that to the test, shall we?" Rose opened her purse and pulled out a piece of paper. "We'll compromise. I'll call the first two numbers on this list. If neither one picks up or is willing to see us, or if they're simply unavailable, we'll switch to Plan B."

"What's Plan B?" Peg asked suspiciously.

"Jason. Norwalk. You going where you want to go and me pretending it's a good idea."

"Ooh." Peg smiled. "I like Plan B."

"Yes, but we're trying Plan A first."

Peg peered over at the list. "What's the first name?"

"Sandy Rivers," Rose read aloud.

"No. Really."

"I'm serious." Rose checked again.

"*Sandy Rivers?*" Peg sighed. "Sandy Shore would have made more sense. Or perhaps Muddy Rivers."

"If those are your idea of decent names, your Poodles should count themselves lucky. At least their names are nearly normal."

"Nearly?" Peg said in a dangerous tone.

"You have a dog named Joker. You named him after a playing card."

"Cards had nothing to do with it. Joker has a wonderful sense of humor."

As if such a thing was possible. This was why Rose could never win an argument with Peg. Because when she was losing, her declarations lost all semblance of logic.

The only way Rose could combat that was by changing the subject. So she got out her phone and entered a number from the list.

To Rose's delight and Peg's chagrin, it took just one call to send them driving back to Greenwich, where Sandy Rivers lived in a cluster of brick town houses not far from Bruce Park. With Peg behind the wheel, they made great time. She parked in a designated visitor's spot, then she and Rose crossed a small central green to reach the row of town houses on the other side.

The attached homes all looked alike. Each was a narrow, two-story building constructed of weathered brick and covered in ivy. Only their doors set them apart. Each one was painted a different color. Sandy Rivers's door was bright yellow.

As they approached, Peg's ears perked up, and she smiled. "Do you hear that?"

"No," said Rose, "I don't hear a thing."

"Sandy has a dog."

"How do you know that?"

"It's barking inside the house. A small dog, I'm guessing a Pomeranian."

Rose stared at her. "Even if there is a dog in there, I refuse to believe you can tell what breed it is by listening to it bark."

"Want to make a bet?" Peg asked as they stepped up onto the stoop.

Rose was tempted, but Peg sounded entirely too confident. She hoped it was a bluff on Peg's part, but she couldn't be sure. Plus, Rose had no idea what a Pomeranian was supposed to look like. So she wouldn't know if Peg was right or not. And she wouldn't put it past her to pull a fast one.

Besides, now that they were right outside the yellow door, Rose could hear a dog yipping too. It sounded as though its feet were scrambling across the floor. So at least Peg had been right about that.

"No thank you," Rose replied primly.

"Good choice," Peg told her as the door drew open and a small, heavily coated dog with a foxy face and its tail flipped over its back came charging out. Peg pointed at it and said, "Pomeranian." Then she hunkered down to say hello to the dog.

It was left to Rose to greet the woman now standing in the doorway. Sandy Rivers was in her sixties. She had a plump body and a friendly smile. Her head barely reached the top of Rose's shoulders. "You must be Rose Gallagher," she said.

"I am. Thank you for agreeing to see us. This"—Rose gestured in the direction of Peg's lowered head—"is my sister-in-law, Peg Turnbull. She likes dogs."

"I can tell," Sandy said with a laugh. The Pom was now trying to climb into Peg's lap so he could reach her face. "Button loves everyone, but I've never seen him be so effusive with a stranger before."

"Peg has that effect on dogs."

"All dogs?"

"I'm afraid so," Rose said. "They flock to her like she's made of prime rib."

"I'm envious." Sandy watched the interaction. "What a wonderful quality to possess. Do you suppose she could teach me how she does it?"

"Teach you what?" Peg rose to her feet with Button snuggled in the crook of her arm.

"Sandy wants to know why dogs are so enthralled by you," Rose told her.

"That's easy. It's because I am endlessly enthralled by them. Is it all right if we come inside?"

"Please do." Sandy stepped back out of the doorway.

The front hall was short, square, and wallpapered in a bright floral pattern. There was a living room on the right. To Rose's surprise, someone else was there. A woman seated on the couch stood up as they entered the room.

"This is Nell Perkins," Sandy said, then finished performing the introductions. "Nell lives just across the way. Last night Gina sent out a memo to our entire group, so we all have a pretty good idea of what you two ladies are

up to. After I heard from Rose, I got in touch with Nell.
She wanted to have her say too. I hope that's all right."

"Of course it is," Peg answered for both of them.

"I wanted to make sure Sandy didn't give you the wrong
idea about Nolan," Nell said. She was a sturdy-looking
woman dressed in dark jeans and a long-sleeved cotton
shirt. Her steel-gray hair was cropped short, and glasses
with oversize frames covered much of her face.

"Peg and I are happy to hear what both of you have to
say," Rose told them as they all took seats.

Sandy joined Nell on the couch. Peg and Rose sat down
in two straight-backed armchairs opposite it. There was a
glass-and-chrome coffee table between them. When Peg
placed Button on the floor, he scooted beneath it and lay
down.

"Good," Nell announced. "Because Nolan Abercrombie was a creep."

"Now, Nell." Sandy laid a hand on the other woman's
arm. "That's no way to begin. What will Rose and Peg
think of us?"

"It's the truth," Nell said. "And since I don't know either of them, I couldn't care less what they think of me."

The comment was meant to put Peg and Rose in their
place. Instead, it had the opposite effect. Peg grinned. Rose
tried hard not to follow suit.

"What's so funny?" Nell asked.

"I like a woman with strong opinions," Peg said. "I
happen to have some myself. And I certainly won't dispute
your assessment of Nolan. Now that I'm learning more
about who he really was, I feel much the same way."

"Gina said one of you ladies dated him." Sandy turned
to Rose. "That must have been you."

"No, I've been married for years," Rose said. "It was Peg."

"That's a surprise," Nell commented.

"Why is that?" Peg asked.

"Most of Nolan's women tended to be docile, agreeable types." Nell glanced at Sandy. "No offense."

"None taken," Sandy replied. "I do like to think of myself as an agreeable person. Perhaps that's why Nolan and I got along so well."

"Or maybe it was because no matter how badly he treated you, you always forgave him."

"Because he always meant well," Sandy said firmly. It sounded like an argument she and Nell had had before. Sandy turned to address Rose and Peg. "Nolan wasn't a bad man. He was a good man who unfortunately had bad ideas. Many of the things that went wrong really weren't his fault."

Nell stopped just short of rolling her eyes. "What went wrong is that your money ended up in his pockets."

"You don't know that for certain." Sandy shook her head. "Nolan thought the offshore shipping company was a sure thing. He and I invested in it together. So I wasn't the only one who lost out. He did too."

Rose smiled at Sandy. The other woman smiled back.

"You're obviously a kind person," Rose said. "How long were you and Nolan together?"

"Oh my." She thought back. "At least a year. Maybe more."

"Sandy *is* a kind person," Nell acknowledged. "Perhaps that's why Nolan let her down gently. Unlike some of us, who got dumped the moment we ceased to be useful to him."

"So you were also a victim of Nolan's bogus investments?" Peg asked.

"My experience was different. I do a lot of charity work here in town. I'm good at fundraising and organizing events," Nell told them. "After my husband died, getting involved in local causes was a way to keep busy. Nolan submitted a grant proposal to a foundation whose board I was on. We met when he brought the proposal to the office and turned it in."

She paused for an ironic smile. "At the time, I thought our meeting was a fortuitous accident. But of course, it wasn't. Nolan had everything planned ahead of time. He'd accounted for every variable. He and I started seeing each other while his proposal was under review."

Peg winced. She could guess what was coming.

"Nolan encouraged me to use my influence as a board member to get the proposal approved, and I did. Stupid me, I believed everything he'd written in it, as well as all the other things he was whispering in my ear late at night."

"Did your foundation offer him a grant?" Peg asked.

"Thankfully, no. Their legal team raised a number of red flags." Nell sighed heavily before continuing. "I assumed those issues could be, and would be, rectified, so I reported the findings back to Nolan. When I did, he just looked at me and laughed. 'Win some and lose some,' he said. In that moment, I had no idea what he meant. I found out several days later, however."

"Nolan withdrew his proposal, didn't he?" Rose said.

"He did. And he ghosted me at the same time. I apologized to the board of directors for my poor judgment, but unfortunately, it wasn't enough to save my position. Or to salvage my reputation in the charitable works community." The expression on Nell's face was thunderous. "But that wasn't the worst part."

"Go on," Peg said.

"The people I'd worked with—worthy people who'd been my friends and colleagues—weren't mad at me. They weren't even disappointed in me. No, it was even more humiliating than that."

Rose sat very still and waited for Nell to finish.

"Instead they saw me as a woman about to turn sixty—a woman who was past her prime—and who'd been willing to trade her integrity for a little attention from a handsome man. *And they pitied me.*"

Abruptly Nell stood up. She brushed past Sandy and headed for the door. When she reached the hall, she paused and looked back at the other women.

"Nolan Abercrombie was a horrible person. He deserved to die. And I hope he rots in hell."

Chapter 18

"It was fascinating," Rose said to Peter that night. The two of them had finished work for the day and left the shelter in Maura's capable hands. Now they were home, sitting in the kitchen of the small ranch-style house they'd rented in the spring. Peter had cooked dinner for them. They were lingering at the table over coffee.

"But it was sad, too. Peg and I were prepared to ask questions, but we never had the chance. As soon as we sat down, Sandy and Nell just started talking. It was as if they couldn't wait to tell us their stories."

"I can understand that," Peter replied. "You and Peg were a fresh audience. One that was happy to listen, and perhaps help them make sense of what had to have been troubling incidents in their lives. There's a reason why people see therapists, you know. Having the opportunity to talk through traumatic events is almost always beneficial."

"Yes, but as it turned out, Peg and I didn't do anything but listen. We weren't able to offer any insight or answers. If anyone was helped by the conversation, it was us."

Rose stood up and walked over to the coffee maker on the counter. She brought the pot back to the table and topped off both their cups. There was a small pitcher on the table. Peter added a splash of milk to his.

"I've been wondering when you'd get around to mentioning that you and Peg had joined forces again," he said as Rose sat back down. "I know you well enough to read the signs. I assume the two of you are looking into Nolan Abercrombie's death?"

Rose flapped a hand in the air as if she were waving away Peter's objection—even though he'd known better than to make one. Sometimes, his ability to read her mind worked in her favor.

"She and I are snooping around a little," Rose admitted. "But, so far, the only thing we've uncovered is a surprisingly large group of disgruntled women."

"I hope Peg isn't among them," Peter said. "How is she coping with all this? After what she went through—first forming the relationship with Nolan, then experiencing the shock of his unexpected death—there are bound to be lingering aftereffects."

"You know Peg. She's tough."

"At least that's what she wants the world to think."

"She told me she was fine."

"I expected nothing less," Peter said with a nod. "But how is she really?"

Rose shrugged. "We talked through some things. She accused me of trying to usurp your role as counselor. Then she drank a cup of tea and didn't eat cake."

"No cake? That sounds serious."

Rose smiled, as she knew she was meant to. "If I had to guess, I'd say Peg is more angry than heartbroken. And her way of working through that anger will be chasing down the person responsible for Nolan's death."

"You're a good friend to help her do that. Please let Peg know that I'm here if she needs me."

"I will."

"What about you?" Peter asked.

"Me?" Rose was surprised. "I barely knew Nolan. I only met him once."

"Yes, but you're the one who encouraged Peg to sign up for that online dating site. I seem to recall that you even created her profile. So maybe you're feeling guilty that you're the person who got Peg mixed up in this."

Rose pushed back her chair and stood up. She'd piled the dinner dishes in the sink and left them for later, so she and Peter could sit and enjoy their coffee. But suddenly it seemed like a good time to get to work. Rose turned on the hot-water faucet and waited, her back turned toward the table, for the ancient water heater in the basement to kick in.

After a few seconds, she sensed Peter standing behind her. Rose slowly turned to face him. "Don't you dare tell me I'm trying to avoid examining my feelings."

"I wouldn't dream of it," he said innocently.

"Peg makes her own decisions. You know that as well as anyone."

"I do," he agreed.

Rose gazed at her husband's face, only inches away from her own. There was a wealth of experience written in the wrinkles that framed his features. The look in his warm brown eyes wasn't judgmental. This man was dearer to her than anything else in the world.

"You know I hate it when you're right," Rose said.

"I do," Peter repeated. Why mess with a good thing? The phrase seemed to be working for him.

"Maybe the dishes can wait until later," Rose said.

She took Peter's hand and twined his fingers through hers. It only took him a moment to realize there was an invitation in the gesture. He smiled. Then he nodded. Rose was still trying to distract him. They both knew that. But at least for now, neither of them cared.

Peg was at another dog show. On a brilliant, breezy, late summer day, she couldn't think of anywhere else she would rather be. This time, her judging assignment consisted of all the breeds in the Toy Group, and then later the group itself. That suited Peg perfectly.

To make the day even better, her ring steward was her good friend Terry Denunzio. Peg had known Terry for years. He'd originally arrived on the dog show scene as assistant to professional handler Crawford Langley. Now the two of them were happily married. Terry was impudent, flamboyant, and always entertaining. His presence was guaranteed to keep Peg on her toes.

Peg had judged occasional shows where the weather was bad, or the entries mediocre, or the exhibitors uninteresting—and the day seemed to last forever. Today, she knew, would fly by. Peg couldn't wait to get started.

When she arrived at her ring, Terry had everything under control. Her judge's table was set up just the way she liked it. The rubber-matted table she'd use to examine the small dogs was already in place. Terry had put two bottles of cold water and a wrapped apple tart beside her chair. When she arrived, he was standing near the in-gate, ready to hand out armbands to early exhibitors.

"Kiss, kiss." Terry smooched both her cheeks in greeting. Then he stepped back and said, "And don't you look lovely today."

Peg smiled, then sighed. As usual on show days, she'd favored practicality over style when getting dressed that morning. Her button-front, midi-length dress had an elastic waist and pockets. Her feet were wearing sturdy, flat-soled shoes. Though it was early, she'd already plopped a cotton sunhat on her head.

Compared to Terry, whose blond-tipped hair curled over the collar of an azure sports coat that he'd paired with a yellow pinstriped shirt and a vermillion tie, Peg felt like a wren standing beside a peacock. A rather large wren, since her height topped Terry's by at least two inches. But still.

"Flattery will avail you nothing today," Peg told him,

though she was nonetheless pleased by the effort. "I still intend to work you like a horse."

"I expected nothing less." Terry waggled his eyebrows suggestively. "You know me, I always aim to please."

"That's not what Crawford says," someone catcalled from outside the ring, where exhibitors and spectators had begun to gather.

Terry's friends were a rowdy bunch, and he didn't miss a beat. Terry looked to see who'd spoken, then stuck out his tongue in response.

Peg's sigh was loud enough to be heard in the neighboring ring. "Decorum," she murmured. "You're in my ring now."

"Yes, ma'am." Terry grinned. He wasn't chastened in the slightest.

It was time to call the first class, Chihuahua Puppy Dogs, into the ring. Two cream-colored puppies came forward, hopping and playing at the end of their handlers' leads. With that, Peg and Terry were off and running. Working together seamlessly, they didn't pause again until the morning's judging was almost finished.

"Papillons," Terry said happily as the last one exited the ring. "I want one. They're such smart dogs, and they excel at agility."

"Agility?" Peg asked. "I had no idea you were interested. Is that going to be the next feather in your cap?"

"Not anytime soon." Terry managed a credible pout. "Crawford keeps me much too busy to think about taking up a hobby."

"Crawford's at the top of his game," Peg said fondly. "Of course you're busy. Most handlers would give their eye teeth to enjoy his level of success. He's worked long and hard for it too."

"You're right, he has. And Crawford deserves every minute of it. But I still wish I could get him to take things a little easier."

Peg felt an unwanted twinge. "Is there a particular reason for that?"

"He's not as young as he used to be," said Terry, who had yet to turn forty.

"None of us are." She looked down her nose at him. Peg and Crawford were of an age. She hoped Terry would consider his next words carefully. "But that doesn't mean we're ready to be put out to pasture."

Terry got the message and changed the subject. "Silky Terriers coming right up," he said before calling the class into the ring.

When the breed was finished, the show photographer came to take the morning's win pictures. Then it was time for their lunch break. Terry was already outside the ring before he noticed that Peg wasn't following him. Instead she was sitting in her chair, thumbing through a catalog.

"Aren't you coming?" he asked.

"In a minute. There's someone I want to talk to first."

"Charlie Vargas."

Peg looked up. "How do you know that?"

"I heard you'd gotten yourself involved in another mystery."

"From whom?"

Terry smirked. "Izzy Hicks told Beth Sharp who told Edmund Bright. When he passed the news along to Crawford, I happened to overhear them."

Peg tried to remember precisely what she'd said to Izzy. She knew they'd spoken about Nolan and Charlie, but she was quite certain she hadn't said a thing about looking into Nolan's death. Had Izzy simply assumed that would be Peg's next step? She hoped not. Peg hated to think that she might be becoming predictable in her old age.

"You *happened* to overhear them?" she said. "I doubt that. Everyone knows you have the biggest ears in the dog world."

"Better than the biggest mouth," Terry retorted. "Charlie has half the Sporting Group today. His ring is down at the other end of the tent."

Peg rose to her feet. "And you know that why?"

"Because a good steward always anticipates his or her judge's needs."

"I suppose I should say thank you." Peg wasn't entirely sure about that.

The last thing she needed was Terry poking his nose into her business. Especially after she'd chided him about decorum. If word got out about her disastrous foray into online dating, she would never live it down.

"No problemo," he replied.

Peg headed toward the gate. "I hope you didn't warn Charlie I'd want to talk to him."

"*Please.* I'm not that much of a busybody."

"Really?" She doubted that claim. "I didn't know there was a quantifiable measurement. Exactly how much of one are you?"

Terry held up his hand with thumb and forefinger less than an inch apart. As she swept past him, Peg rearranged his fingers, widening the gap considerably. Then she leaned down and smacked a kiss on his cheek. "But we love you anyway."

"I should hope so," Terry said.

Peg walked down the tent-covered center aisle that ran between the double rows of rings. When she came to a group of Irish Setters gathered outside a ring, their owners intent on the action taking place within, she knew she'd found the right place.

Charlie Vargas was holding court inside the ring. He was an attractive man, tall and hearty, several years older than Peg. He judged his class with an effortless air of authority, gained through his many years of experience in the dog world. Unless Peg missed her guess, Charlie was about to award Best of Breed. Half a dozen handlers and dogs were standing in front of him, each one working hard to convince him that their red Setter was the best.

Automatically, Peg's gaze skimmed down the line. The Winners Dog and Winners Bitch were at the end, and she dismissed them immediately. Both were nice specimens of their breed, but neither was as impressive as the four champion Irish Setters in front of them. Before Peg had time to make her choice, Charlie was already pointing to his winner. The crowd around the ring whooped its approval. The handler at the head of the line moved his dog over to stand beside the BOB marker. Best of Opposite Sex and Best of Winners went to the Winners Bitch.

Charlie spent the next ten minutes posing for pictures. When he finished, Peg was still waiting patiently. By then most of the spectators had dispersed. Charlie exited the ring carrying a small backpack. He seemed surprised to see her standing there.

"Hello, Peg," he said. "This is an unexpected pleasure. Were you looking for me?"

"Yes, I was hoping we could talk."

Charlie and Peg's husband had been good friends. Peg had fond memories from years ago, the three of them getting together for post-show dinners, along with whichever of Charlie's wives he'd been married to at the time. Peg seemed to recall that there had been at least three.

She nodded toward his backpack. "Is that your lunch?"

"It is. Years of eating dog show food gave me ulcers, so I started bringing my own. It's a huge improvement."

Peg wondered if Charlie was currently married. Perhaps the succession of wives had more to do with his abdominal upset than the food he'd been eating. Peg had no intention of asking about that.

Charlie gestured toward an empty picnic table under a nearby tree. "You're more than welcome to join me, but I'm sorry to say I didn't bring enough for two."

"Don't worry about me. My steward was kind enough

to bring me an apple tart this morning, and I'll grab something from the hospitality tent before I head back to my ring."

They sat down across from each other at the rustic table. Peg waited for Charlie to unpack his lunch. He went about the chore methodically, setting out a bottle of Gatorade, a wrapped sandwich, an orange, and an energy bar. There was also a napkin, a straw, and a moist towelette for his fingers. The meal was so organized that Peg found herself wondering if Charlie might have another new wife and whether she'd been the one who packed it.

Charlie held up his orange and offered it to her. Peg shook her head. She had no intention of getting sidetracked by sticky fingers.

"I'm wondering what you might be able to tell me about Nolan Abercrombie," she said.

"Who?"

He unwrapped his sandwich and quickly took his first bite. Call Peg cynical, but she was pretty sure he'd shoved the ham-and-cheese on rye into his mouth in order to give himself time to consider how he wanted to respond.

"Nolan Abercrombie," she said again. "He told me he knew you. That the two of you used to do business together."

"No, that's wrong." Charlie hadn't even finished chewing, and he was already shaking his head. "Nolan was just a guy I met somewhere along the way. He said he was interested in getting a Vizsla. I might have brought him along to a show once or twice."

Peg nodded as if that made sense. Which she was quite sure it didn't. Charlie seemed intent on convincing her that he'd barely known Nolan. That wasn't the impression she'd gotten from Izzy or from Nolan himself.

"Did you sell him a dog?" she asked.

"No. He would have been a terrible home. As I recall, he lived in an apartment and led a mostly sedentary lifestyle. A high-energy dog like a Vizsla would have been a horrible choice for him. I told him that."

Charlie opened his Gatorade bottle and took a long swallow before reaching for his sandwich again. "I haven't thought about Nolan Abercrombie in years. Why are you interested in him?"

"He's dead," Peg said bluntly.

Charlie slowly put the sandwich back down. "That's too bad. Was he a friend of yours?"

"We'd just met recently. And no, due to a variety of reasons I wouldn't characterize Nolan as a friend. But I do find myself curious about why someone might have wanted to kill him."

"Kill him?" Charlie sounded shocked. "How did he die?"

"Someone ran over him with a car." Peg gave him a minute to absorb that information. Then she added, "Since then, it's come to light that Nolan was a bit of a con man. Did you know anything about that?"

"Of course not. Like I told you, he and I never did business together. He was an accountant, and I had no need for his services."

Peg frowned at yet another version of Nolan's "truth." Either the man had concurrently held a variety of jobs, or he'd told everyone he met a different story. Most likely the latter.

"Apparently he was skilled at keeping track of other people's money," she said drily. "Whether they wanted him to or not."

"I wouldn't know anything about that. Nolan and I mostly just talked about dogs."

That was interesting, Peg thought. Considering that she and Nolan had spent almost no time talking about dogs. It hadn't seemed to be a subject Nolan cared much about.

"Izzy Hicks sends her regards," she said suddenly.

"Izzy." Charlie started to smile, then paused and went still.

Peg hoped he was making the connection she intended him to. It seemed he had, because before he spoke again Charlie began to gather up the remains of his half-eaten lunch.

"Please tell her I said hello the next time you see her."

"I will," Peg promised.

"I hate to eat and run," Charlie said. The table between them was empty. He'd already stuffed everything back inside his backpack. "I just remembered I told the show secretary I'd stop by during my break."

"That sounds important," Peg said. "I won't detain you any longer."

"Nice to see you, Peg." Charlie stood up. "I enjoyed our chat."

"Me too," she replied to his departing back.

Peg watched him stride across the open field and disappear beneath the tent. "Show secretary, my foot," she said.

Chapter 19

Rose used the phone number Barbara had given Peg to find Jason Abercrombie's address. He was still living in Norwalk. Google Maps showed her a picture of a plain brick apartment building, located on the edge of an industrial zone. Rose relayed the information to Peg when she got home from her dog show. They decided to visit Nolan's son the following morning.

Rose awoke to a rumble of thunder. Sheets of rain were driving against the windows of her bedroom. Still sleepy, she turned over and saw that Peter's side of the bed was empty. The clock on the night table said seven-fifteen.

Rose's eyes opened wide. She threw back the covers and jumped out of bed. It had been years since she'd slept this late. Peter had an early counseling session scheduled. She knew he'd be long gone by now. Why hadn't he awakened her before he'd left?

"Drat, drat, drat," Rose muttered as she stubbed her toe on the way to the shower. Peg was due to pick her up shortly. Knowing nothing about Jason's employment situation, they'd concluded that their best chance to catch him at home might be first thing in the morning.

At least that had seemed like a good idea the night before. Now Rose wasn't so sure. By the time she went dashing out of the house with damp hair, a mis-buttoned blouse, and her raincoat flung over her shoulders, Peg who was sitting by the curb outside, had already honked twice.

Rose yanked open the door to the minivan. Several fat drops of water landed on her head as she jumped up onto the seat. Then her raincoat snagged on the door handle and slid off her shoulders. Rose just managed to snatch it up before it landed in the gutter. She slammed the door and glared at Peg.

"If you were so impatient, why didn't you come inside to wait?" she growled.

For several seconds, Peg simply stared at her. Then she started to laugh.

"What's so funny?" Rose demanded.

"You."

"This"—Rose waved a hand to encompass her entire bedraggled appearance—"isn't funny."

"From here it is." Peg's hair was dry. So were her clothes. A neatly folded umbrella lay on the floor between their seats. Presumably the minivan had been parked in Peg's garage when she'd gotten behind the wheel.

And Peg was still laughing. *Dammit.*

"Now what?" Rose snapped.

"I can't remember the last time I saw you lose your temper. So pardon me if I'm enjoying watching you let off steam. You're the most mild-mannered person I've ever met. You never have a bad day. Do you have any idea how annoying that is?"

Rose opened her mouth. No words came out. She closed it again.

As Peg turned the key, the windshield wipers began to slap back and forth. "All hell can be breaking loose. I'll be running around like a lunatic—and you just sit there like an island of calm in an ocean of chaos. Placid. Composed. Unperturbable. It's unnerving."

Rose blinked several times as she processed that. A bead

of water slid down the length of her nose, then dropped off to land in her lap.

"It's not normal," Peg added, as if she hadn't already made her point.

"It is for me," Rose replied in a small voice. "I hate to lose control."

Peg looked at her, then frowned. "I suppose that's another thing they trained out of you in the convent."

"Possibly."

"Well, you're out in the big world now. You should try yelling at someone once in a while."

"I don't want to yell at anybody." Rose shuddered at the idea.

"Are you sure?" Peg asked. "You came close to yelling at me a minute ago."

"That doesn't count. You're different. If anyone knows where to find my last nerve, it's you."

"I think I'll take that as a compliment," Peg said.

Rose navigated while Peg drove. On the rain-slick roads, the trip to south Norwalk took half an hour. As they were approaching the block where Jason lived, the clouds finally began to part. The rain stopped, and a small slice of sun peaked through. By then, Rose had rebuttoned her blouse and fluffed her hair. She was trying to remember if she'd had time to brush her teeth when Peg pulled the minivan over to the curb and parked.

"You stay here," she said.

Rose was already reaching for the door handle. "What? Why?"

"Think about it. There's a good possibility Jason will be reluctant to talk about his father. We shouldn't take a chance on spooking him by both of us showing up unannounced. He might refuse to see us altogether."

Peg had used similar logic when Rose had proposed calling ahead to ask Jason if he'd be willing to meet with them. Yet here they were anyway, sitting outside his apartment building on a mission that was suddenly beginning to look like an ambush. And, as usual, Peg thought she should be the one who got to do the interesting stuff and have all the fun.

That was so not happening, Rose thought. She hadn't come all the way to Norwalk just to wait in the car.

"If you think both of us together might be a problem, then you stay behind and I'll go talk to him," she said. "Besides, everybody knows you're the spooky one. Look what happened at the funeral. I seem to recall Jason couldn't get away from you fast enough."

"Bygones," Peg said.

Rose thought not.

"At least Jason will recognize me," Peg said. "He might not even open his door to you."

That was backward thinking if Rose had ever heard it. Why would Jason open his door to someone who had already annoyed him? Rose, meanwhile, was an unknown quantity. And a delightful one at that.

As Rose was framing her rebuttal, Peg barged ahead and took matters into her own hands. Assuming Rose's acquiescence, the exasperating woman hopped out of the minivan and strode across the sidewalk, heading toward the paved walkway that led to the front of the building.

Fuming silently, Rose watched Peg's progress through her side window. Maybe the door to the squat, unadorned building would be locked. Maybe Peg would need to be buzzed inside and no one would come to her aid. Then she'd be forced to turn back and they could come up with a new plan. *Together.* One in which Rose figured prominently . . .

No such luck. Peg opened the front door without a hitch and stepped inside the building. Rose sighed. And resigned herself to waiting.

She spent the next two minutes listing all the reasons why this situation was unfair. Rose and Peg were supposed to be partners. Granted Peg was the one with more experience in these matters, but that was no reason for Rose to assume a subordinate role. She could think on her feet. Not only that, but she'd acquitted herself admirably during their previous case.

No, the real problem was that Peg was a bully and Rose wasn't being forceful enough in standing up to her—

Abruptly Rose sat up in her seat when a movement next to the apartment building caught her eye. Peg was still inside somewhere, probably pounding on Jason's door. Meanwhile, a man was walking toward the street in the alleyway between this building and the one beside it. When he reached the end of the alley, he paused to cautiously look both ways.

Rose had only caught a brief glimpse of Jason at the funeral. But that was enough for her to recognize him now. He was dressed in worn jeans and a long-sleeved T-shirt that looked as though it had been pulled on in a hurry. A dark baseball cap was pulled low over his chiseled features. Now that Rose knew that Jason was Nolan's son, it was easy for her to see the resemblance between them.

Rose cast a quick glance back to the building's front door. There was still no sign of Peg. Rose chuckled under her breath. Peg probably thought she had Jason cornered in his apartment. Instead, he'd managed to slip out the back to avoid her.

Fate—or Peg's arrogance—had handed Rose a chance to show what she could do. She felt like an understudy who'd unexpectedly been given the starring role. Rose wasn't about to blow this opportunity.

She grabbed her purse, opened the door, and casually stepped out onto the sidewalk. Jason didn't even glance her way as he strolled across the scraggly lawn in front of the brick building. Reaching the sidewalk, he turned and headed in the opposite direction from where Rose was standing.

Up ahead, stores and businesses lined either side of the street. Rose saw a welding company, a cabinetry design store, and an auto-supply shop. She suspected Jason wasn't interested in any of them—he was merely trying to escape. He pulled out his phone and began to scroll through something on the screen as he walked along. Thankfully, that slowed his steps enough that Rose was able to catch up.

"Excuse me, Jason?"

He lifted his gaze just long enough to glance back at her. "Yes?" he said without breaking stride.

Rose thought fast, then said, "I was a friend of your father." Okay, that was stretching things a bit, but Rose knew it was what Peg would have done under the circumstances. "Can we talk?"

Jason stopped. When he turned around, the expression on his face made Rose's heart sink. The young man looked hopeful, as if he thought maybe she'd come to convey a last message of love or acceptance from Nolan.

Obviously Rose had nothing of the sort to offer. And she hated having to be the person who would dash his hopes. All at once she found herself wishing that she'd stayed in the minivan.

The two of them stared at each other for a long moment. Rose realized she'd waited too long to say something when Jason's expression abruptly hardened. He shoved the phone back in his pocket and resumed walking.

Rose stared after him briefly. Then resolve stiffened her shoulders. She refused to believe she'd missed her chance already. She jogged to catch up, then fell into step beside him.

"My name is Rose Donovan," she began.

Jason shrugged. He didn't care. "How did you know my father?"

"We met through a mutual friend." That answer seemed safe enough.

"Nolan had lots of friends," Jason said dismissively. "Most of them were women."

"Yes," Rose agreed. "He liked women."

"Probably because they let him take whatever he wanted from them."

"You seem to have a rather clear-eyed view of your father's flaws," Rose said. It was hard enough trying to hold a conversation talking to the side of Jason's head. If he didn't slow down, pretty soon she was going to be out of breath from trying to keep up.

"I should. I've been keeping track of his exploits for a long time."

"That's interesting."

Jason flicked a glance her way. "Why?"

"Because someone was angry enough with him to want to kill him. Maybe you'd have some idea who that might be."

"Maybe I would," he said. "What's it to you?"

Rose's phone buzzed in her purse. She ignored it. No doubt Peg had arrived back at the minivan and was wondering where she was. Rose wasn't about to interrupt the conversation to offer an explanation.

"Don't you want to answer that?" Jason nodded in the direction of the sound. He was probably hoping to get away while she was distracted.

"No." Rose reset the shoulder strap so the purse was now behind her. "It's not important."

"It's that other old lady, isn't it?"

"What other old lady?"

"The busybody who accosted me at the funeral."

"Peg didn't mean to accost you," Rose said. "She just wanted to say hello."

"Yeah, right."

The sidewalk was buckled and broken in spots. Rose should have been looking where she was putting her feet. Instead, she'd turned to gaze up at Jason. So when her toe caught in a rut, her leg went right out from under her. As she started to stumble, Jason reached out a strong hand to grab her upper arm and steady her.

"Whew." Rose blew out an unsteady breath. "Thank you."

He shrugged. "Don't mention it."

She pressed on. "Peg was in a relationship with your father when he died. She didn't realize it at the time but if his scheme had gone according to plan, she could have become his latest victim."

"Then I guess it was lucky for her that he got run over," Jason said. "It sounds to me like she had a pretty good motive. Do the police have her on their suspect list?"

Rose laughed in spite of herself. "No."

He didn't look amused. "Why not?"

"Because Peg and Detective Sturgill are friends. Peg might get herself into trouble from time to time, but the detective knows perfectly well that she would never kill anyone."

"That doesn't seem fair," Jason muttered. "When I get into trouble, the law comes down on me like a ton of bricks."

"Is that so?" Rose said. "What kinds of trouble do you get into?"

"Nothing that you need to worry about." He stopped and turned to face her. "Look, are you going to follow me all the way to work or what?"

Rose shrugged. "Maybe I will. I'm enjoying our conversation. Where do you work?"

"I pick up odd jobs here and there. Today I'm filling in as an electrician's assistant. Guy has an office up the block. He's expecting me any time now."

"Then we should keep going," Rose said. There was something about this young man with the tough exterior that she was beginning to like. By mutual consent, they started walking again. "I wouldn't want to make you late. What other kinds of jobs do you do?"

"Whatever people need, I'm pretty much up for it as long as they're willing to pay."

"I hope you're not talking about lawbreaking," she said, remembering his earlier comment.

"Sheesh." Jason shook his head. "Who are you? My mother? I'm talking about normal stuff. Plumbing, painting, home maintenance, mechanical crap. Give me a set of tools and I can fix almost anything."

"You sound like a useful person to have around."

He peered at her suspiciously, as if he was afraid she might be making fun of him. "I like to think so."

"How come you don't have a steady job?"

"Because I don't have a high school diploma." His voice assumed a hard edge. "Which apparently makes people think I'm stupid."

"You don't sound stupid to me," Rose said.

"Thank you. I think. So what's the deal with you and the other lady?"

"We're trying to figure out who killed your father." Rose had thought her answer might surprise him, but Jason just nodded and kept walking.

"Why do you want to do that?"

"Because Peg and Nolan had become close. Peg thought she knew who he was. And now she realizes there were aspects of Nolan's life that she never even suspected. It's a puzzle she wants to solve."

Jason didn't look impressed by that answer. "You think you two old ladies can scoop the police?"

"We might. And if you're as smart as you think you are, you'll stop calling me an old lady."

"Will do." Jason grinned.

"You said earlier you might know of someone who had a grudge against Nolan. Will you give me a name?"

"Joe Danson."

"Who's he?"

"He used to be Nolan's best friend."

Rose committed the name to memory. "But not any-more?"

Jason shook his head.

"Why not?"

"You'd have to ask him."

"I'll do that," she said. "Where would I find Mr. Danson?"

"Probably at the Greenwich Library. Last I knew, the guy was like a permanent volunteer there."

Jason stopped outside a small office building at the end of the long block. The names of several businesses were stenciled on the front window. "This is me."

Rose nodded. "Thank you for talking to me. Do you have time for one last question?"

"If it's a quick one."

It wasn't, but Rose gave it a shot anyway. "Would you accept a full-time handyman position at a women's shelter if it was offered to you?"

Jason stared at her. "*What?*"

"My husband and I are co-proprietors of the Gallagher House in Stamford. The offer of employment would be subject to his approval, of course. But I think we could use someone with your skills."

"What?" Jason said again.

Rose reached out and patted his arm. "There's no need

to make a decision now. Just think about it, okay? I'll check back with you in a few days."

"I don't understand," he sputtered.

"That's all right. I'm not sure I do either."

"Are you for real?"

"I believe so," she said with a smile.

Jason looked utterly bewildered. He spun around, shoved open the door to the building and went inside. Rose couldn't blame him for his response. She was feeling a bit off-kilter herself.

She'd always believed in following her gut. Time would tell whether this was a brilliant idea or one of the dumbest snap decisions she'd ever made.

Chapter 20

Peg was looking distinctly disgruntled when she picked up Rose outside the electrician's office.

"What do you mean you had a long conversation with Jason Abercrombie?" she asked, as Rose climbed in and fastened her seat belt. "How did that happen? He wasn't even home. And if that wasn't bad enough, I came out of the building and discovered that the minivan was empty. For all I knew, you could have been abducted by aliens."

Of course, that would be Peg's first guess. Apparently, she'd never heard the old adage about hoofbeats and zebras.

"Jason *was* home," Rose replied. "But he saw you coming and ducked out before you could nab him."

"Why would he want to do that?"

Rose assumed that wasn't a serious question.

"He gave me the name of someone we should check out," she said. "Joe Danson. Apparently he was Nolan's best friend. Until he wasn't."

"I'd imagine that kind of thing happened to Nolan a lot." Peg glanced over at Rose. "Are you sure it's a real lead? Maybe Jason just fed you a line to get rid of you too."

"Jason didn't want to get rid of me. He and I were having a lovely chat."

"A lovely chat," Peg muttered. "That sounds unlikely. He didn't even want to talk to me."

"Which is why you and I make good partners," Rose said mildly. "We complement each other. I'm good with people who require a soft touch, and you—"

"Aren't?" Peg finished for her.

"I was going to say that you have other strengths. Which you know perfectly well you do." Rose settled back in her seat. "By the way, I offered Jason a job."

"*What?*"

Funny thing, Rose thought. That was Jason's first reaction too.

"A job at the shelter," she said. "Sort of a general handyman position. Subject to Peter's approval, of course."

"No wonder Jason was willing to talk to you." Peg sounded annoyed all over again. "You offered him a bribe."

"I did not. The idea for the job was totally separate. One thing had nothing to do with the other. Now the next move will be up to him."

Peter's reaction to Rose's job offer wasn't any more positive than Peg's had been. Even worse, Maura got involved in the discussion too. Pretty soon it began to feel as though everyone thought Rose was off her rocker.

Maura had been vacuuming in the living room when Peg dropped off Rose in front of the shelter. Peter was working in the office. When Rose went to talk to him, Maura tagged along. All three of them were stuffed inside the small room when Rose began to explain about Jason. It didn't go over well.

"Let me get this straight." Peter was sitting at the desk. He'd closed his computer when Rose and Maura entered and prepared to pay attention to what they needed. Now, however, he just looked perplexed. "You met this man for the first time this morning, spoke with him for perhaps ten minutes—and at the end of that time, you felt inspired to offer him a job. Working *here* in a capacity which I have yet to discover."

Marmalade was reclining in her favorite spot, on top of the file cabinet. Rose reached up and lifted the orange kitten down into her arms. Peg had said numerous times that she thought better with her hands on a dog. Maybe something similar would work for Rose.

"Yes, *here*," she replied firmly. "Jason could take care of all the things that have been eating up your valuable time: painting, rewiring, fixing the shutters, repairing the radiators. You know perfectly well that this house has been one problem after another since we moved in. And considering its age, we can reasonably expect the need for repairs to continue. While he's doing that, your expertise could be put to much better use in other areas."

Peter nodded. Rose wanted to believe that he'd conceded her points, but she knew her husband better than that. Peter was an analytical and deliberate man. He never rushed headlong into anything. More likely, he was simply considering what she'd said.

"Tell me more about him," he said.

"I didn't hear this from Jason, but apparently he had a rough start in life. His parents never married. He was rejected by his father and raised by a single mother. Both his parents have since passed away. Jason's had to make his own way in the world. He supports himself by picking up odd jobs, which has made him proficient at any number of skills."

Peter appeared to be softening. Rose had thought he might when he heard about Jason's background. "It seems you've learned a great deal about this man in a short amount of time," he said thoughtfully.

"You two are way too easy on people." Maura was still skeptical. She'd pulled a tissue from her pocket and was polishing the upper leaves of the rubber plant. "This guy you're talking about is an adult, right?"

Rose nodded.

"Then the fact that he doesn't already have a real job is a red flag. How old is he?"

"Young," Rose replied. "In his thirties. Like you."

"Young." Maura snorted, but she didn't look displeased. "And yet I, like most people my age, have a job. You see where I'm going with this, right?" Before Rose could reply, she added, "Would I have to train him?"

Rose laughed. "Not unless you're much more mechanically inclined than you've previously led us to believe."

Marmalade butted her head against the bottom of Rose's chin. They both enjoyed it when the kitten then rubbed her ears from side to side.

"Let's be realistic," Peter said. "As you know, our budget is already stretched thin. We don't have extra money lying around that we can use to hire someone just because we feel sorry for him."

"That's true," Rose replied. "But what if Jason could take over all the time-consuming projects that pull you away from more important things that you'd rather be doing?" She'd mentioned that earlier, but it didn't hurt to say it again. "I know you've been wanting to expand your counseling practice. If you had more free time, you could think about bringing in outside clients. That's something you've considered doing."

"You're right," Peter acknowledged. "But before we go too far down that path, there's something else we need to take into account. Is this young man still considered to be a suspect in his father's death?"

"Yes," Rose admitted unhappily. Somewhere along the way, she seemed to have lost sight of that complication.

"Then I propose that we table this discussion for the time being. I'd be happy to meet with Jason, but we should postpone any decision making until after the police have solved the crime. Does that meet with your approval?"

"It does," Rose said.

"That makes sense to me." Maura's reply was even more emphatic.

Marmalade added a loud purr to the proceedings. It seemed that they were all in agreement.

It felt like much too long since Peg had taken Hope for a ride in the car. Once, when they were both a good deal younger, she and the big Poodle had taken biweekly outings to dog shows, where Peg had handled Hope to both her championship and an obedience degree. They'd both enjoyed those excursions enormously.

But then time had moved on. Hope had produced two litters of puppies. Peg had been busy exhibiting Hope's offspring, and then her grandpuppies. After Peg was granted a judge's license, it meant that her trips to dog shows were mostly, of necessity, solitary jaunts.

Hope wasn't a youngster anymore. She wasn't as sprightly as she'd been, and her hearing wasn't as sharp. Once, their days together had seemed nearly limitless. Now Peg couldn't help but be aware that too much of that time was behind them. If Max's premature death had taught her anything, it was not to take the company of loved ones for granted. With that in mind, she was determined for Hope to enjoy as many special moments as possible.

"We're going to Bedford," Peg announced, even though Hope hadn't asked. The Poodle was sitting on the back seat of the minivan, staring intently out the window. She was just happy to be along for the ride. "Helen Woodruff lives on a small horse farm there. She said you were welcome to come with me as long as you behaved."

Hope wagged her tail happily. She wasn't worried. She'd been a model of decorum since birth. Besides, they both understood that of the two of them, Peg was the one more likely to misbehave.

When Peg and Rose had split up earlier in the day, Peg requested a copy of Rose's list of contacts. Rose had emailed it to her swiftly and without complaint, probably because she was still gloating over her success with Jason. Rose had certainly stolen Peg's thunder there.

Not that the two of them were in competition, of course.

Having been left behind once today, Peg wasn't about to let it happen again. Nor did she have any intention of consulting with Rose about her next move. Rose obviously hadn't asked her opinion before leaping into action earlier. Peg was merely following suit when she took out the list and began making calls. On her third try, she'd spoken to Helen Woodruff, who was available to meet with her this afternoon.

Peg had expected a horse farm to be located in the countryside. To her surprise, once she'd reached Bedford, GPS directed her to a suburban neighborhood. Peg slowed down when a post-and-rail fence came into view. The number on the mailbox matched the one she'd been given, and she turned into a gravel driveway that was bordered on either side by an acre of pasture.

Peg glanced around but didn't see any horses. Hope, however, was up on her feet, dancing back and forth across the seat and whining under her breath. Clearly she'd spied something interesting.

The driveway ended in front of two small structures: a cape-style house and a compact barn, both painted in a matching shade of moss green. As Peg paused to fasten a leash to Hope's collar, a woman emerged from the barn. Dressed in a faded denim shirt, dark jeans, and paddock boots, she was wiping her hands on her pants as she approached the minivan.

Helen Woodruff was a few years younger than Peg and

looked like someone who'd spent the majority of her life outdoors. Her skin was tanned, her boots were scuffed, and her gray-blond hair was fastened back in a low bun at the nape of her neck. Her bright blue eyes cast an appraising glance at Peg. Then she smiled when Hope hopped out of the van.

"That's a pretty Poodle," Helen said. She stooped down to cup her palms gently around Hope's muzzle. "I was expecting something smaller. What's her name?"

"Hope." Peg was happy to be upstaged by her dog.

Helen glanced up. "Was that meant to be a prediction or a promise?"

"Both."

"I can probably guess the answer by looking at her, but did she live up to your expectations?"

"That, and more," Peg replied.

"Are you her breeder?"

"I am."

"Then well done." Helen levered herself back to her feet.

"Thank you." Peg had a feeling she and Helen were going to get along just fine. "Where are your horses?"

The woman gestured toward the field Peg had just driven past. "In this weather, they mostly live outside. It's better for them. Plus they're happier out there. Do you want to go have a look?"

"Yes, please." Peg followed Helen across the driveway to a gate. She still didn't see any horses. The pasture wasn't that big. Surely they should have been visible by now.

Hope tugged at her leash. She poked her nose between the fence rails and woofed softly. Her tail began to wag. Peg moved in closer and took another look. Abruptly, she realized that she needed to adjust her gaze downward.

Out near a copse of trees, and half-hidden in the shade, was a herd of a dozen tiny horses. Peg saw pintos, palominos, and dappled grays. As Helen unlatched the gate and they entered the field, she realized that none of the small equines appeared to be much bigger than Hope.

The horses had been grazing, but now several lifted their heads to check out the visitors. With their large eyes, sculpted muzzles, and copious forelocks, they looked like something out of a fairy tale.

"How adorable," Peg said. Then she began to laugh. "When you said you had a small horse farm, I thought you were referring to acreage, not the horses themselves."

"Actually, I said I had a Miniature Horse farm," Helen corrected with a smile. "These are Miniature Horses. We can walk over and say hello, if you like. They're very friendly."

"I'd love that."

They reached the edge of the compact herd and were immediately surrounded. The mini horses were both affectionate and curious. They were particularly interested in Hope, who was similarly fascinated. The Poodle touched their muzzles with her nose, much as she would have done to greet another dog.

"What do you do with them?" Peg asked as she patted the withers of a friendly mare. "I assume they're too small to be ridden?"

"Only by very tiny children," Helen told her. "But they pull carts quite handily. I show them in Pleasure Driving and Halter classes. And I breed them to try and improve upon my stock." She glanced down at Hope. "Much as I suspect you do with your Standard Poodles?"

"Absolutely," Peg replied. "It looks as though we have more in common than our association with Nolan Abercrombie."

"That poor man." Helen sighed. "I didn't go to his funeral, you know. I should have, but I couldn't bring myself to do it. I knew there was bound to be acrimony, and women who'd chosen to attend for the sole purpose of venting their bitterness. I just didn't want to subject myself to that."

"It sounds as though your feelings for Nolan must have been different from theirs," Peg commented. She was keeping a close eye on Hope, but the Poodle appeared to be getting along splendidly with the horses.

Helen nodded. "I met Nolan at a particularly vulnerable time in my life. I'd lost my husband to cancer six months earlier. After he passed, I fell into a deep depression. To be perfectly frank, I wasn't sure I could see the point of continuing on alone."

"I'm sorry," Peg said. "I understand all too well how you felt." Thank goodness when Peg had found herself in a similar situation, she'd had Melanie and their collaborative search for her missing stud dog to assuage her dejection.

"Nolan was the perfect antidote," Helen said with a fond smile. "He was handsome, erudite, and utterly attentive to my needs. He was everything I needed at that point in my life."

"And maybe you fell in love with him?"

"Oh yes, I most definitely did that." Helen reached down and scratched a small pinto between its brown-and-white ears. "I was blindly, perhaps foolishly, head over heels in love."

"Foolishly?" Peg echoed. "Did Nolan try to take advantage of you too?"

"He didn't just try, he succeeded." Helen didn't seem unduly perturbed by that fact. "I considered the money I lost on Nolan's investments to be a small price to pay for the pleasure of his company. When Nolan moved on, I wasn't upset about that part. I was only sad that our time together had come to an end."

Peg couldn't imagine that. It occurred to her that Nolan must have been awfully good in bed to inspire that kind of devotion, despite everything else he'd done. Perhaps it had been a mistake not to find out for herself.

"Nolan took your money, then broke up with you, and you weren't angry about that?" she asked.

Helen chuckled at Peg's expression. "You sound like my son. Harry was utterly outraged on my behalf. He threatened to hunt Nolan down and make him pay."

"Harry," Peg said carefully. "Considering what happened, are you sure he didn't do just that?"

"Quite certain. He works for the State Department, and he's currently posted to Shanghai. He was thousands of miles away when Nolan died." Helen winked at her over the backs of the two ponies between them. "I may have been a fool in love, but in other matters, I'm quite astute. If there was any possibility Harry had been involved, I would never have told you about him."

Ten minutes later, Peg and Hope were on their way back to Greenwich. "What did you think?" Peg asked over her shoulder. "Was Helen's story about being in love with Nolan credible? I believed her until the very end. Then suddenly, she made me wonder if everything she'd previously said was a well-crafted fabrication."

Hope sat up and pricked her ears, so Peg kept talking. "It would be terrible if I was turning into a pushover. It's bad enough that I allowed myself to be duped by Nolan. Do you suppose I've done the same with Helen?"

Hope woofed happily. Peg knew what that meant.

"You don't care about any of that, do you? You just liked Helen's little horses."

Tongue hanging out of the side of her mouth, the Poodle grinned in agreement.

Peg turned her gaze back to the road in front of her. "I'm glad to see somebody's pleased about the way that worked out," she grumbled.

Chapter 21

Rose had always loved the Greenwich Library. Located just west of downtown, it was housed in a multistory concrete building with large windows and plenty of open space. The facility had thousands of books, numerous databases, and a collection dedicated to local history and genealogy. As a Connecticut resident, Rose was able to access the library's services, even though she lived in neighboring Stamford. She often made good use of its resources.

It was midafternoon when Rose parked in the lot outside the library. Several hours had passed since Peg had dropped her off at the shelter, and though she'd been tempted, she had so far resisted the impulse to call and offer the apology she was sure Peg was waiting for. It wasn't her fault that she'd succeeded with Jason where Peg had failed.

Rose would never have admitted this out loud, but she was feeling quite proud of herself. The morning's accomplishment had given her a sense of satisfaction she was still savoring. Maybe by the time she was finished at the library, she would have scooped Peg again. That would really make her day.

Rose skipped up the library steps and went directly to

the welcome desk. She offered her best breezy smile to the woman who was waiting there to help her and said, "Where might I find Joe Danson at this time of day?"

The woman smiled in return. "Are you a friend of his?"

"Yes," Rose fibbed. "He told me I should drop by and say hello when I was in the neighborhood."

"He's probably in the children's reading room. We finished hosting an event not too long ago. I'd imagine he's still straightening up and reshelving all the books that got pulled out and dropped on the floor." She lowered her voice to a whisper. "We love having the little ones come and visit, but sometimes it's a relief when they go home."

"I know what you mean," Rose said. "Thank you. I'll go look for him."

Having just stated that she knew the man, Rose could hardly ask now what he looked like. Fortunately, when she reached the children's section of the library, it was mostly empty. A lone older man was attempting to push two wooden tables together to form a single large workspace. Rose strode over to the far table, dropped her purse on top of it and shoved it toward him. The tables came together with a sharp click.

"Thanks," he said. "That's easier to manage with two people."

The man straightened and rolled his shoulders. He was taller than Rose and slender in build. His deep brown eyes stood out beneath a head that was entirely bald and somewhat sunburned. A handmade sign reading I'M HERE TO HELP! was affixed to the right side of his button-down shirt.

"You must be Joe," Rose said.

"That's me. Tell me what you're looking for, and I'll show you where to find it."

"I need information."

"That's easy." Joe nodded. "I can direct you to our card catalog, to a computer, or to our information desk. Your choice."

"Actually, I was hoping that you might be free for a few minutes to chat. My name is Rose Donovan. My associate and I are looking into the murder of Nolan Abercrombie."

By implication, that was another fib. This day was turning out to be full of them. Rose hoped she wouldn't have to go to confession by the end of it.

He stared at her. "You don't look like you're from the police. Who's your associate?"

"Peg Turnbull." Of course the name wouldn't mean anything to him. Rose rushed on before he had time to think about that. "I understand that you were Nolan's best friend."

"Used to be," he said with a frown. "Not anymore. Who'd you say you work for again?"

"I didn't say. It's a private matter."

The answer felt inadequate to Rose, but to her relief, Joe was satisfied by it. "I guess I could take a short break," he said. "But we probably shouldn't talk here."

"What about downstairs in the café?" Rose asked. "Can I buy you a cup of coffee?"

"Add a raisin scone to that, and you've got yourself a deal."

The lower-level eatery was doing a brisk business in midafternoon, but Joe managed to snag them a table near the front window. Rose bought two cups of coffee and a scone, then joined him there. She waited until Joe had added two sugars to his coffee, then taken his first sip. When he began to unwrap the raisin scone, she was about to speak but Joe beat her to it.

"It occurs to me that I'm sitting here with a woman

whom I conned into buying me a snack," he said, sounding bemused. "And since that reminds me of Nolan, it also makes me wonder. What's your connection to the guy?"

"I believe you have that backward," Rose replied. "I was the one who offered to buy you coffee. So consider yourself absolved of guilt in that regard. You should also consider my motives—and that my offer was probably made in an attempt to con you into answering my questions."

"Yeah, but so far it isn't working out very well for you." Joe grinned, then stuffed a large piece of scone into his mouth. It didn't appear to impede his ability to talk. "I'm munching on a free and tasty pastry over here, and I still haven't answered a single question."

Rose sampled her coffee. The dark brew was hot and delicious. "I'm hoping that's about to change."

"Shoot," Joe invited.

"You and Nolan used to be friends, and now you're not. What happened to change that?"

"Which version do you want?" Joe asked. "The long or the short?"

"I'll take the long one if you have time."

"Considering that I'm a volunteer here at the library, I'd say I have just as much time as I want. And if you were inclined to get me a second scone, you might find yourself getting even more answers."

Rose glanced over toward the counter. The line had disappeared. She could probably be there and back in less than two minutes.

However there was something about Joe's flippant manner that made her suspect he wasn't entirely trustworthy. Rose was sure Peg would know what to do in a situation like this. Thanks to her experiences with Melanie, she was accustomed to dealing with smooth talkers like Joe. While Rose most definitely was not.

"You're not going to disappear when I turn my back, are you?"

Joe's brown eyes twinkled. "You look like a lady who enjoys a challenge. Go ahead and try me, and we'll both find out."

It wasn't the most encouraging answer she'd ever heard. Then again, it wasn't the worst one either. Rose stood up and strode over to the counter. She completed the transaction without taking so much as a single backward glance. When she finally turned around, Joe was still seated at the table where she'd left him.

He lifted one hand and saluted her with a small wave.

"I'm not sure you're a nice man," Rose said. She handed Joe his second scone and sat back down.

"I'm not sure I ever said I was." He smirked.

"But that doesn't necessarily mean you're a murderer."

"*Whoa.*" Joe glanced up. "How did that idea get on the table?"

"You offered me two versions of your story." Rose sat back and crossed her arms over her chest. "So far, I haven't heard either one. So now I'm just trying to move things along. Someone killed Nolan Abercrombie. Was it you?"

"Of course not."

"Why not?"

"What do you mean 'why not?' " His brow lowered in a ferocious frown. "Because I'm not a murderer, that's why."

"But you might have had reason to want him dead."

"No. Yes. Maybe." Joe stopped and shrugged. "Not dead. Just gone from my life."

"Why?" Rose asked.

They were finally getting somewhere. It was about time. If she had to go back and buy Joe a third scone, she was going to get one for herself. Because it was beginning to look like she might be here through dinner.

How did Peg manage to wrap up her interrogations in such a timely manner? Rose had no idea. Maybe she ought to ask. If Peg was still speaking to her, that is. Apparently that was still to be determined.

Then it occurred to her that Joe had yet to answer her question. This seemed to be the continuing theme of their conversation.

"Go on," she prompted with a flick of her hand. "Say something."

"I'm not guilty," Joe blurted out.

"I never said you were."

"If not, you certainly implied it."

"That's because you're making me do all the talking. This conversation would be much easier if you'd speak up every now and then."

Joe swallowed and took a breath. It looked like he might finally be ready to tell his story. "Nolan and I used to be pals," he said. "Fellow sports enthusiasts. Drinking buddies. We hung out together."

"Good start," Rose replied. "Keep going."

"I thought I knew most of what there was to know about him. I mean, I'd been pretty candid about my own life: a failed marriage, kids grown and gone, a small inheritance that enabled me to think about retiring early. As far as I was concerned, we were just two guys keeping each other company rather than drinking alone. If that meant I was Nolan's best friend, it was only because—as I realized afterward—the guy didn't really have any friends."

"After what?" Rose took another sip of her coffee. It was beginning to grow cold. She wasn't about to get another.

"Nolan introduced me to a lady friend of his. Said she was a widower and alone like me. Since we seemed to have a lot in common, he thought maybe we'd get along. At

first I wasn't interested. I'm way past the age where someone should be setting me up on blind dates, you know?"

Rose nodded.

"But Nolan could be persistent when he wanted something," Joe continued. His fingers were turning his scone
into a crumbling mess. "And eventually I caved in. When
he introduced me to Barbie, we immediately hit it off.
Man, I thought she was something special."

"Barbie?" Rose repeated. A suspicion took shape in her
mind.

"Yeah, like the doll. And the name suited her. Blond
hair, big blue eyes, and . . ." Joe held up his hands and
traced a curvaceous figure in the air. "For a couple of
months, I thought I was the luckiest man in the world."

"I'll bet," Rose said.

Joe peered at her across the table. "You asked me to tell
you my story, and now you sound skeptical. What gives?"

"I think I've met your Barbie. Only her name was Barbara. And she said she was Nolan's sister."

"His sister?" He looked surprised. "That's not right.
Nolan didn't have any close family."

"Nolan told a lot of people lies," Rose said mildly.
"Probably including you. I'm guessing Barbie did too?"

"You could say that," Joe admitted.

"Did she convince you to let Nolan invest money
for you?"

"Nolan?" Judging by the look on Joe's face, Rose had
surprised him again. "Hell no, he never asked me for anything. It was Barbie who did that. She told me she was
about to make a killing on a real estate deal in the Cayman
Islands. After we got to know each other a little, she offered me a chance to get in on it. But only if I acted fast.
She said she was doing me a favor."

Rose winced slightly, hopefully not enough for Joe to
notice. She wasn't about to admit that she'd nearly been

convinced by Barbie's Little Miss Innocent act too. Now his tale was putting a whole new spin on things. Rose supposed she shouldn't have been surprised to hear that the woman who'd claimed to have been one of Nolan's victims had been running scams of her own.

Joe gazed out the window into the distance. There was a faraway look in his eyes. "Barbie knew just what she was doing. She spun this whole yarn about how once the deal had gone through, we'd go down there with the money we'd made and buy a condo on the beach. She and I were going to spend the rest of our lives with our toes in the sand and piña coladas in our hands. Man, I couldn't transfer the money fast enough after hearing that."

Rose regretted having to pull him back to reality, but it couldn't be helped. "I assume things didn't work out the way you expected."

Joe's head snapped back around. "I'd call that an understatement," he growled, "because they didn't work out at all. The money I'd given Barbie disappeared. She told me that the deal fell through at the last minute because some island mob boss got involved. Once he moved in and took over, the other investors scattered, leaving their assets behind."

"And you believed her?" Rose asked curiously.

"At first, sure. I mean, why not?"

"Her story didn't sound improbable to you?"

Joe shrugged. "I'm a simple guy. I lead a normal life. I don't go looking for trouble, and I like to think that it's not looking for me. Yeah, the story sounded a little crazy, but Barbie assured me it was true. I'd seen her big house and her fancy clothes. I figured she had money and knew how to handle it. Besides, we'd been happy together for several months by then, so what else was I to think?"

Maybe that a beautiful, affluent woman like Barbara might possess an ulterior motive for being attracted to a self-described simple man like Joe? The thought seemed terribly rude. Rose had no intention of voicing it aloud.

"I know what you're thinking," Joe said.

Rose certainly hoped not.

"I was a fool to believe her, wasn't I?"

"It wasn't your fault," Rose said. "Barbara is very good at making people believe what she wants them to. I'm guessing you're not still together?"

Joe sighed. "Not since last year. After everything went south, it was never the same between us. It was probably inevitable that she'd break up with me."

"And what happened between you and Barbara soured your relationship with Nolan too?"

"Not exactly," Joe told her. "Nolan did that all on his own."

"How?"

"I told him everything. Maybe I was looking for a little sympathy, or at least some understanding from someone I thought was a pal. But instead Nolan cussed me out. He told me I was stupid for letting a great gal like Barbie slip through my fingers. He made it sound like everything that had gone wrong was my own fault. Talk about kicking a man when he's down."

Joe shook his head. "I can still picture the scene. Nolan and I were sitting side by side on a pair of barstools. When he said that, I looked over and thought, 'I don't need to take this crap from him.' Everything started to go downhill when Nolan introduced me to Barbie. Now my life was ruined, and he was the one to blame."

"I'm sorry," Rose said softly.

Joe didn't seem to hear her. He snatched up the empty wrappers and crumbled them into an angry ball in his fist. "I was down in the dumps. I'd lost Barbie, not to mention a boatload of money, and Nolan couldn't even be bothered to throw me a bone. In that moment, I understood what people mean when they say they saw red. I was so angry at that jerk, I could have killed him."

Rose swallowed heavily. She had no response to that. She wasn't even going to try.

Joe suddenly went still, as if he'd just realized what he'd said.

"That's just a figure of speech," he added quickly.

"Of course it is," Rose agreed.

Chapter 22

Peg supposed she owed Rose an apology.

She wasn't happy about that. In fact, if she thought about it long enough, she could probably talk herself around to believing that Rose owed her one instead. She liked that idea much better.

If experience had taught her anything, however, it was that she and Rose couldn't allow issues between them to fester. Last time they'd had a problem, she and Rose hadn't spoken to each other for thirty years. Well, neither one of them had that kind of time to spare anymore. Peg figured that meant she had to be the bigger person.

Then her phone rang. And it was Rose. Which annoyed Peg all over again. Once again, Rose had beaten her to the punch.

Peg picked up and said, "Can I call you back in ten minutes?"

"Sure," Rose replied. "I'll be here."

Peg tucked her phone in her pocket, then collected Joker and headed downstairs to her grooming room. The basement space was small but well designed. Two rows of track lighting illuminated the rubber-matted grooming table in the center of the room. A nearby wall of shelves held all the grooming tools Peg could possibly need.

Joker, who'd recently turned a year old, was in a continental trim. That meant there was a long coat of dense black hair covering the front half of his body. The coat needed to be brushed regularly to keep it from matting. Line brushing was a mindless chore. Peg's fingers could be flying through the hair while her brain was busy elsewhere.

Like talking to Rose.

Peg hopped the big dog up onto the table and laid him down on his side. Joker knew what to expect. For him, the process would be easy. Within minutes, he'd probably be asleep. Peg selected a pin brush and a greyhound comb and lined them up on the rubber mat. Then she hung a spray bottle of water from the lip of the table.

Once everything was in place, Peg dialed Rose and put her on speaker. She set the phone down on the counter beside her. When it began to ring, Joker raised his head quizzically.

"That's not for you," Peg said, smoothing the dog back down into place.

"What's not for me?" Rose asked, having picked up.

"Sorry, I was talking to Joker," Peg told her. "We're in my grooming room. I thought I'd take the opportunity to brush him while we spoke."

"Is this one of those conversations where you talk to your Poodles, they answer you, and everyone knows what's going on but me?" Rose asked. "Because if it is, I'll call you back later."

"No, Joker's going to sleep, I'm going to work on his coat, and you and I are going to talk," Peg retorted. "Does that suit?"

She'd intended to apologize, but now she was losing her temper again. Rose often had that effect on her. Especially when they were discussing Peg's Poodles.

"Fine," Rose replied. "I'm calling to apologize. I should

have texted you when I saw Jason sneaking out of his building rather than just jumping out of the van and disappearing like that."

"Yes, you should have." Peg made her first part down the middle of Joker's back. "But I should apologize too. It was a good thing you took off after him when you did. Because if you hadn't, we would have lost him. Plus, you were able to get Jason to open up to you. I'm not sure I could have managed that. Did you really offer him a job?"

"I did." Rose laughed. "It was a spur-of-the-moment decision. I guess because I felt sorry for him. It turned out that Peter and Maura were as skeptical about the idea as you are."

"The man is a murder suspect."

"Yes, I know. And Peter pointed that out too."

Peg tamed Joker's flyaway hair with a quick spritz of water. "I hope your husband succeeded in talking some sense into you."

"He tried. We agreed to wait until after the police have solved Nolan's murder before making any decisions regarding the position."

"I should hope so," Peg said. "Now that we're finished apologizing, I have a confession to make. I called several of the women on your list and ended up visiting one of them earlier today."

"Which one?"

"Helen Woodruff. She lives in Bedford on a Miniature Horse farm."

There was a pause as Rose considered that. Then she asked, "How small is it?"

"That's what I wondered," Peg replied with a chuckle. "But it turns out that the farm is a normal size, and it's the horses that are little. Even more unexpected than the tiny equines was the fact that Helen claimed she still loved Nolan even after he'd scammed her out of her money and dumped her."

Peg put down her brush. She needed both hands to un-tangle a snarl behind Joker's elbow. The dog opened one eye and gazed at her reproachfully.

"I know," she murmured. "I'm sorry."

"Sorry about what?" Rose asked.

"Nothing. Just a tangle in Joker's coat. Helen and I had a perfectly pleasant conversation. As I was getting ready to leave, she mentioned her son, Harry, who's in Shanghai."

Peg heard Rose sigh. It was probably justified. Peg was allowing her account to meander all over the place.

"Why do we care about Harry?" Rose asked.

"Because although Helen continued to have warm and fuzzy feelings for Nolan, Harry was outraged by what he'd done. He threatened to make Nolan pay."

There was another pause. Then Rose said dubiously, "So you're telling me that the best suspect we've found so far is in China?"

"Something like that," Peg grumbled. She picked up her pin brush and went back to work.

"Then it's a good thing I managed to come up with something useful. I spoke with Joe Danson."

"The lead Jason gave you?"

"Precisely." Rose sounded more than a little pleased with herself. Under the circumstances, Peg couldn't blame her. "He's a volunteer at the Greenwich Library."

"Good for him," said Peg. "Why does that matter?"

"I don't know, maybe because it made him easy to find? I was just giving you some background detail to set the stage. Anyway, Joe and Nolan used to be friends, and now they're not."

"I already knew that." Peg tapped Joker's shoulder and the dog sat up. She then turned him onto his other side and started the whole process over again.

"You did know that, but you don't know why."

"I can guess," Peg said. That was a no-brainer. "It had something to do with money."

"Yes, but in this case, Nolan was only peripherally involved in the fraud that took place. Barbara was the one who shook Joe down."

"*Barbara?*" Peg's hand stilled. Then she thought about what Rose had said and snorted under her breath. "Shook him down?"

"Isn't that the right lingo?" Rose sounded unsure. "Now that you and I are investigators, I'm enhancing my vocabulary. I want to sound like I fit in."

Peg would have laughed, but she was afraid Rose would hear. "I hate to tell you, but anyone who uses a phrase like 'enhancing my vocabulary' is never going to fit into the sordid underbelly of society. Now tell me about Barbara."

"Since you brought it up, I'd rather hear more about the sordid underbelly of society," Rose said wistfully. "But I suppose that will have to wait for another time. As for Barbara, apparently she was lying to us."

Peg reached for her spray bottle again. "By now, it feels as though we've been told so many lies that it's hard to keep them all straight. What's the problem this time?"

"Barbara didn't just support Nolan when he was running his scams. She was swindling people too. Joe Danson became one of her victims after Nolan set them up."

"I can see how that would ruin a friendship," Peg mused. "And maybe it explains how Barbara's able to afford that house and her designer clothes. If that is her means of support, she must be better at larceny than Nolan was."

"Well, she succeeded in fooling us," Rose said.

Peg disagreed about that, but the point wasn't worth debating. Besides, Rose was still talking.

"Barbara not only told us a story that would gain our sympathy, she was also smart enough to seed it with enough nuggets of truth to make it believable."

"That's true," Peg conceded. She was still brushing.

"But I'm thinking we should look on the bright side.

We're far from the only ones who got taken in. And we're way better off than Helen and Joe, who were taken advantage of, yet still seem to harbor fond feelings for Nolan and Barbara. So we could be doing worse."

"The bar you've set for the bright side is so low it might as well be sitting on the ground," Peg pointed out. Sometimes she wished Rose wasn't such a Pollyanna. "Now keep going. You still haven't told me what destroyed Nolan's and Joe's friendship."

"Rather than placing the blame for what happened on Barbara where it belonged, Joe became furious with Nolan. He said Nolan had ruined his life."

Peg brightened. "That sounds like a perfectly good motive for murder. And Joe isn't in China, which is enormously helpful."

"Except . . ." Rose said.

"Go ahead. Wreck my good mood. What now?"

"Actually, it's *why* now? Barbara broke up with Joe last year. And everyone else we've spoken to had a relationship with Nolan that was in the past. Since then, they all seem to have picked up their lives and gone on. What we need to figure out is whose life Nolan was ruining just before he died."

Peg wondered if she'd heard correctly. Surely Rose couldn't be serious. She did, however, seem to be waiting for Peg to reply. So Peg did.

"Hellooo!"

"Hello to you too." Rose sounded puzzled.

Once again, she was missing the point. Peg rolled her eyes, which thankfully Rose couldn't see. "It's me."

"Yes, I know it's you. I called you, remember? We've been talking for twenty minutes. Peg, are you feeling all right? Have you hit your head recently? Should I come over?"

Peg waited until the flood of words had petered out, then said, "I'm fine. I was merely trying to indicate that you are concentrating so hard on the details that you are missing the big picture."

"Which is?"

"*I* was supposed to be Nolan's most recent victim, remember? That's why we're talking to people from his past. Because I was Nolan's present."

"Oh, that's right." Rose sounded chastened. As well she should.

"I have an idea," Peg told her. "You're not going to like it. Hang on for a minute."

Peg had finished working on Joker's coat. She set her brush and comb aside before waking him up. Joker scrambled to his feet on the tabletop. Then he gave his hair a long, leisurely shake.

"Good boy!" Peg said.

"I assume that wasn't directed to me?" Rose's voice floated across the room from the phone on the counter.

"No, not yet. I need to get Joker down off the table and give him a treat. Then it's your turn again."

"In the meantime, I'll just sit here and think about ideas I don't like," Rose commented. "Starting with sitting here twiddling my thumbs while you play with your dog."

"Oh pish," Peg said. "I know perfectly well your time in the convent taught you forbearance. I'll only be another moment."

She handed Joker a biscuit from the jar on the counter. Rather than stopping to eat it, the Poodle ran out of the room and dashed up the stairs. Peg knew what that meant. In less than a minute Hope and Coral would appear, wanting to know why they didn't have a biscuit too.

Oh well, Peg thought. Maybe by that time she'd be off the phone.

"Back to you!" she said cheerfully.

Rose muttered something Peg was sure was uncomplimentary. Peg decided to ignore it.

"I think we should talk to Detective Sturgill," she announced.

"You're right," Rose snapped. "That's a terrible idea."

"I didn't say it was a bad idea, only that you wouldn't like it."

"Of course, I don't like it. And with good reason. Even aside from the fact that the man treats me like I'm an idiot, you know perfectly well that he gets annoyed when you go poking around in his cases—"

"When *we* go poking around," Peg corrected her.

"Either way," Rose said. "Why would you want to purposely antagonize him?"

"Maybe I like to live dangerously." Peg laughed.

"That's a given." Rose laughed with her. "But seriously, why?"

"Because maybe we've learned some things that he'll find useful. Or maybe he'll share some useful information with us."

"Good luck with that. Detective Sturgill isn't a sharing kind of guy. Here's my counter idea. Considering how many people close to Nolan we've spoken to, I think our best plan is to keep a low profile."

Peg heard the sound of thundering feet coming down the stairs.

"What the heck is that?" Rose asked. "It sounds like you're under attack."

"Only my Poodles," Peg assured her. "They're coming to let me know that I owe them a biscuit."

"How did that—" Rose began, then stopped. "Never mind. I don't want to know."

"Sleep on it," Peg said, "and we'll talk tomorrow. At some point we should touch base with Rodney. And it's probably better for our sakes if we don't leave it too late."

Chapter 23

Saved by the bell, Rose thought gleefully.

It was the following morning, and she'd just gotten off the phone with Gina Malone. Since their walk in the Waveny woods, Gina had continued to think about Peg's and Rose's quest. Now she told Rose that she'd asked the women in the support group if they would be open to the idea of holding an impromptu meeting with Rose and Peg as guests. The women's response had been favorable, and Gina wanted to know if eight o'clock tonight would work.

Rose quickly confirmed that would be perfect. She had nothing scheduled that evening, and she was sure Peg would also make herself available. Unless something dog-related was happening, in which case Rose would attend the meeting on her own.

Best of all, that meant there was no point in going to see Detective Sturgill until after she and Peg had heard what these women had to say. Maybe she was only postponing the inevitable, but Rose didn't care. Any day that ended without her and the detective being in the same room was a good day as far as she was concerned.

"You look happy," Maura said.

The housekeeper had come up the shelter's back steps and entered the kitchen, carrying a basket that was filled with yet more tomatoes. The plants had seemed so small and scraggly when Rose put them in the ground. Now she was beginning to wonder if they'd ever serve another meal that didn't include the red fruit.

"I am feeling rather pleased," Rose admitted. She put her phone down and took the basket from Maura.

The kitchen was small, with limited counter space. Its appliances were a mismatched group, and judging by its groovy appearance, Rose suspected the worn linoleum beneath her feet had been installed in the nineteen-seventies. An upgrade was on the schedule for someday. Until then, they all made do.

"Windowsill or fridge for these?" she asked.

"Windowsill for this batch," Maura replied. "I'm making spaghetti sauce this afternoon. I guess you weren't talking to Peg, then."

"Why do you say that?" Rose set the basket down beside the sink. She began to take out the tomatoes one by one.

"Because you always seem to be frowning when she's around."

"I do not," Rose said. Then she paused. "Do I?"

"Yup. In fact, you're frowning right now, just thinking about her. If my mother were here, she'd tell you you're going to get ugly grooves on the sides of your mouth from doing that."

"If your mother were here," Rose replied, "I'd tell her that she raised an impertinent daughter."

"Too late." Maura laughed. "She already knows that. And it's her recipe I'll be using today, so don't say anything mean about her."

"I would never do that. I'm sure she's a lovely woman." Rose finished unloading the tomatoes and tucked the basket into a low cabinet. When she straightened and turned around, Maura was still standing there. "Is there something else?"

"I've been down to Mabel's house a couple of times this week," Maura said. "She and I are friends now."

"Thank you for checking on her. And for taking the time to get to know her better. Mabel seems like she could use some new friends."

Maura leaned back against the counter. "I don't like her grandson much. Nor those guys he hangs around with."

"So they've been back," Rose said unhappily. She'd become so immersed in the search for Nolan's killer that she hadn't noticed. She should have been paying more attention.

"A few times," Maura confirmed. "They treat her house like it's their own place. They show up and eat her food, put their feet all over her furniture, and generally make a nuisance of themselves."

"What does Mabel say about that?" Rose asked.

Maura shrugged. "She's an old softie. Just because Donny's family, she seems to believe he's entitled to do whatever he wants. Also, I think she's a little afraid of him and his freeloading buddies. They're young, they're loud, and although I've never seen them push her around, it wouldn't be a big stretch to imagine that they might. Even if Mabel wanted to stand up to them, I'm not sure she'd be brave enough to do it."

"I don't like the sound of that at all," Rose said. "Have you told Peter about your concerns?"

"Not yet. I figured I'd start with you."

Rose nodded. "Thank you for caring about Mabel. You're a good person, Maura Nettles."

Maura smiled. "So you and Peter will figure out how to help her?"

"We most certainly will," Rose promised.

That evening, Rose assumed the role of driver for a change.

She and Peter only had the one vehicle between them. So if possible, she liked to leave it available for Peter's use. Which meant she usually caught a lift with Peg. Unfortunately those rides often left Rose clutching her seat with white-knuckled hands and praying for deliverance as Peg hurtled them toward their destination.

Tonight, Peter had no other obligations. Since Rose was going out, he decided to stay late at the shelter and catch up on some paperwork. Rose would stop back and pick him up when the meeting was finished.

Peg came from Greenwich and left her minivan parked in front of the Gallagher House. She professed to be delighted to have Rose act as chauffeur for the trip to Gina's house in New Canaan. Her appreciation didn't last long.

"You drive like an old lady," Peg complained five minutes later. She couldn't see the speedometer, but she was willing to bet that it hadn't been north of thirty mph since they'd headed out.

"If you're trying to insult me, you'll have to do better than that. In case you haven't noticed, I *am* an old lady. And I would like to arrive at Gina's house in one piece."

"And I would like to get there sometime before midnight," Peg groused. Suddenly she shot forward in her seat as if she was about to launch herself through the windshield. "Don't let that man cut you off! You had the right of way!"

"He didn't cut me off, he was merging," Rose said mildly. "And letting him go ahead of us cost us no more than a few seconds."

"Seconds add up," Peg muttered, leaning back again. "Soon they become minutes."

"I see your dilemma," Rose said. "Because minutes in a car with you can feel like hours."

"Until you and I started riding around together, nobody ever complained."

Rose found that hard to believe. "They were probably just being polite. Or maybe they were too afraid of you to open their mouths."

"Thank goodness I don't have to worry about that with you."

Was Peg's comment meant to be ironic? Rose wasn't sure. She hoped not, because otherwise it sounded suspiciously like an insult. Either way, she wasn't about to ask because she was probably better off not knowing.

Gina lived in a split-level house on a tree-lined street that was within walking distance from the center of town. Her short driveway was already filled with two rows of cars when Rose and Peg arrived. Rose parked on the street, being careful to not block access to either of the neighboring houses. Although it was barely dusk, Gina had already turned on the lights on the front of her house. A brick walkway led to her arched front door.

"This looks like quite a turnout," Peg said as they approached the house. "How many women did Gina say she was expecting?"

"She didn't say. And I didn't think to ask. I believe there are more than a dozen women in the group, although, of course, we've already spoken to some of them. I wouldn't necessarily expect all the remaining women to be here tonight, especially not on such short notice."

"*We're* here on short notice," Peg said.

"For a gathering that was put together on our behalf." Rose hardly thought she needed to point that out. "It makes sense that *we* would juggle our schedules to make it. Gina is doing us a favor tonight, so be sure to be properly grateful."

"I'd be especially grateful if one of the women we meet tonight decides to break down in tears and offer us a confession."

"No, you wouldn't." Rose snorted. "That would make your life entirely too easy. Offered the path of least resistance, you always opt for the more challenging route."

"You might be right," Peg considered.

"I am right—" Rose stopped speaking as the door opened in front of them.

Gina stood in the doorway. She was holding a glass of red wine in her hand, and her brows were raised halfway to her hairline. "Goodness," she said, "I could hear you two squabbling from in here." She glanced at Rose. "I recall Peg being quite spikey at the funeral. Is she always like that?"

"Peg does enjoy a good argument," Rose said. "But she's going to be on her best behavior tonight."

Gina laughed. "I certainly hope not. There's plenty of alcohol on hand, and I've promised the ladies an entertaining evening. I would hate to disappoint them."

"Bring on the wine!" Rose said happily as she and Peg stepped through the doorway together. "I don't get out much. I'm more than ready to be entertained."

"I like your spirit." Gina shut the door behind them. "White or red? Pinot Grigio or Cabernet, if that matters."

"Surprise me," Rose said.

A selection of bottles and glasses had been set out on the table in the dining room that opened off the front hall. As Gina headed that way, Peg hung back. She grabbed Rose's arm when she started to follow.

"What is the matter with you?" she demanded under her breath. "We're here to ask probing questions and uncover clues, not to take part in a bacchanal."

"In vino veritas," Rose whispered. She hoped Peg was up on her Latin.

Apparently she was, because Peg straightened, then said, "Oh."

Rose patted Peg's arm. "Try to keep up, sweetie. It may be a long night."

Sweetie? Peg stared after Rose, who went to join Gina at the table. This was a side of Rose Peg hadn't seen before. And she wasn't at all sure she liked it.

Minutes later, Peg, Rose, and Gina were standing in the doorway that led to Gina's living room. Each was holding a glass of wine that was filled nearly to the brim. Rose looked pleased by that development. Peg most assuredly did not. She'd already decided she'd be the one driving them home later.

The room before them had a high ceiling and a big picture window in the rear wall. It was large enough to comfortably accommodate the eight women who were milling around within. Peg let her gaze skim from one face to the next. Most of the women looked familiar; she knew she'd seen them at the funeral. That day, some had been forlorn, while others stood by the gravesite with stiff backs and dry eyes. Tonight, however, the mood was jovial.

At first glance, the room appeared to be crammed with furniture. Then Peg realized that extra chairs had been brought in from the dining room to ensure there would be plenty of seats for everyone in attendance.

"Ladies!" Gina said in a loud voice. The buzz of conversation died down. Everyone turned to face them. "I know we like our meetings to be informal, but I need to interrupt your conversations to introduce you to Rose Donovan and Peg Turnbull. They'll have some questions for you, and I hope you will also have questions for them. If everyone wouldn't mind taking a seat, I'll finish the introductions."

All the women were similar in age to Rose and Peg, but beyond that they had little in common: not their physical attributes, nor the clothes they were wearing, nor the expressions on their faces. Several of the women looked curious. Three were smiling. Two were clearly reserving judgment. Rose pegged them as the potential trouble-makers of the group.

When everyone was sitting down, Gina gestured toward the woman seated at the left of the room. "Aimee," she said. The woman tipped her head to one side and nodded. *Gray hair, red lipstick, yellow blouse,* Rose told herself. She was determined to commit each name to memory.

"Dani." *Big smile. Butterfly tattoo on her wrist.*

"Trudy." *Brown hair, no makeup, wary eyes.*

"Erin." *V-neck sweater. Beautiful nails.*

"Ashley." *Another smile. Friendly face.*

"Blythe." *Gold bangles jingling on her arm. Skinny.*

"Sara." *Looks like she'd rather be anywhere else but here.*

"Connie." *Long gray hair, twists it around her fingers.*

"Got all that?" Gina asked at the end. She smirked as though she was quite sure they didn't.

"I hope so," Rose said.

"Yes," Peg replied firmly.

Of course this would be child's play for her, Rose thought. She'd seen Peg handily judge a large class of dogs that all looked alike, sorting them from best to worst in mere minutes. Indeed, Rose wouldn't be surprised to learn that Peg had sorted these women into some preferred order too.

"Excellent," Gina said. "Then let's get started."

Rose had assumed she and Peg would be the ones lead-ing the conversation, but that wasn't what happened. As soon as Gina opened the floor, questions came at them from all sides of the room.

"How do you solve a murder?"

"Are you working with the police?"

"Who inherited Nolan's money when he died?"

"Where do you look for clues?"

"Why is what happened to us any of your business?"

Rose and Peg shared a startled glance. Rose looked taken aback. Peg just grinned, then swallowed a gulp of her Cabernet.

"If you give us a chance to get a word in, we'll be happy to answer all your questions," she said. "This is going to be fun."

Chapter 24

From that moment on the discussion never slowed, even briefly. Someone was always either making a point, sharing an experience, asking a question, or complaining about the way she'd been treated by Nolan. There was plenty of the latter to go around.

At some point, Gina tired of people running back and forth to the dining room to refill their glasses. She gathered up the remaining wine bottles, brought them back to the living room along with a corkscrew, and set them on the coffee table for easy access. After that, the conversation became even more raucous.

Peg was elated that Nolan's women had a lot to say. That made her job easier. By unspoken accord, she and Rose decided their best course of action was to mostly keep quiet and listen. It didn't prove to be a problem. The women in the room needed little encouragement to speak their minds.

Connie leaned in and said to Peg, "I met Nolan on a dating site, too. That guy had his approach down pat. He'd have Googled you before you even met. While you were staring dreamily at his picture, he was busy calculating your net worth to the penny."

"And debating how smart you were," Trudy added. "Nolan preferred his women on the dumb side."

"Hey!" Blythe cried. "I resent that."

"Resent it all you like," Trudy said. "But you can't refute it. Remind me again, how much did you lose to him?"

"My entire jewelry collection," Blythe said with a sigh. "And a . . ." Her voice trailed away.

"A what?" Rose leaned forward curiously.

"A 1972 Bentley," Blythe admitted. "Say what you will about Nolan, but the man had a real appreciation for beautiful things."

"Hunh." Sara snorted. "Let's not sugarcoat this. What Nolan had was an appreciation for *other people's* things. And beauty had nothing to do with it. All he cared about was how much they were worth."

"And how easily they could be converted to cash," Dani said as she gazed around the room. "So that's why we're all here, even those of us who had close calls. We're the women who survived Nolan and lived to tell the tale."

"Which is more than can be said for him." Erin snickered and held up her wineglass. "I think we need to make a toast."

"To Nolan?" Gina asked dubiously.

Erin sputtered another laugh. Peg was pretty sure the woman was on her third glass of wine. Or maybe her fourth. "No, of course not. To us."

"To us!" They all raised their glasses for the toast, even Rose who'd barely known the man. It was hard not to be carried away by the booze-fueled camaraderie in the room.

"And to whoever gave him what he deserved!" Trudy cried.

Ashley held out her hands, formed a fist, and slapped it into her other palm, creating the sound of a crash. For several seconds, everyone looked shocked. Then the room dissolved into giggles, and they all toasted again.

More wine was poured. Every glass was topped off. Peg

was having a fine time, getting into the spirit of things. She was about to share her story when Gina rose to her feet.

"Let me just say that if anyone here would like to stand up and take credit for a job well done, I would be the first to applaud."

"Me too!" Aimee added.

"Me three!" That was Dani.

Of course nobody stood up. To Peg's disappointment, no one even squirmed in her seat. It seemed a shame to let all those potential accolades go to waste.

"But it's not as if we haven't fantasized about it," Erin said. "Admit it, ladies. Right here in this room, we've had some hair-raising discussions about all the various ways we wanted to do Nolan in."

"Fire," Trudy said. Peg suppressed a shudder.

"Poison." Ashley nodded.

"I wanted to toss him off a cliff," Sara admitted.

Dani chuckled. "I was hoping he'd be eaten by a shark. Slowly. Bite by bite."

"You're a bloodthirsty woman," Blythe said with admiration. "If we could have figured out a way to make that happen, it would definitely have gotten my vote."

"And then after we came up with all those wonderfully inventive ideas, Nolan went and got hit by a car." Connie sounded disappointed. "It just seemed so . . ."

"Pedestrian?" Rose offered, and the group broke out in another chorus of giggles.

"Yes." Erin nodded. "Underwhelming. I think we all figured Nolan was the kind of man who would go out with a big bang."

"For all we know, he did," Gina said. That occasioned more peals of delighted laughter. By then, they'd consumed so much wine that everything had begun to seem funny.

"Now that we're talking about Nolan's death, it occurs

to me that we missed our opportunity," Ashley mused. "What we should have done was make a plan and then take care of him ourselves."

"All of us together?" Connie sounded skeptical.

"Yes, that's why it could have worked. Since all of us would have been equally guilty, no one would have been able to figure who the real culprit was."

"That sounds familiar," Gina said. "Didn't some famous mystery author write a story about that?"

"Agatha Christie," Aimee piped up. "So that's out. Because who wants to be derivative?"

Seriously? Rose thought. That *was her problem with the plan?*

"Here's an even better idea," Dani proposed. "Why should we let Peg and Rose have all the fun? I think we should help them solve the crime."

"We'd appreciate that," Peg said, speaking for both of them. "Rose and I need all the help we can get. Who has information for us?"

"Maybe it was someone from Nolan's sordid past," Sara ventured.

"Did Nolan have a sordid past?" Ashley asked with interest. "Do tell."

"How should I know?" Sara replied. "I'm just tossing out a guess. Based on his sordid present, it seems like a good possibility."

"I vote for a family squabble," Trudy said. "Maybe his sister did it."

"You mean Barbara?" Peg asked.

Trudy nodded. "Maybe she killed him for his money."

"No way." Blythe shook her head. "She's already rich."

"Not only that," Peg told them, "but Barbara isn't Nolan's sister."

"She's not?" Aimee gasped. "Dammit, I liked Barbara. Then who the hell is she?"

"Apparently she was Nolan's partner in crime," Rose

said. "And quite accomplished in running scams of her own."

"Another illusion shattered." Erin sighed loudly. She peered down at her wineglass, which was nearly as empty as the bottles scattered across the coffee table. "All this Pinot is making me maudlin. How many glasses have I had anyway?"

"Four," Connie told her. "But who's counting?"

"On that note, I think it's time to bring tonight's meeting to a close," Gina said, looking at her watch. "There's coffee in the kitchen for anyone who wants a cup before they leave. I'd also be happy to call Uber for anyone who would rather leave their car in my driveway overnight."

The women slowly stood up. No one seemed in a hurry to go. Sara helped Gina pick up the empty wine bottles and carry them out to the kitchen. Dani and Trudy gathered up the glasses and followed after them. Peg and Blythe grabbed chairs and took them back to the dining room where they belonged.

As they slid the chairs back beneath the table, Blythe said, "I believe you and I have a friend in common."

"Oh?" Peg asked. "Who's that?"

"Izzy Hicks."

"Izzy?" Peg smiled. "She's a lovely woman." She paused, making the connection. "You must have met her through Nolan?"

"No." Blythe looked surprised. "Was she involved with him too?"

"She was."

"I had no idea. It was a friend of my late husband, a man named Charlie Vargas, who introduced us."

"Charlie?" Now it was Peg's turn to be surprised. "What a coincidence."

"Is it?" Blythe shrugged. "I don't know about that. I was in the market for a Bulldog puppy, and Charlie put me in touch with Izzy."

"You can't go wrong with a puppy from Izzy," Peg said.

"You're right about that," Blythe agreed with a smile. "Bruno is just what I wanted."

When she and Blythe had finished returning all the chairs, Peg was ready to leave. She went to find Rose, who was helping Gina and Dani clean up in the kitchen. A pot of coffee was brewing on the counter. Peg noted it was almost empty. She hoped Rose had chugged at least a cup of it while she was working.

"There you are." Rose saw Peg in the doorway. "Let me just say thank you to Gina, and we can be on our way."

Gina and Dani were at the sink, rinsing out glasses. "How's Meredith's treatment coming along?" Dani was asking Gina as Rose approached.

"As well as can be expected," Gina replied. "We're doing the best we can." She turned and saw Rose. "Are you and Peg leaving?"

"Yes. I didn't mean to interrupt. Is everything all right?"

Gina nodded, but her expression was bleak. "My daughter is battling cancer. Dani was just asking after her."

"I'm so sorry," Rose said. "I had no idea. Now I feel incredibly insensitive to have bothered you with Peg's and my problem."

"Don't worry, it's not your fault," Gina replied. "I don't talk about it much. But these are my ladies." She smiled over at Dani. "We support each other through thick and thin."

"It was a pleasure meeting you," Dani said to Rose. "I can't remember the last time we had such a lively meeting. I hope you'll keep us apprised of future developments?"

"We will," Rose replied. "Gina, thank you for taking the time to host us this evening, especially under the circumstances. It was lovely having the chance to meet everyone."

"I'm glad you enjoyed yourselves." Gina gathered Rose into a warm hug. "Don't be a stranger. We still need to sit down and figure out how my camp and your shelter can work together to support those in need."

"Yes, please," Rose said. "I definitely want to do that."

By the time Rose and Peg let themselves out the front door, Gina's home was nearly empty. When they reached the minivan by the side of the road, both women walked around to the driver's side.

Rose had been fishing the keys out of her purse. Now she looked up. "What?"

"I hope you don't think I'm letting you drive, Miss I-Don't-Get-Out-Much. I've never seen so much liquor poured and drunk in such a short amount of time. That group went through wine like it was water."

"As I recall, you drank your share," Rose commented.

"I'm bigger than you. I can handle a drink or two when the situation calls for conviviality," Peg said loftily. "Whereas your feet are probably sloshing around in your shoes as we speak."

"For someone who prides herself on paying attention, you certainly missed the boat tonight." Rose was inordinately pleased to have answered Peg's liquid metaphor with one of her own. To her disappointment, Peg didn't even seem to notice.

"What do you mean?" she demanded. "I paid particular attention to everything that went on. Nothing escaped my notice."

Rose laughed and reached for the door handle. "Except perhaps for the fact that I nursed a single glass of wine through the entire evening. I'm perfectly fit to drive us home." She leaned closer and peered into Peg's eyes. "Which is possibly more than can be said for you."

Peg harrumphed under her breath and walked around the other side of the van. "You're not just trying to one-up me, are you?" she asked as she climbed inside.

"Of course not. I'm not stupid. I wouldn't drive if I was impaired. Now fasten your seat belt, and prepare for a safe and sedate trip back to the shelter. While I drive, you can tell me what you think we learned tonight."

For once in her life, Peg did as she was told. She waited until the minivan was rolling—sedately—down the road, then said, "Nolan must have been quite gifted when it came to making women fall in love with him." She leaned back in her seat and sighed. "I suppose I wanted to believe those women would be a bunch of pushovers, easy marks ripe for the plucking. But they weren't. They struck me as both thoughtful and discerning. They were all women who should have known better, but somehow didn't."

"That's because they were also women who wanted to believe in love," Rose said. "And who hoped they might be lucky enough to find their happily-ever-after. Unfortunately, Nolan knew exactly how to prey on those dreams."

"Nolan was a chump." Peg stared straight ahead through the windshield. "He didn't deserve any of those women. Or me, for that matter. Maybe this is the wine speaking, but I had a delightful time getting to know all of them."

"I did too," Rose agreed. "It's a shame that it took their personal disasters to bring them together."

"I refuse to give Nolan any credit for that," Peg muttered. "Now that I've met those women, I'll be very disappointed if one of them turns out to be our killer."

It was dark by the time they arrived back at the shelter.

There were no streetlamps in this part of Stamford, but lights were on at the Gallagher House, both inside and out. It wasn't unusual for Maura to be roused from her apartment in the middle of the night to admit someone who'd fled an untenable situation. As they drew near, Rose was pleased to see how welcoming the place looked after dark.

"We'll talk tomorrow," Peg said. Impatient to be on her way, she'd hopped out of the van the moment it stopped.

"You're sure you're okay to drive?" Rose knew what Peg's answer would be, but she felt obliged to check anyway.

"Of course," she replied. "I'm always fine. You know that."

Inside, Rose expected to find Peter in the office. Instead he was sitting at the dining room table. Stacks of paper were piled all around him. The majority of the table's considerable surface was littered with them.

Peter's back was to the door. Rose walked over, leaned down, and dropped a kiss on the top of his head. Peter still didn't look up. Instead he lifted a single finger, indicating that he needed a minute. He was staring down at the documents in front of him with such concentration that Rose half-expected them to spontaneously combust.

"Problem?" she asked, when he finally lifted his gaze.

"No more than usual." He smiled up at her. "How was your meeting?"

"Quite entertaining, actually."

"You sound as though you didn't expect that."

"I didn't," Rose admitted. "Peg and I were just talking about how much we liked the women Nolan chose."

Peter chuckled. "So what you're saying is that for all his faults, Nolan was a man with good taste."

"Something like that. Are you almost finished for the night?"

"Give me five more minutes." Peter looked down at the papers and frowned. "Maybe ten. I should have things wrapped up by then."

"There's no hurry," Rose assured him. "Maura was picking tomatoes earlier, so I know we have plenty on hand. I'll go put some in a paper bag to take home with us."

"Good idea," Peter said absently. He'd picked up his pen again.

Rose left him to it. Humming under her breath, she passed through the swinging door into the kitchen. There was a stack of reusable paper bags under the sink. Rose took one out and opened it up. Maura had made her sauce that afternoon, but there were still a half dozen large, juicy tomatoes left over. Rose packed them all in the bag. She and Maura could always pick more tomorrow if they needed them.

She walked back through the dining room to the hall. Peter was still busy scribbling away. Even though he couldn't see her, Rose smiled fondly. She thought about how different her life was now from those years she'd spent in the convent.

She loved coming home, knowing that Peter would be there waiting for her. She loved having someone to share her days with. And her nights. Peter was the other half of her heart. Until she'd met him, Rose wouldn't have believed such a thing was possible. Now she couldn't imagine her life without him in it.

Rose opened the front door and walked out onto the porch, leaving the door open behind her. She'd be back in just a minute. Shifting the unwieldy bag to one side, she maneuvered her way carefully down the dark steps. Cars were parked nose to tail down the length of the road. Her minivan was beside the curb in front of a neighboring house.

Rose looked both ways, then stepped out onto the street. There was virtually no traffic this time of night, and its smooth surface was easier to navigate than the crumbling and uneven sidewalk. She'd started to hum under her breath again when the sound of a car engine revving behind her made her stop and turn.

Rose threw up a hand as she was suddenly blinded by headlights. The bag wobbled in her other arm. Tomatoes began to spill out. For a moment, Rose stood frozen in place. The car had come out of nowhere and was now flying down the street, heading straight toward her.

Rose's head whipped around. On one side she was blocked by her van, parked between her and the safety of the sidewalk. She didn't dare flee in the other direction—that would place her directly in the car's path. What was wrong with the driver? How could he not see her?

Rose heard someone shriek. It might have been her. Now the car was only a length away. And still the driver was making no attempt to avoid her.

Rose had no choice. At the last moment, she flung herself sideways. Her hip and shoulder bounced off the front of the van. The remaining tomatoes went flying. Rose did too. Pain radiated down the side of her body as she slithered into the narrow space between the van and the car parked in front of it. Seconds later, she landed in a tangled heap on the pavement.

With a squeal of tires, the car went speeding past. Still seeing spots, Rose caught only a vague impression of a dark sedan. She couldn't make out who was behind the wheel. Good Lord, her head hurt. She closed her eyes briefly and wondered how badly she was injured.

One thing Rose was sure of, however. The driver of the car had never braked, much less tried to steer around her. Rose's breath suddenly caught in her throat. Her heart was pounding like a jackhammer in her chest.

This near miss had been no accident.

Chapter 25

"Rose!"

As she tried to sit up, Rose dimly became aware that Peter was calling her name. She opened her mouth to reply, but no sound came out. Instead she tasted blood. Rose was pretty sure she'd bitten her tongue.

"Rose! Answer me! Where are you?"

Once again, she attempted to get up. Rose's arms felt like jelly. Her legs did too. And why was her head spinning? Surely that wasn't normal. If only she could stand up, or even say something, maybe Peter would stop yelling. At this rate, he was going to wake the whole neighborhood.

Rose grasped the bumper of the car behind her and pulled herself upward. Now she was sitting on the pavement. That was somewhat better.

Footsteps went pounding past on the sidewalk, then abruptly stopped. A door slammed, and she heard Maura call out, "Peter, what's the matter?"

"Call an ambulance!" he yelled.

Then suddenly Peter was there, right beside her, kneeling on the hard road and gently wrapping his arms around her. Rose hadn't realized she was shivering until that moment when his warmth enveloped her and she was able to close her eyes and lean into it.

"Blasted driver," he growled. For Peter, that was profanity. "Please tell me the car missed you. Please, Rose, talk to me. Tell me you're all right."

"I think I'm mostly okay." Her voice was shaky. There didn't seem to be anything Rose could do about that. "I'm definitely better now that you're here."

"Where are you hurt?" Peter asked softly. He drew back to have a look at her. Even in the dim light, Rose could see his face grow pale. "Oh my God, you're covered in blood."

"Not blood." Rose managed a wan smile. "Tomatoes."

"Tomatoes?" Peter repeated incredulously. He leaned in close and took a sniff. "Not blood. No blood?"

"I hope not." To Rose's surprise she was currently calmer than her husband was. "The car came close, but it didn't hit me. I managed to squeeze in here."

In truth, she'd somehow flown through the air, ricocheted off the van, then cartwheeled a bit before going splat on the hard ground. But perhaps Peter would do better without having to hear all the details.

"Any broken bones?" He gently felt his way down each of her arms. Then he shifted her to one side so she could untangle her legs. "Don't try to move if anything hurts. We can stay right here as long as you need to. Maura's gone to call an ambulance."

"I don't think that will be necessary." Rose closed her eyes briefly. "I've really just taken a tumble."

"That was no tumble," Peter said grimly. "That was a horrifyingly close call. The driver must have been crazy to be speeding like that on this small street. You could have been badly injured. You could have been killed. If it was one of those damn hooligans who hang out at Mabel's place . . ."

Peter was still talking, but Rose had stopped listening. As soon as he'd said the words "close call," she'd realized something. She'd heard that expression earlier in the evening—

that time with regard to relationships with Nolan. The man who was now dead, killed by a hit-and-run driver.

"Rose! What's the matter? Talk to me! Are you losing consciousness?" Peter had realized she'd ceased paying attention. Now it sounded as though he was getting upset all over again.

"I'm fine," Rose said quickly, a necessary white lie. "I'm beginning to feel a bit better. Maybe you should help me up."

"Are you sure?" he asked solicitously. "Help is on the way. You probably shouldn't move until a doctor or a paramedic has had a chance to examine you."

"Peter, listen to me. I'm a sixty-eight-year-old woman who's sitting in a dirty gutter and covered in squished tomatoes. I've lost a shoe somewhere, and I'm pretty sure my dress is ripped. I have no doubt that my body will be covered in bruises tomorrow. But right now, while I'm able to stand up, I would like to greet the ambulance crew on my feet.

"Otherwise, you know perfectly well that they'll treat me like an old lady who has no idea what's what. I'll find myself being shuffled off to an emergency room, where I'll wait for hours to be seen by an overworked resident, who will take my temperature and pronounce me fit enough to go home. Given the choice—which I would like to think I still possess—I have no desire to experience any of that."

"Yes, ma'am," Peter replied.

"Don't toy with me," Rose grumbled.

"After that lecture, I wouldn't dare."

Peter carefully released her, then shifted away before standing up. The sound of approaching sirens was audible in the distance. If Rose was going to be on her feet before the ambulance arrived, they needed to get moving. Nevertheless, Peter refused to hurry.

He extended a hand down to her. "We're going to do this slowly and cautiously," he said. "I will help you up, and you will let me. If at any point, you feel unwell, or something hurts, or you start to become dizzy, speak up immediately and we will stop and wait for help."

"Apparently I'm not the only one who knows how to give a lecture," Rose said crisply.

"Has anyone ever told you people that you talk entirely too much?" Maura was holding Rose's missing shoe. She slid herself in between the car and the van on the other side. Her gaze raked up and down Rose's body. "You look like an extra in a horror movie. The dumb blond who went down into the basement anyway."

"It's only tomatoes," Rose said.

"That's what I figured." Maura reached down to support Rose's other side. "Good thing we have plenty."

Peter stared at her. "In the midst of this situation, *that's* what you're concerned about?"

Rose started to laugh. Even though it made her ribs hurt, it still felt good. After a few seconds, Maura joined in. Peter and Maura slowly hoisted Rose to her feet. She wobbled for a few seconds, then found her balance. Maura leaned down and slipped Rose's shoe onto her foot.

As they emerged from between the two parked vehicles, an ambulance turned the corner onto their road. A plain sedan, equipped with a flashing light, was just behind it.

"Who is that?" Rose asked, squinting toward the following car.

For the second time in fifteen minutes, she was nearly blinded by headlights. This time, however, both vehicles slowed to a crawl before approaching. This time, they were there to help.

"I don't know," Peter replied. "Maybe the police?"

"Umm . . ." Maura bit her lip. Both sets of eyes swung her way. She hesitated, then said, "After I called 9-1-1 and reported your accident, I called Peg. Because . . . you know."

Peter groaned softly. Rose couldn't blame him. For once, it would have been nice to be in the middle of a crisis and not have to also deal with Peg. But apparently that decision had been taken out of their hands.

"We know what?" Rose asked.

Maura grimaced. "Peg would have killed me if I hadn't told her what happened."

Peter looked resigned. "She has a point."

Then all conversation stopped as the doors at the back of the ambulance flew open. A pair of paramedics hopped out and took over. They surveyed the scene and asked for details about the accident. Rose and Peter both supplied those. Maura chimed in too, even though she'd been the last to arrive.

The initial questions were followed by a physical examination of Rose that was practiced and thorough. The EMTs asked about her medical history and what medications she was taking. Allergies? Visual impairment? Had she ever had a stroke? They checked the size of her pupils and took her blood pressure. They asked her if she knew what day of the week it was.

Maura laughed out loud and the paramedics glanced her way. "Sorry," she said. "Rose is always mixed up about that."

"Saturday," Rose guessed. She was nearly right.

Thankfully, the physical exam revealed no broken bones. Rose had major bruising around her ribs and hip. Her right shoulder and knees were already turning colors. One ankle had a slight sprain. There was a strong possibility of a concussion. Considering her age, the paramedics recommended that Rose take a ride to the hospital in the back of their ambulance.

She thanked them gratefully for their time and expertise and declined.

While the EMTs were busy poking and prodding her, Rose had watched Detective Sturgill climb out of the second car and walk over. Standing just outside the circle of light provided by the headlights, he'd folded his arms over his chest and observed the activity taking place in front of the shelter impassively. His expression was grim.

Then again, Peg's friend, Rodney, always looked grim to Rose.

Now the detective stepped forward. "I think you should reconsider, Mrs. Donovan. A quick trip to the hospital to get things checked out would be reassuring to your family." He glanced toward Peter and Maura for support.

"Detective Sturgill," Rose spoke up before anyone else had a chance. "I appreciate your concern on my behalf. I didn't expect to see you here tonight."

"Peg called me," he said.

Rose sighed. *Of course she had.*

"I let the station know I'd respond so they didn't have to send a car. Which means I'm going to have some questions for you. But let's make sure you're finished with medical support first."

"I am," Rose said firmly.

Sturgill looked at Peter for confirmation. Rose wanted to smack him. The detective, that was. Not Peter. Her husband was an innocent bystander.

"Rose can speak for herself," Peter said. *Brilliant man.* "I'll keep a close eye on her overnight. If anything doesn't seem right, I'll take her straight to the emergency room."

"Your call," one of the paramedics said.

They'd already packed up their gear. They closed the back of the ambulance, then climbed into the cab and pulled away. As that vehicle was leaving, another one arrived. Rose recognized Peg's maroon minivan.

Oh joy.

She wondered how many speed limits Peg had broken on her way back from Greenwich. Maybe she should make a citizen's arrest and hand Peg over to Detective Sturgill. While the two of them were hashing that out between them, Rose could disappear into the shelter and go to bed. That would simplify her night enormously.

Rose savored that thoroughly unattainable pipe dream for the minute it took for Peg to hop out of her minivan and come over to join them. At least she hadn't brought a Poodle with her. Rose supposed that was something to be grateful for.

"That's not blood, is it?" Peg said by way of a greeting.

"No," Rose replied. "Tomatoes."

Peg nodded. "Better." She turned to the detective. "I understand someone nearly succeeded in running Rose down. Have you caught the culprit yet?"

He looked at her and held up his empty hands. "I just got here."

"No," Peg said deliberately, "*I* just got here. You've probably been here for at least twenty minutes."

At some point Maura had left the group and gone back inside the shelter. That left four people now standing in the middle of Digby Avenue. In the dark. Late at night. Making noise.

It wasn't the kind of neighborhood where the sound of sirens and the appearance of flashing lights would bring people outside to see what was going on. Here, the opposite was true. At the first sign of trouble, neighbors locked their doors and closed their curtains. That didn't mean they weren't watching, however. And listening.

"Let's move this discussion inside, shall we?" Peter proposed. He was ever the voice of reason.

"Good idea." Peg leaned over and kissed his cheek. "Pardon my manners, I should have said hello but I was too concerned about Rose to stop and observe the proprieties. It's lovely to see you, Peter. As always, I'm sure you have the situation well in hand."

"If only that was actually true," Peter said. He began to herd everyone onto the sidewalk, in the direction of the shelter.

Luckily, no women were in residence at the Gallagher House at the moment. The group wasn't disturbing anyone when they congregated in the living room. Having preceded everyone else inside, Maura had taken the initiative to brew a pot of fresh coffee. She'd also remembered that the reason there was Earl Grey tea in the pantry was because Peg refused to drink coffee. As soon as they'd all gotten settled, refreshments were served. Then Maura sat down to join them.

"Start at the beginning, and tell me everything that happened," Detective Sturgill said to Rose.

He was gazing wistfully at the tray Maura had used to bring in the drinks. Peg always served him cake. He looked as though he was wishing for some now. Maura hopped up again and disappeared back into the kitchen. She returned toward the end of Rose's recital with a plate of Peter's favorite shortbread cookies. The detective helped himself to two.

"I know you said it happened so fast that you couldn't identify the car or the person who was driving it," he said. "But I'd like you to stop and think back for a moment anyway. Are there any small details you might have noticed? Maybe something hanging from the rearview mirror, or a reflection off the driver's glasses? Consider the car too. Was there a dealer plate on the front, or maybe a bumper sticker?"

"I'm sorry," Rose replied unhappily. "By the time I saw the car, it was already coming straight at me. The high beams were shining in my face. I could barely see a thing. And I guess I was sort of . . . panicking."

"That's understandable," Sturgill replied gently. "Anyone would have felt the same way. Especially being trapped out there in the road like you were. It was quick thinking on your part to wedge yourself between those parked vehicles."

This was a side of the detective Rose hadn't seen before.

At least not directed toward her. Sturgill was going out of his way to be kind, and even compassionate, as he probed for answers. She only wished she had better feedback to offer him.

"In that moment, I'm not sure I was thinking at all," Rose admitted. "It was just instinct to get out of the way by any means possible."

Detective Sturgill nodded. He ate another cookie. Then he turned and looked at Peg. "The way I see it, this is your fault."

"My fault?" Peg had been sipping her tea, which she'd liberally laced with sugar. She stared at him over the rim of her cup. "How do you figure that?"

"You and I had a conversation about this. You assured me you weren't going to get involved in police business again."

Peg blinked in surprise. She put her cup back down in its saucer. "I'm quite certain I did nothing of the sort."

"Then you should have done," Sturgill persisted. "Because when you don't listen to me, this is what happens. People get hurt."

If Rose had been feeling up to par, she might have broken in to tell him that he shouldn't feel singled out by Peg's resistance. She never listened to *anyone's* advice. But the conversation moved on, and her chance was lost.

"You're blaming Rose's near miss on me?" Peg's tone skated dangerously close to outrage.

"Perhaps we should all take a deep breath," Peter interjected. "It's been a stressful night. It's understandable that tempers are on edge. But we won't accomplish anything by arguing with each other."

Detective Sturgill frowned. Peg opened her mouth, then snapped it shut. Maura looked as though she might be enjoying herself.

Peter waited a beat, then said, "Detective, it sounds as

though you're assuming that what happened here tonight is related to a case of yours, the death of Nolan Abercrombie."

"That's right, I am."

"If I may, I would like to introduce a different theory."

"I'm listening," Sturgill said cautiously. He looked like he was wondering if there might be yet another murder Peg and Rose had gotten themselves mixed up in.

"We've recently had some problems on this block with a group of delinquents who've attached themselves to a house at the end of the street. The home is owned by one of the young men's grandmother. These men come and go whenever the mood suits them, and observing safe driving practices is the last thing on their minds."

The detective straightened in his seat. "You think this could have been one of those men?"

"It's a possibility," Peter replied. Rose and Maura both nodded.

"Do you have a name for me?"

"Mabel Mayberry is the home's owner. Her grandson's name is Donny," Maura said. She was already rising from her seat. "If you want, I can write down Mabel's address and phone number."

"I'd appreciate that." Sturgill nodded. "We'll check into it."

He finished his coffee, then stood up. "Mrs. Donovan, I'm glad your injuries weren't more serious. But I still want you to think carefully about what I said earlier. This thing that you and Peg do together is putting you at risk. Possibly both of you. Maybe what happened here tonight wasn't related, but I wouldn't bet on that. I need you to promise me that you'll be careful."

"I will," Rose said solemnly.

"Good. I hope you mean that." He turned and started for the door.

Peg stood up and followed him. Maura was coming from the office with a piece of paper. Before she reached the detective, Peg stepped between them.

"I've been wondering about something I didn't see reported in the media," she said. "Who were Nolan's heirs?"

Sturgill turned back to face her. His glower would have intimidated a lesser woman, but Peg stood her ground. "You never give up, do you?"

"Not if I can help it." She jutted out her chin. "Look at it this way. The more information Rose and I possess, the safer we'll be."

He accepted the paper from Maura's outstretched hand, then reached for the doorknob. Peg thought he wasn't going to answer her question.

At the last moment, he glanced back. "There was only one heir. Abercrombie had a son named Jason. Never married the mother, but I guess he knew the kid was his. It wasn't a huge estate, but whatever there was went to him."

Chapter 26

"Jason?" Peter said after Maura had closed the door behind Detective Sturgill, then gone downstairs to her basement apartment. "That name sounds familiar."

He waited for Rose to comment. She didn't. Peg, for once, also remained silent.

"This would be the same man to whom you offered a job?"

Much as she wanted to, Rose couldn't dodge her husband's questions forever. "Yes, that's him."

"It appears he now has a motive for wanting his father dead."

"Jason already had a motive," Peg said unhelpfully. "Several, in fact."

"I see." Peter considered that.

Whatever conclusions he reached, he didn't share them with Rose and Peg. Instead, Peter piled the cups and saucers back on the tray, then picked it up and left the room. Peg stared after him.

"You have him very well trained," she said. "Max could barely find his way to the kitchen, much less figure how to wash a dish."

"Peter came that way, so I can hardly take any credit," Rose replied. Now that Detective Sturgill had left, she wondered why Peg had remained behind. "Besides, we have a dishwasher."

"Even so."

Peg strolled over to the fireplace. There was a row of inexpensive figurines on top of the mantelpiece. She ran her finger over them as though she was checking for dust. Rose doubted she'd find any. Maura was very good at her job. Much better than Rose had ever been when it was her duty to wield the dustcloth.

"Peg, what are you doing?" she asked.

"Stalling."

That was unexpected. When Peg had something to say, she usually couldn't wait to blurt it out.

"Why?"

Peg turned slowly. "Because I owe you another apology. And this time I'm really sorry."

"For calling Detective Sturgill?"

"Heavens no. That was a good idea."

"Then what? Would you please stop wandering around and come and sit down? If you don't, I'll have to get up, and considering that I feel as though I've been run over by a truck, I'd just as soon not."

"For *that*," Peg replied. "Rodney was right, you know. Not that I would give him the satisfaction of hearing it from me. But what happened to you tonight is my fault."

"How do you figure that?" Rose threw Peg's own words from earlier right back at her.

"Because if it wasn't for me, you wouldn't be sitting there turning black and blue even as we speak."

"First of all," Rose said firmly, "I'm your partner, not some minion who does whatever you tell me. And second, if I hadn't pushed you to sign up for that dating app, neither one of us would be here. Now sit!"

Rose pointed toward the chair opposite her. Peg frowned. Rose didn't care. She didn't stop pointing until Peg's fanny was in the seat.

"It doesn't seem fair," Peg mused.

"Now what?"

Rose was too tired for this conversation. What she really wanted to do was show Peg the door, collect Peter from the kitchen, go home, and sink into a dreamless sleep in her own bed. It didn't look as though any of those things would be happening anytime soon.

"Last time we did this, the culprit came after me. My kitchen window being shot out was bad enough, but at least I didn't get hit."

"Fortunately I wasn't hit either," Rose pointed out. "The car missed me when I jumped out of the way."

"Precisely," Peg retorted. "And that's the problem. You're too old to have to go jumping around like that."

"At the risk of stating the obvious, I didn't have a choice. And I don't understand what you're getting at. What's your solution here? Do you think we should stop looking for Nolan's killer?"

Peg slowly shook her head. "No, not now. Not when it feels like we're getting close."

"So . . . what then?"

"I want you to be more careful. You scared me half to death tonight. I would hate for something truly terrible to happen to you."

That sounded familiar. Hadn't Detective Sturgill tried to extract the same promise from her earlier? *Sheesh*, Rose thought. She had one little accident and suddenly everyone was treating her like an invalid. Or an old lady. She wasn't sure which was worse.

She reached across the small expanse between them, took Peg's hand in hers, and squeezed it. "I will if you will."

Peg's gaze dropped to their joined hands. She tried for a flippant tone. "Why, Rose, I didn't know you cared."

"Of course I care. Who else can I depend upon to drive me crazy at least once a week?"

Rose softened the words with a smile. After a moment, Peg smiled too.

"Do we have a deal?" Rose asked.

"Deal," Peg agreed.

Peg awoke the next morning with her head buzzing with ideas.

Chief among them was the conviction that it was time to figure out who killed Nolan Abercrombie before Rose had a chance to put herself in harm's way again. Peg wasn't worried on her own behalf—she was strong as an ox. But Rose was like a fawn lost in a forest. She assumed all the other animals were on her side, even the ones with big teeth and hungry eyes.

The first thing Peg did was pull out Rose's list. She ran her finger down the row of names until she came to Blythe Cummins. There was a phone number too. A quick call to Blythe confirmed a suspicion she'd been mulling over since she'd left Gina's house the previous evening.

Then Peg had a chat with Izzy Hicks. Having received the answers she'd expected on both counts, her next step was to bid the Poodles goodbye, get in her minivan, and drive across the state line to New York.

Charlie Vargas lived in Dutchess County. The trip took a bit more than an hour. That was nothing for Peg. She routinely drove much longer distances to dog shows. This time, however, she found herself drumming her fingers impatiently on the steering wheel for nearly the entire drive.

She hadn't dared to call ahead to see if Charlie was available. Given the chance, she was reasonably sure he'd try to avoid her. Instead she'd checked his judging schedule, then relied upon her own experience as a popular dog show judge. Peg and her peers all spent an inordinate amount of time on the road, which meant they prized their quiet days at home when they didn't have a far-flung assignment.

Peg hadn't been to Charlie's home in a long time—at least a dozen years—but she still remembered the way. The last time she was here, she'd come with her husband, Max. He and Charlie had been good friends. Since Max's death, however, Peg's and Charlie's socializing had been confined to brief conversations at occasional shows.

Peg hadn't stopped to consider that before, but now she did. She had many friends in the dog show community, fellow breeders and judges with whom she spoke frequently. To all appearances, she and Charlie had once been close, but without Max to provide a bridge between them, their friendship had simply withered away.

Maybe that was because there'd always been something about Charlie that Peg didn't entirely trust. He was the kind of man whom other men admired: energetic, slightly loud, always sure of himself, and often the center of attention. He bought rounds of drinks, slapped men's backs, and ogled pretty women with the same hearty enthusiasm. But sometimes his air of genial bonhomie felt forced. As if it was an act he put on to make a sparkling impression on everyone around him.

Charlie hadn't been sparkling the last time they'd spoken, Peg realized. Maybe he hadn't felt she was worth the effort. That was a lowering thought. And probably also an accurate one. It occurred to Peg that her main problem with Charlie was that she'd simply never been as impressed with the man as he was with himself.

Despite her feelings for its owner, Charlie's house was lovely. Compact in size, it was made of stone and nestled on a small corner lot that was heavily shaded by mature trees. His lawn was freshly mowed, and his front walk was bordered on both sides by colorful summer flowers. There was a Jaguar sedan parked in the driveway—an older model with classic lines and the iconic hood ornament. Seeing it now, Peg recalled that Charlie had always been inordinately proud of that car. She pulled in behind it and parked.

He answered the door wearing pressed khakis, tasseled loafers, and a blue shirt that matched his eyes. Peg had pasted a friendly smile on her face. Even so, Charlie looked shocked to see her. He quickly recovered, however.

"Well." He swallowed heavily. "This is a surprise."

"I could lie and say that I was in the neighborhood, but the truth is that you and I need to talk," Peg said. "May I come in?"

Charlie didn't issue an invitation, but he did step back out of her way. Peg figured that was close enough. As he closed the door behind her, she cast a surreptitious glance around. The house was very much as she remembered it. That, combined with its general untidiness, suggested that there wasn't a fourth wife out of sight in another room.

Good. Considering the questions Peg intended to ask, she'd rather hold this conversation in private.

"What's this about?" Charlie asked when they'd taken seats in a comfortable living room whose walls were lined with numerous pictures of Charlie and his Vizslas.

"Nolan Abercrombie." Peg hadn't driven sixty miles in order to waste time mincing words.

"Again?" He scrubbed a hand over his face. "I thought we settled that."

"We didn't settle anything. We just stopped talking. Or at least you did."

"That's because I'd said all there was to say."

"I don't think so."

Peg looked around the room again. So many gorgeous Vizslas on the walls, and not a single live one here in the home. There wasn't even a dog bed or a rawhide bone on the floor. She counted that as another strike against him.

"I first heard your name in connection with Nolan from Izzy Hicks," she said.

"Okay." Charlie wasn't about to give anything away.

"She told me you were the person who'd introduced her to Nolan."

He shrugged indifferently. "I may have done so. I don't remember, but if Izzy says it's so, I suppose it is."

"Let me jog your memory again, then. Do you remember introducing Blythe Cummins to Nolan?"

"Who?" His confusion wasn't entirely credible.

"Blythe Cummins. You and her husband, Harold, were friends."

"Oh." Charlie's expression cleared. "*That* Blythe."

"Yes," Peg agreed mildly. "That Blythe. The one you set up with your good buddy, Nolan, after her husband passed away."

"Nolan and I were hardly buddies," he corrected her quickly. "I believe I told you that before."

"You did. You also told me that the two of you hadn't been in business together. But it turns out you were lying."

"Don't be ridiculous. Why would I lie about something like that?"

"Maybe because after you got Nolan and Izzy together, he tried to scam her out of a rather large sum of money. Fortunately for Izzy, he didn't succeed. Unfortunately for Blythe, Nolan had more success conning her."

Peg fixed him with a beady glare. "You know. *That* Blythe. The one you introduced to Nolan out of the goodness of your heart."

"You're making it sound as though I did something wrong," Charlie said irritably. His fingers were curled around the arms of his chair. "Blythe was lonely after Harold died. She was despondent, on the verge of becoming a recluse. I figured Nolan might cheer her up. Or at least he'd get her out of her house and make her go places. I introduced Blythe to Nolan for her own good."

"How good do you think she felt after Nolan made off

with all her jewelry and her deceased husband's vintage Bentley?"

"I don't know what you're talking about." Charlie's eyes shifted from side to side. Not only was the man a liar, he wasn't even a good one.

"Really?" she prodded. "An automobile aficionado like yourself? Someone with an appreciation for fine older cars? I'm sure Nolan must have shown off his classic Bentley to you. I wonder if he asked you to appraise it for him before he sold it?"

"Of course he didn't ask me to do that!" Charlie snapped.

Peg settled back in her seat. She let Charlie think about what he'd just said.

"You don't understand," he said after a minute.

"Oh, I think I do. You and Nolan were doing business—"

"We were not. If he were here, you could ask him yourself. I never swindled anyone."

"You didn't have to," Peg said angrily. "All you had to do was scout out well-to-do older women, hand them over to Nolan, and let him do the rest."

"Look," Charlie growled. "The only thing I did was make an introduction or two. Women thanked me for that. I'd imagine you know why. It's because the ratio of older women to older men in this country is totally skewed against them."

Peg nodded as if he'd made a good point.

"Thousands of women your age are hoping for a chance to go out and flirt, and make themselves feel young and pretty again. Nolan gave them all that and more."

By "more," Peg assumed he was talking about sex. She nodded again.

"Those women who helped Nolan financially? That

was *their* choice. They didn't have to give him access to their money. They *chose* to."

"It wasn't an informed choice though. Most of them didn't understand the ramifications of letting Nolan handle their investments."

"That's hardly my fault," Charlie replied. "In fact, none of what you're talking about is my fault. I was performing a service by bringing people together. I was doing a *good* thing."

Peg didn't share his optimistic view. Not only that, but if she allowed him to continue throwing out these flowery rationalizations, pretty soon they'd be having a kumbaya moment. It was time to retake control of the conversation.

"I assume you were being paid for your *services*," she said. "Maybe a cut of the proceeds every time you delivered a new pigeon that was ripe for plucking?"

"Now you're just being crude." Charlie shoved himself to his feet. "You've always been outspoken, Peg, but these accusations are outrageous. I never understood why Max didn't do a better job of taking you in hand."

Peg bristled at that. Just as Charlie had no doubt intended. She refused to let herself be distracted.

"Max would be ashamed of himself for calling you a friend if he knew what you'd been up to," Peg snapped back. "Don't kid yourself that Nolan did all the dirty work while you remained blameless. What you were doing was damn dirty too."

"That's slander, and you'd better not repeat it." Charlie stalked toward the door. "Whatever you might think you know about Nolan and me, I'm certain you don't have any proof. I was much smarter than his legions of silly women. I made sure to cover my back."

Peg followed him across the room. She had no intention of letting him have the last word.

"Your concerns are misplaced," she said as Charlie

yanked open the door and she stepped outside. "Those stupid schemes you were part of are just a side issue now. Everyone already knows Nolan was a horrendous partner. And that anyone who trusted him to look out for their interests did so to their detriment.

"The only question now is whether or not someone Nolan had dealings with killed him as a result. I hope for your sake that person wasn't you."

Chapter 27

Rose was at home, sitting in her living room, when her phone rang. She had a book in her lap that she wasn't reading. There was an apple on the table beside her chair that she didn't feel like eating. She set the book aside and reached for the phone, grateful for the diversion.

"If I wanted to call on you, where would I find you?" Peg asked.

Rose perked up. It was hard to feel sorry for herself when Peg was sounding so chipper. Suddenly, it felt as though her life was about to become more interesting.

"I'm at home, sitting around moping. Peter and Maura both think I should be resting, which is ridiculous. Everyone is treating me like I'm made of glass and might break if I try to do something useful."

"I can fix that," Peg said. "Do you feel well enough for an outing?"

Rose smiled her first real smile of the day. "That sounds like just what I need."

She rose from her chair as though Peg's arrival might be imminent, although surely that wasn't the case. Nevertheless, Rose was itching to be up and moving. Any sedentary tendencies she might once have possessed had been put aside during her days at the convent, where indolence was considered to be nothing short of sinful. Even years later, Rose was unaccustomed to cosseting herself.

"Are we going somewhere interesting?" she asked. "How soon can you be here?"

"Less than ten minutes. I'll tell you all about my morning and where I think we should go next when I get there. If you happen to have something on hand for lunch, that would be a plus."

Rose rolled her eyes. How like Peg to arrive hungry. And to have already decided what their next move should be. As if Rose's input was immaterial. She'd hoped Peg would have learned better than that by now.

Having stood up, Rose stretched her body carefully. New bruises had bloomed overnight, and she'd retaped her ankle that morning. A generous dose of ibuprofen was making her feel better than she looked. Luckily, her brain was working just fine. Rather than sitting around wallowing, she felt more than ready to do *something*. Even if that meant starting by making lunch.

Nine minutes later, Peg was at the front door. She knocked, then let herself inside.

"I'm in the kitchen," Rose called. She had slices of bread in the toaster and a bowl of tuna salad on the counter. She'd also found baby carrots in the crisper and an unopened bag of chips in the cabinet.

Peg walked around the corner, then stopped dead. "You look like hell," she said. "Are you sure you should be out of bed?"

"Not you, too." Rose groaned. "I'm bruised, not half-dead."

"Hard to tell that by looking at you." Peg walked over to the counter and helped herself to a carrot. She wrinkled her nose at the nearby bowl. "Tuna fish?"

"People who invite themselves to lunch on short notice

get what's on hand." The toaster popped up. Rose grabbed the first two pieces of toast, then put in two more. "There are chips too."

"Thank goodness for that." Peg grabbed the bag, headed for the tiny table in the corner of the room and sat down. "I spent the morning talking to Charlie Vargas."

Rose frowned and glanced at Peg. "Why do I know that name?"

"He's a dog show judge. He was an old friend of Max's. And apparently Nolan's too."

"That's right. Nolan mentioned him when we were at the dog show. He was the guy who had dogs with a name that made me think of the Gabor sisters. Were they Zsa Zsas?"

"Vizslas," Peg corrected. "Close though, same country of origin. Are those sandwiches ready yet? I'm starving."

"Coming right up." Rose carried two plates over to the table. Each held a sandwich, cut in half diagonally, and a small mound of carrots. She sat down opposite Peg. "Aside from knowing Nolan, what does Charlie Vargas have to do with anything?"

"It turns out that Charlie also knew another dog show friend of mine named Izzy Hicks. Then last night, Blythe happened to mention him in passing."

Rose looked up from her sandwich. "He's beginning to sound like a man who gets around."

"That's what I thought. Especially since both Izzy and Blythe told me that Charlie was the one who introduced them to Nolan."

"That's interesting. What did Charlie have to say about that?"

"Not much of anything until I backed him into a corner." Despite wrinkling her nose at tuna fish, Peg had already finished her sandwich. Now she was munching on a carrot. "Eventually he all but admitted that he and Nolan were in cahoots."

"Cahoots," Rose repeated. "Great word. It's too bad it doesn't come up more often. So Charlie was another partner in Nolan's scams?"

"Yes, but differently than Barbara. Charlie was procuring for Nolan, then taking a cut of the proceeds."

"Yuck. In case you ever wondered, men like Nolan and Charlie are the reason why women become nuns."

"Noted." Now Peg was eyeing the second half of Rose's sandwich. Rose picked it up and passed it over.

"Do you think Charlie had something to do with Nolan's death?"

"Possibly. Although I haven't yet figured out what his motive would have been. Which brings me back around to our upcoming outing."

"Motive?" Rose inquired.

"Right. As in who had one. And the newest suspect to fill that role is . . . ?"

"Jason Abercrombie," Rose said unhappily. "And I hope your suspicions are wrong. He seemed like a nice guy."

"Ted Bundy seemed like a nice guy too. That's how he got away with killing all those women."

"Jason didn't kill anyone."

"Says you," Peg retorted. "I'd like to hear what Jason has to say for himself. As you may remember, I never had a chance to talk to him."

"As you may remember, that was your own fault."

Peg ignored that. She stood up, picked up her plate, and carried it over to the sink. "What's for dessert?"

Rose didn't have a good answer. She'd been thinking about Jason's problems. "More carrots?"

"Surely you can do better." Peg was scanning the small room as if she was hoping a piece of cake might leap out of a cabinet and land in her hands. *Good luck with that.*

"An apple?" Rose tried.

"Keep going."

"I would, but I'm running out of options."

Rose took her plate over to the sink too. The bowl she'd used for the tuna salad was already soaking. The dishes could wait until later. Right now, she was concerned about Jason. She realized she needed to hear him tell his side of the story again.

Peg was right about motive. It now appeared that Jason had not just one, but possibly several. Nolan had been remarkably adept at fooling women with his lies. Rose hoped Jason wasn't following in his father's footsteps.

Peg and Rose caught Jason on his lunch break.

At least that was what he told Rose when she called to see if they could get together. Rose, who was too soft-hearted for her own good, believed him. Peg wasn't so sure. She thought it was equally likely that Jason wasn't employed at all, but thought this answer would go over better.

They arranged to meet at a diner in Norwalk. Peg figured that meant they'd probably be buying Jason lunch. On the other hand, the diner probably had cake. So there was that upside to look forward to.

"I just realized why you brought me along," Rose said once they were on their way. "It's because you were afraid Jason wouldn't agree to see you if you were on your own."

"Maybe that was part of it."

"What was the other part?" Rose asked suspiciously.

"Apparently when I leave you alone, you get into too much trouble. Someone should be keeping an eye on you."

Rose snorted out a laugh. "You're a fine one to talk."

"I'm not the one who looks like she went ten rounds with Mike Tyson."

"Be glad I'm not still covered in tomato juice," Rose muttered.

Denton's looked like a classic 1950s diner. The building was long and low and covered in aluminum siding. A row of windows revealed a U-shaped counter in the back of the room, while a long line of booths wrapped around the front. Music was not only playing inside, it was also piped out into the parking lot.

"Cool," Peg said.

Rose gave her a look. "Just so you know, people who still say 'cool' aren't."

"Speak for yourself," Peg replied haughtily. She led the way inside.

The diner was crowded, but Jason had already arrived and commandeered a booth. He was perusing a laminated menu that was decorated with colorful pictures of the available dishes. Peg was immediately sorry that she'd already settled for tuna fish. She and Rose slid onto the plastic-covered seat across from him.

Jason lifted his gaze to Peg and scowled. "You didn't tell me she was coming," he said to Rose.

"And you didn't tell me that you were Nolan's heir," Rose replied. "So we'll call it even."

"If I had told you that, you'd have thought I was the one who killed him."

"We suspected as much anyway," Peg said.

Rose kicked her under the table, but the damage was already done.

Jason slapped his menu down on the Formica tabletop and began to slide out of the booth. Rose reached a hand across to stop him. "Please stay. Let us treat you to lunch, and I'll do my best to keep Peg under control."

"She's twice your size." He started to smile, then he looked at Rose more closely and his amusement faded. "Holy crap! What the hell happened to you?"

"Rose had a near miss with a speeding car," Peg told him. Jason went still. "You mean like Nolan did?"

"Exactly like that. Luckily, this time there was a different outcome. Now maybe you'll understand why finding your father's killer has suddenly begun to seem imperative to us."

Jason nodded. "Have you seen a doctor?" he asked Rose. "If not, I know where there's a clinic that only makes you pay what you can afford. I'd be happy to take you there and introduce you around."

"Thank you for that," Rose said. "I appreciate your concern, but I've already received medical care. I know I look pretty bad, but I mostly just need time to heal."

"Got it. Sorry." He looked back down at his menu. "I didn't mean to intrude."

"You folks know what you want?" A middle-aged woman with an order pad and a cheery smile paused at the end of the booth. "Today's special is a pulled pork sandwich on a kaiser roll with melted Swiss cheese and double fries."

"That'll do it for me," Jason said, handing back his menu.

Peg ordered a cup of tea and an extra-large slice of chocolate cake. Rose was about to ask for coffee when a bright pink image on the menu caught her eye. "I'll have a strawberry milkshake," she said instead. "With a spoon and a straw, please."

"Got it." The waitress spun around and left.

"Good for you," Jason said.

"What?" asked Rose.

"Ordering a milkshake. You look like you could use a treat."

"Oh?" Peg gazed down her nose at him. "And what do I look like?"

"Like you could probably take me down with one hand tied behind your back." He grinned at her across the table. "I assume you do that on purpose."

"Do what?"

"Intimidate people. So they'll give you what you want."

He wasn't entirely wrong. Not that Peg was about to admit that. And especially not to this cocky young man who somehow thought he knew everything about her.

"And what is it that you think I want?" she asked.

"Answers." His tone implied that was obvious. "Isn't that why we're here?"

"I don't know about you," Peg replied, "but I'm here for the cake."

Rose began to laugh. She should have known better because that made her ribs feel like they'd been hit with a hot poker. Abruptly she stopped and sucked in a breath. Peg looked at her in concern. Then Jason did too.

Thankfully, before anyone could inquire about the state of Rose's health for the umpteenth time, the waitress reappeared. She set Rose's milkshake and Peg's cake down on the table. Jason sat back and crossed his arms as both women paused before reaching for their food.

"Dig in," he told them. "I'm sure my sandwich will be along any minute. And once I'm finished eating, I'm out of here. So if you've got something to say to me, you'd better get to it."

"Right." Rose scooped a spoonful of whipped cream off the top of her milkshake. She held it in the air while she said, "When you and I spoke about your relationship with your father, you had ample opportunity to mention that he'd left his estate to you. Why didn't you?"

Jason frowned. "I already answered that question."

"Your first answer was too glib. Try again."

"Let's be clear about something. It's not like Nolan was rich or anything. He was probably spending money just as fast as he was making it."

The waitress returned to the booth with his pulled pork sandwich. Jason eyed the tall mound of fries with approval as she slid the plate in front of him. "Thank you," he told her. "That looks great."

"Even a small amount of money is meaningful to someone in need," Peg pointed out as Jason nabbed a french fry and popped it in his mouth.

"Don't get me wrong. I'm not saying I wasn't happy to have it. But him leaving me money after he was gone felt like 'too little, too late.' I'd rather have had a real relationship with him while he was still around."

Rose nodded. She could see that. And as long as she didn't have to talk, she could enjoy her strawberry milkshake. It was too thick for her straw so she was eating it with a spoon.

"Another thing," Jason said. He'd already wolfed down nearly half his sandwich. "I had no idea about the bequest until Nolan was already dead and his lawyer contacted me. So if you're looking for motives, you can count that one out."

Even with a big piece of cake in front of her, Peg didn't look pleased by that development. "That assumes you're telling us the truth," she said.

"If you're not going to believe my answers, why are you bothering to ask me questions?" Jason said practically. Now he was hoovering his way through the pile of fries. Rose hadn't seen anyone eat that quickly since she'd returned from her mission trip.

He glanced up. "Since time's passing, I'll help you ladies along. What you should be asking is, what about my car?"

"Okay," said Peg. "What about it?"

"I don't have one."

Rose didn't bother to hide her surprise. "I thought just about everyone who lived in the suburbs owned a car."

"Not everyone I know." Jason lifted a hand and ticked off several items on his fingers. "Registration, insurance, license, gas. Even if it's a junker, a car costs more money than I have. I get around on public transportation." He paused, then added, "As far as I know Nolan wasn't hit by a bus."

"No," Peg admitted unhappily. "He wasn't."

Jason turned to Rose. His plate was nearly empty. "Before I go, I have a question for you."

Rose scooped up the last of her milkshake with her spoon. She swallowed blissfully, then licked the spoon clean. She should indulge herself more often. That was the best treat she'd had in a long time.

"Go ahead," she said.

"That stuff you said before about offering me a job at your shelter, was that for real, or were you just stringing me along so I'd talk to you?"

"I was perfectly serious. And I still am. I told my husband about you, and he's eager to meet you . . ."

"But?" Jason prompted when her voice trailed away. He looked as though life had taught him that there would always be a catch.

"Under the circumstances, Peter thought it would make sense to take our time before moving forward—"

Jason was shaking his head. "By circumstances, you mean me being a suspect in Nolan's death. Right?"

When Rose hesitated, Peg answered for her. "Yes."

"I didn't kill him. I'm sure I already told you that." Jason sighed. "But it doesn't matter, does it? Because someone like me—a guy without enough education or a steady job— will always look suspicious to people who already have everything and take it all for granted."

He plucked the napkin off his lap and dropped it on the

tabletop. Then he slid out of the booth. "Thanks for lunch, Mrs. Donovan. And for giving me a glimmer of hope—even if only briefly—that someday my life could change."

Peg and Rose watched Jason stride out of the diner. He walked across the parking lot and disappeared around the side of the neighboring building.

"That's a man with a chip on his shoulder," Peg said.

Rose winced at that description. She was irritated by how the meeting had ended.

"Can you blame him?" she asked.

Chapter 28

When Peg and Rose left the diner, Rose insisted she felt well enough to go to work, so Peg dropped her off at the Gallagher House. Peter was surprised to see her. They walked into the living room together and sat down.

"You're supposed to be taking it easy," he said.

"I am. I lounged around home all morning, and Peg and I just had lunch."

Marmalade came over to wind herself around Rose's legs. When Rose reached down to give her a scratch, the kitten hopped up onto the couch cushion beside her.

"By yourselves?"

In all the years Rose had known Peter, he'd never been suspicious about her choices or activities. Then Rose had teamed up with Peg, and now it seemed like he was always full of questions. Unfortunately for Rose, more often than not they were justified.

"Actually we met up with Jason Abercrombie," she admitted.

"The man who needs a job?"

Rose nodded. "He asked about that."

"Is he still a suspect in his father's death?"

"Less and less all the time. It turns out he doesn't even own a car."

Peter wasn't convinced. "That's hardly a reason to eliminate him. He might have borrowed a car. Or, for all you know, he could have stolen one."

"I don't think so," Rose said as Marmalade snuggled in along the length of her thigh and flicked her tail. "But you don't have to take my word for it. Once this is over, you can meet him and judge for yourself."

"Let's hope I'm able to interview him here at the shelter and not uptown at the police station," Peter muttered.

"Where's Maura?" Rose asked, changing the subject. It was unusual for the housekeeper not to be on hand.

"At the end of the block with Mabel Mayberry. Mabel taught her how to play canasta, and the two of them spent several hours yesterday playing for pennies. Maura won nearly a dollar, but Mabel refused to pay up. She made Maura roll her winnings over into today's game. I think Mabel may be cagier than she lets on. I'm waiting with bated breath to see if Maura gets fleeced today."

"Tell her I'll cover her losses if she does," Rose said with a smile. "Especially now when we're not busy, I'm happy she's taken it upon herself to keep an eye on things at Mabel's house."

"Me too," Peter agreed. "But you can tell her yourself. I'm sure she'll be back before we leave for the day."

"I would, but I think I'd like to go out again if you don't need to use the van for anything."

"Are you sure you feel well enough?"

"Yes, of course." Rose tried not to grumble. She knew Peter meant well, but she was tired of everyone trying to manage her life for her. "Besides, I'm only going north of the parkway."

"Melanie's house?"

"Not exactly." Rose dropped her gaze and rubbed Marmalade's soft tummy.

Peter sighed. "The fact that you and I appear to be playing twenty questions isn't entirely reassuring. Not to mention that you're no longer looking at me. Are you planning on doing something dangerous?"

"Definitely not." Rose lifted her eyes. "I just want to talk to one of the women from Nolan's group. She said something at the meeting last night that I'd like to clarify."

"I see." Peter didn't look happy. "Is it anything I can help with?"

"No, but thank you. If Dani's available to talk, I shouldn't be gone more than an hour."

"I'll hold you to that." Peter reached over and picked up the kitten so Rose could stand. "Text me Dani's address and phone number. One hour, tops. Then I'm coming after you."

Dani was happy to talk to Rose again. Apparently, she and several of the other women had spent much of the morning comparing notes about the previous night's meeting. Peg's and Rose's investigation had been the subject of much curiosity and speculation, not to mention amusement. Now Dani was pleased to be singled out for round two. She invited Rose to her home in North Stamford.

Dani's house was perched high on a hilltop overlooking the Mianus Reservoir. Surrounded by trees and constructed of glass and cedar, the A-frame building blended seamlessly into its surroundings. A cathedral ceiling, paired with numerous windows and an open floor plan, offered a spectacular view of the steep hillside and sparkling water below.

"Wow," Rose said as she stepped inside. "This place is amazing."

"I know, right?" Dani had answered the door in a well-worn gardening smock, cut-off jeans, and sneakers. Her blond hair was cropped short in a symmetrical bob that highlighted her elfin features.

She gave Rose an odd look before continuing. "My husband and I had it built to spec in the seventies when A-frames were all the rage. We always thought we'd have to sell it and get something bigger when the kids came along, but . . ." Dani stopped and shrugged.

"You didn't have any children?" Rose asked.

"Nope. It didn't happen for us. You?"

"Me either." Rose declined to elaborate.

She followed Dani into a large center room. Area rugs were scattered around the hardwood floor, and the furniture was low and unobtrusive. Everything was decorated in muted earth tones. Nothing detracted from the panoramic vista outside.

Dani waved Rose to a seat on a flannel-covered couch. "I know we barely know each other, so I hope you won't think I'm interfering. But last night you appeared to be fine. And now you look as though something's gone terribly wrong in the meantime. So I'm asking as one woman to another—do you need help?"

For a moment, Rose didn't understand. Then suddenly she did. "Oh. No. It's not what you're thinking," she said quickly. "In fact, my husband and I run a women's shelter—"

Dani nodded. "Yes, I think Gina mentioned something about that. But that doesn't mean you're immune."

"Of course, you're right," Rose conceded. "And thank you for your concern. But Peter had nothing to do with this. Last night after I got back from the meeting, I was almost hit by a car."

"Almost?" Dani paused to consider that. "Was it an accident?"

"I don't think so," Rose replied.

"Could it have been related to what happened to Nolan?"

"There's a strong possibility that it was. Although other alternatives exist too."

Dani stared at her. "You don't look like much of a badass, but it sounds like you run with a tough crowd."

The Sisters of Divine Mercy would have a good laugh about that, Rose thought.

"You should talk," she replied. "As I recall, you were the one who wished Nolan had been eaten by a shark."

"Wishing is one thing. Doing is another," Dani replied crisply. "Last night's meeting was interesting. And illuminating. You said you had more questions for me?"

"Yes." Rose settled back in her seat. "I wanted to ask about something you said to Gina afterward. You inquired about her daughter's health?"

"Yes, Meredith. Sadly, she's been fighting esophageal cancer since last year. It's beginning to look as though she may not make it. Gina tries to stay upbeat, and she always puts on a brave face, but she worries about Mere constantly."

"What a terrible thing to have to go through," Rose said sympathetically. "For both Gina and her daughter."

"Meredith's treatment has been especially debilitating recently. She had to give up her own place and move in with Gina. She was probably asleep upstairs last night while we were there. Gina hides it well, but I think she's pretty much at her wit's end. The doctors here are running out of options. There's an experimental treatment in France that Mere could have qualified for, but Gina didn't have the money to make it happen."

"That's a shame. I'd imagine something like that must be terribly expensive."

"I guess so," Dani said. "Gina doesn't go into specifics with the group. Obviously as the cancer's progressed, the topic has become even more upsetting for her. Mostly we try to spare her by not talking about it."

Rose hadn't slept much overnight. Instead, she'd passed the long dark hours turning over ideas in her mind—and speculating about all the things she'd learned. Now those suspicions were beginning to crystallize into a solid theory. She still needed additional information, however, before she could be sure.

"I got the impression Gina was one of the driving forces behind the formation of your group," Rose said. "I know she lost a great deal to Nolan. She called it a blow to her self-esteem."

Dani nodded.

"Her financial loss must have been a hardship too."

Dani's expression hardened. "I'm not sure why that would be any of your business."

Rose disagreed. She recalled the conversation she and Gina had shared while walking in the woods. The one where Gina had outlined—in a surprisingly detailed manner—all the reasons why she wasn't Nolan's murderer. One had concerned the timing of his death. Gina stated that she wouldn't have waited years to take her revenge.

Her assertion had seemed like a compelling argument at the time. *Why now?* Rose felt as though that question had haunted her and Peg in one form or another ever since. Until today. When Rose finally believed she knew the answer.

She was considering what her next move should be when the doorbell rang. The sound of its loud chimes bounced off the tall windows and hardwood floors. Dani didn't look surprised. She immediately rose to her feet.

"Are you expecting someone else?" Rose asked.

"You'll see." Dani smiled. "This will smooth things along. You want to know stuff about Gina, and last night she requested that none of us meet again with you or Peg unless she was present. When I found out you'd be dropping by, I called and let her know. Perfect, right?"

No, Rose thought wildly. *Not perfect at all.*

Just when she thought she'd found answers, more questions suddenly arose. Why hadn't Dani found Gina's request suspicious? Was it possible that she and Gina had planned Nolan's murder together? Either way, Rose was in trouble. It appeared she'd made a serious misstep by coming alone to this house hidden in the woods.

Dani was already on her way to the door. Rose quickly grabbed her phone out of her purse. Peg's number was at the top of her recent contacts. *SOS*, she texted, her fingers flying over the keypad. *At Dani's house. Bring the cavalry!*

As Dani opened the door, Rose stood up. On her feet, she felt as though she had slightly more control over the situation. Her phone was still in her hand. Maybe there was time for one more call. She dialed 9-1-1 and listened to the number ring on the other end.

The call had just connected when Gina suddenly appeared in front of her. She plucked the phone from Rose's hand. They both heard a voice say "Nine-one-one, what's your emergency?"

Gina held the phone away from Rose as her thumb severed the connection. Then she dropped the device into her own purse.

"You don't need that," she said. "We're all friends here, right?"

"Sure," Dani agreed, but she looked uncertain as Rose's phone disappeared. "Let's sit down and chat."

Rose resumed her seat on the couch. Gina and Dani took chairs opposite her. Rose knew she wasn't imagining the undertone of hostility Gina had brought into the room. Staring at the two women across from her, Rose suddenly felt like she was on an opposing team. And she was outnumbered.

"We were just talking about you," Dani told Gina.

"Why am I not surprised?" Gina looked annoyed. "You should have waited until I arrived."

"Don't worry, it was nothing important," Rose said.

She hoped Peg had gotten her message. Either way, her best bet now was to stall for time. That meant keeping the conversation going for as long as possible. Eventually Peter would come looking for her. And if she was lucky, she might uncover even more answers in the interim. Gina obviously thought she was the smartest person in the room. Rose was about to put that theory to the test.

"Dani and I were discussing your relationship with Nolan," she said. "We wondered whether the financial losses you suffered with him meant that you were short of money now."

"That's not true." Dani glared at Rose. "I wasn't wondering any such thing."

"My bad." Rose shrugged. "Maybe it was just me."

"Maybe that's none of your business," Gina snapped.

"That's what I said," Dani interjected. No one was listening to her.

"I thought Nolan's murder was about unrequited love," Rose mused. "But all the time it was just about money."

"Everything's about money," Gina said with a snort. "I'm surprised you haven't learned that before now. My daughter is dying. Day by day, I have to watch her fade away. And because of *money*, there's nothing I can do to stop it. Nolan Abercrombie ruined my life."

"Nolan ruined lots of lives," Dani agreed.

Rose ignored her and kept her eyes on Gina. "I'm very sorry that your daughter is losing her battle with cancer. I know she doesn't deserve that, and I can only imagine how helpless it must make you feel. I understand how you might have felt desperate enough to strike out—"

"Is that so?" Gina snapped. "Because from where I sit, it looks as though you don't understand much of anything. How easy your life must be for you to feel the need to spice things up by interfering in other people's problems. No one asked you to get involved in Nolan's death. How do you think I feel watching you and Peg stir up trouble for your own amusement and entertainment?"

"That's not what we're doing," Rose said, but her cheeks went pink all the same. "Peg and I believe that people who commit murder should be brought to justice—"

"*Justice.*" Gina glowered at her across the low table between them. "I did what needed to be done. Nolan was a vile man. He'd injured scores of people in his life. Left alone, he'd have injured scores more. He had to be stopped."

Dani was squirming uncomfortably in her seat. Her gaze darted back and forth between them.

Rose wondered if she was just now realizing that Gina had taken retribution for Nolan's sins into her own hands. She hoped that was the case. Because if Peg didn't arrive to intervene, Rose was going to need someone to be on her side.

"That wasn't your decision to make," she said to Gina. "And where was the justice in trying to run me down? Or did you decide that I needed to be stopped too?"

Dani gasped. She stared at Rose's bruises, then turned to Dani. "You were responsible for *that*?"

Gina shrugged, but didn't bother to answer. Once again, she'd only been doing what needed to be done.

Rose gritted her teeth. Gina's attitude was infuriatingly nonchalant. As if she knew something Rose didn't. Rose hated to think what that might mean. She'd had more than her share of unpleasant surprises recently.

"When we spoke before, you said that a car wouldn't have been your weapon of choice," she said. "You didn't want to have to deal with a smashed bumper. What changed your mind?"

Gina smirked. "I'm surprised you'd even remember a silly comment like that. As it happens, I don't have to worry about making repairs. My daughter's car has been sitting in my garage. It was a wonderful bit of symmetry to use it against Nolan. Wouldn't you agree?"

Rose didn't say a thing. Neither did Dani, who'd shrunk

down into her seat as though she was wishing she could disappear. Rose knew just how she felt.

"Enough chitchat," Gina said abruptly. She shot to her feet. "It's time to tie up loose ends."

"What loose ends?" Dani asked faintly.

Gina sighed. "It would have been so much easier if Rose had simply died last night. Instead she'll have to suffer yet another accident today. What a shame that Rose didn't realize that she wasn't well enough to drive. I'm sure she must have a nasty concussion."

Once again, Dani remained silent. She seemed frozen in place.

Gina's gaze went to Rose. "Headache? Blurred vision? Loss of cognitive ability? You poor dear. I feel for you. But don't worry. It will all be over soon."

Rose could hardly think of a less reassuring sentiment. Mildly concussed or not, she was thinking clearly enough to realize that Gina was ten years younger than she was, and in much better shape physically. And that was before Rose had injured her shoulder and cracked her ribs. She hoped she'd be able to count on Dani as an ally, but that didn't seem to be happening.

"We'll say she must have blacked out when she tried to turn her van around in your driveway," Gina continued. "All we could do was watch in horror as it tipped over the ledge, then went flying down the slope and crashed into the water below. Such a shame that she hit her head on the windshield and drowned before we were able to reach her."

"That's a terrible plan," Rose said, her voice quavering. "You'll never get away with it."

Gina glanced at Dani, who still wasn't moving. Then she smiled complacently. "Watch me," she said.

Chapter 29

Before Rose could respond, Gina had circled a hand around her upper arm and yanked her to her feet. Rose stumbled and hissed out a gasp.

"Sore shoulder?" Gina inquired with mock sympathy.

"You should know," Rose snapped. "It was your car that sent me flying."

Even healthy, Rose was no physical match for Gina. Now she didn't stand a chance. Rose tried to dig in her heels, but her resistance did no good. Gina continued to march across the room, pulling Rose along behind her.

Rose glared at Dani. "Don't just sit there. Call the police."

"Don't!" Gina snapped over her shoulder. "This is a private matter between Rose and me."

"Listen to me," Rose said to Dani. "There's about to be another murder. Gina's second one. You heard what she admitted to. And this time you'll be an accessory."

Finally Rose had gotten through to her. Dani jumped to her feet. It was about time.

"Gina, stop this," she said. "Let her go. You need to think about what you're doing."

"I've already thought about it," Gina replied, but her footsteps slowed. Rose caught a quick breath as Gina kept speaking. "You know you have too. Every woman in the group talked about it, fantasized about it . . ."

"That was about Nolan," Dani said grimly. "He was different. He hurt all of us."

Rose swiveled to face her. "Wait a minute. You already *knew?*"

"No, of course not," Dani replied quickly.

"That's not what it sounds like."

"Okay, maybe I suspected a little. Maybe we all did. But Nolan got what he deserved. None of us were upset by that."

Rose choked back another gasp. "You suspected there was a murderer in your midst and *none of you were upset by that?*"

"You have to understand; by the time we knew about it, the deed was already done. Maybe some of us had private concerns, but no one felt the need to ask unnecessary questions. Why would we, when all of us were feeling that justice had been served?"

"Why would you?" Rose echoed faintly. This was unbelievable.

"Besides," Dani began to backpedal, "we weren't the only ones who hated Nolan. He had plenty of enemies. Anyone could have been driving the car that hit him. Once he was gone, there was no point in worrying about the details of how it happened. It's not like it would have changed anything."

Yes it would have! Rose wanted to shout. If the women hadn't willfully looked the other way, Nolan's murder would have been solved days earlier and Rose wouldn't be in this situation.

She turned back to Gina. They were within an arm's length of the front door. But as long as Gina was distracted by the conversation, she wasn't reaching for the knob. That meant Rose had to keep talking.

"I don't understand," she said to Gina. "Holding that meeting was your idea. You invited Peg and me to attend."

"I don't know why you're surprised about that." Gina shook her head at Rose's stupidity. "I needed to find out how much you and Peg knew. Which, as it turned out, was entirely too much. You hadn't managed to put all the pieces together yet, but I figured it was only a matter of time. And I was right about that, wasn't I?"

Rose didn't need to reply. They both already knew the answer.

Gina smiled malevolently. "That's enough talk. It's time to get this done."

"Dani, I need some help over here!" Rose cried.

Dani was already on her way across the room. "Gina, stop—" she began as Gina yanked the door open.

Peg was standing outside on the porch. Her hand was raised, about to knock. She took in the situation in a glance. Rose, her face white with pain, was being manhandled by Gina. That was all Peg needed to know. Her fingers were already curled in a fist. She shot her arm forward and punched Gina in the nose.

The woman shrieked and fell backward. Gina's grip on Rose loosened as she stumbled to find her footing. Blood spurted from her nose. Peg grabbed Rose and held her steady as Gina tripped over the edge of a rug and crashed down on the hardwood floor.

Rose was trembling, equal parts horrified and elated by what had just happened. When Peg wrapped an arm around her shoulders, Rose allowed herself to be pulled out onto the porch. She and Peg both heard the sound of sirens in the distance.

"And you think I'm the troublemaker." Peg surveyed the scene with satisfaction. "I'd say I got here just in time."

* * *

A minute later, Detective Sturgill arrived and immediately took charge. He looked around slowly. Gina was still on the floor. Both her hands were cupped over her nose, and she was wailing as though she'd been run over by a car rather than merely knocked down. Dani had backed away, distancing herself from all of them. Peg looked triumphant. Rose had never felt more relieved in her life.

The detective's gaze passed over each of their faces in turn before pausing on Peg's. Rose swallowed a frustrated sigh. After all the brilliant deductions she'd made, and everything she'd gone through as a result, Sturgill still believed that Peg was the only one of them with a brain.

Then Peg surprised her. She stepped back and ceded the floor to Rose. But before Rose could say anything, Gina leaped to her feet and pointed at Peg.

"I want her arrested for assault!" she cried.

"Assault," Sturgill repeated. He noted that Peg happened to be holding her hands behind her back.

"Gina assaulted me first," Rose said.

That finally turned the detective's attention her way. "Last night?"

"Yes."

"Are you sure?"

"Yes," Rose replied firmly.

"Can you prove it?"

Rose nodded. "Gina killed Nolan Abercrombie too. Dani and I both heard her confess."

"Is that right?" he asked Dani.

She hesitated for so long that Rose thought she might try to deny it. But then she finally nodded too.

"There's something else," Rose said. "The car that Gina used to kill Nolan belongs to her daughter, Meredith. It's parked in Gina's garage. I'm sure you'll be able to find evidence there too."

Detective Sturgill's brow rose slightly as if he hadn't expected her to be the one to supply him with crucial information. He nodded his thanks, then quickly reassumed his usual poker face. Sturgill turned and motioned to the officers standing beside the patrol car parked next to his sedan. One came to confer with him. The other immediately got on the radio.

"You bitch," Gina muttered under her breath. "I befriended you. I invited you into my home."

"Only for your own devious purposes," Rose retorted. "So I hardly think that counts for anything."

Peg sidled over to stand beside Rose. "Are you sure you're all right?" she asked under her breath. "You look even more ghastly than you did last night."

"It was touch and go for a few minutes, but I'm much better now," Rose replied. "Gina planned to stuff me in my van and shove it down the slope into the reservoir."

Peg looked shocked. "Seriously?"

Rose nodded.

"I should have hit her harder," Peg growled. "Not that she would have succeeded. I know you better than that. You'd have fought like hell."

Rose's body was suffused with a warm glow. That was the second vote of confidence she'd received, and it felt great. "Yes, I would have," she agreed. "But I'm just happy it didn't come to that."

To nobody's surprise, Peg's compliment was followed by a complaint. "Why didn't you call me? What were you thinking, coming here alone?"

"I know it seems stupid in hindsight. But I had no idea everything would go haywire so quickly. Gina wasn't even supposed to be here. All I wanted to do was ask Dani a few questions about something she said last night."

"About Gina's daughter?" Peg guessed. "I hadn't even heard of her until you mentioned her name a minute ago."

Rose explained about Meredith's illness, then said, "I probably should have realized something wasn't quite right when I met with Gina last week. Seemingly off the top of her head, she listed all the ramifications Nolan's killer would have had to consider. At the time, I thought she was just being clever."

"She *was* clever," Peg said. She glanced at Detective Sturgill, who was still with the other officers. "Unless I'm mistaken, the police were several steps behind us in figuring things out. Gina had a good chance of getting away with it until you got her to confess."

"I hope she's in for big trouble now," Rose said as Sturgill returned to where the women were standing.

He looked at Rose, Peg, and Dani. "The three of you need to come down to the station and make statements," he told them. Then he turned to Gina. "We're expediting a search warrant for your home and garage. In the meantime, I'm detaining you on suspicion of manslaughter and attempted murder."

Rose felt like punching a fist in the air. Automatically, she restrained the impulse. It would have been both boastful and undignified. Instead, she and Peg shared a gratified glance. That felt like more than enough.

Chapter 30

By the end of the week, Gina Malone had been arrested for Nolan Abercrombie's murder. She retained a lawyer who got her out on bail, then began making a case in the media for extenuating circumstances. Gina lay low, took care of her daughter, and talked to no one. The women's group was summarily disbanded.

Peg deleted her Mature Mingle account and declared that she was done with dating forever. Rose refused to believe that. Nevertheless she decided to let Peg make her own choices about her love life from now on.

Jason Abercrombie arrived for his interview with Peter wearing a sports coat and tie. His hair was neatly combed, and he had a hopeful expression on his face. Rose had intended to sit in on their conversation—and perhaps to plead Jason's case, if necessary. She was never given the opportunity. Once the introductions had been made, Peter ushered Rose out of the office and shut the door behind her.

Maura and Rose stood in the hallway and stared at the closed door for several minutes. Constructed of solid wood decades earlier, it didn't allow sound to carry, even when they pressed their ears against it. Eventually, the two women sat down in the living room to await the outcome of the meeting.

"Peter will like him," Rose said. She hoped that wasn't wishful thinking on her part. "Jason is a sensible, well-mannered man who'd be useful to have around."

"And not bad to look at," Maura replied.

"If we have someone on-site who knows how to rewire things when they go bad, Peter can stop watching how-to videos on YouTube, and I can stop worrying that he's going to accidently electrocute himself," Rose added.

"How old do you think he is?" Maura mused.

"Maybe mid-thirties?" Rose guessed. "Definitely young and limber enough to climb up on the roof and nail down those loose shingles that keep flapping in the wind."

Maura nodded. "Married?"

"I don't think so," Rose said absently. "He probably would have mentioned that. He did mention knowing a bit about plumbing, however, and there's a clog in the third-floor bathroom he could get to work on right away."

"The guy sounds promising," Maura decided.

"Good. I'm glad you agree with me." Rose frowned as she was roused from her home-repair reverie. It suddenly occurred to her that she and Maura might not be admiring the same set of qualifications.

Before she could explore that problem further, they heard the office door open. Rose and Maura hurried around the corner to see Peter and Jason standing in the hallway shaking hands.

Both men were smiling. Peter's left hand was gripping Jason's shoulder in a paternal fashion. Marmalade, who must have been in the office with them, was purring as she wrapped herself around Jason's legs.

Rose couldn't think of a better set of endorsements.

"Well?" she asked, already smiling.

"Jason and I have decided on a monthlong trial period to see how we all get along," Peter informed her. "Paid, of course. If everyone is in agreement at the end of that time,

Jason will become our second employee, and we'll have a discussion about insurance and other benefits."

"Benefits," Jason said with a grin. "Nobody's ever offered me those before."

"Perhaps you've been undervaluing your skills," Peter said. "And with regard to that, I think it would be a good idea for you to study to get your GED while you're working here. Rose and I will be happy to help."

"Me too," Maura chimed in.

Jason started two days later. Within a week, he was halfway through the shelter's to-do list, Peter had booked two new counseling clients, and Maura was wearing lipstick and humming under her breath as she worked. Rose wasn't about to say, "I told you so," but she certainly thought it.

Indeed, everything in her life was going so well that she decided to press her luck. She informed Detective Sturgill that he owed her a favor. At first he was amused by the notion. But after Rose expanded on what Peter had told him about Mabel's situation and explained why she needed assistance, he nodded thoughtfully and told her he'd get right on it.

Overnight, their neighborhood was added to the roster of downtown areas that were regularly patrolled by police cruisers. The next time Mabel Mayberry's grandson and his friends came to visit, a vigilant officer ran their car's license plate and discovered that the vehicle had more than a dozen outstanding parking tickets.

Rose and Maura happened to be outside in front of the shelter when Donny came swaggering out of Mabel's house to discover the boot on his front tire. His stamping and swearing were amusing to watch, but Donny was livid and looking for someone to blame. When Maura made the mistake of laughing out loud, the sound immediately drew his attention.

He was halfway down the block, stalking toward them

angrily, when Jason opened the door to the Gallagher House and stepped out onto the front porch. He folded his arms over his chest and watched Donny's approach. When Jason decided he'd come close enough, he descended the steps, then walked down the sidewalk to meet him.

The two men spoke in heated tones for less than a minute. Rose and Maura caught only snippets of the conversation, but judging by the men's body language, it wasn't hard to tell which one of them was in charge. Within moments, Donny had turned back around and scuttled away.

"That's settled," Jason said with satisfaction. He came over to join Rose and Maura in front of the shelter. "From now on, he and his friends will only be visiting Mrs. Mayberry by invitation."

"Well done," said Rose. Jason was proving to have even more talents than she'd expected. He wasn't just good for the shelter; he was going to be a fine addition to the whole neighborhood.

He turned to Maura. "I'd like to invite Mrs. Mayberry for tea tomorrow afternoon. I figure you could discuss the new rules with her then. Is four o'clock okay?"

Maura favored him with a wide smile. "That sounds perfect," she said.

"Why would I want to accompany you to a dog show?" Rose asked Peg a few days later.

"Because I'll be judging all the breeds in my favorite group. And it will give you the chance to sit outside on a beautiful day and watch me do what I do best."

Rose considered the offer. It seemed as though Peg was still miffed that Rose had not only taken the lead in their investigation, she'd also beaten Peg to the solution. Apparently, being the person who'd ridden to Rose's rescue wasn't enough compensation for Peg.

"You do many things well," Rose said.

"Of course I do," Peg agreed. "But this one is the most fun. Besides, I wouldn't mind having the company."

"Company? I've watched you judge before. Your attention is riveted on the dogs in your ring. You won't even know I'm there."

"Maybe not for part of the day," Peg allowed. "But the show site is nearly two hours away. That's four hours in the car. It would be lovely to have someone to talk to."

Rose was quite certain Peg had never used the word "lovely" in connection with her before. Not in any context she could think of. So that was new. And unexpected. If Peg was making an honest attempt to deepen their friendship, far be it from Rose to shy away.

She still had one question, however. "Who's driving?"

"That's a tough one," Peg said.

"Is it a deal breaker?"

"Not if you're willing to compromise. I'll drive on the way there, and you can drive coming home."

Rose thought for a moment, then held out her hand. "I'm in," she said.

Please turn the page for an exciting sneak peek of
Laurien Berenson's next Senior Sleuths mystery
PEG AND ROSE PLAY THE PONIES,
coming soon wherever print and ebooks are sold!

Chapter 1

"Have I ever mentioned that I own a horse?" Peg Turnbull asked.

She'd arrived at the Gallagher House to visit her sister-in-law, Rose Donovan, and had been directed around the back of the narrow, three-story building in downtown Stamford, Connecticut. Originally a home, the house now served as a women's shelter that was owned and operated by Rose and her husband, Peter.

"No, you haven't." Rose looked up as Peg walked around the side of the building and used the question to announce her presence. Trust Peg to make an unusual entrance.

Rose was a slender woman in her late sixties, with angular features and short gray hair that she wore tucked behind her ears. At the moment, she was holding a rake in her hands. Peg had no idea why.

The tiny yard behind the shelter consisted mostly of hard-packed dirt with a few scraggly tufts of grass. The only spot of color was a row of tomato plants growing near the tall fence that separated the property from its neighbor. Peg couldn't see anything in the area that called for the implementation of a rake.

Then again, she'd just arrived. Perhaps enlightenment would be forthcoming.

"And now that you are mentioning it," Rose continued, "I'm not sure I believe you. I've been to your house on numerous occasions. If you had a horse there, I'm quite certain I would have noticed."

"Lucky Luna doesn't live with me," Peg replied. "In fact, she doesn't even live in Connecticut."

"Good." Rose nodded. "At your age, you shouldn't be galloping around anyway."

Peg was in her seventies, a few years older than Rose. Apart from that, the two women had few similarities. Peg was taller in stature and broad through the shoulders. Not only did she possess a bigger build, Peg also had the forceful personality to match.

"No one is galloping anywhere on Luna," Peg said. "She's a Thoroughbred broodmare, boarding at a farm in Kentucky. Every year or so, she produces a foal."

"That sounds like more than one horse," Rose commented. "Years add up, you know."

Peg's lips flattened. They were both well aware of that.

"Are your foals adding up too?"

"No, and that's actually why I'm here."

"So there's a reason for your visit." Rose smiled to soften the words, which had come out sounding sharper than she'd intended. Then she abruptly went still. "Please tell me you're not offering me a horse."

"Would you accept if I were?"

"Of course not." Rose was half-afraid Peg might be serious. When she was around, you never knew what might happen next.

Though they'd been related for more than fifty years, Rose and Peg had spent the majority of that time pointedly not speaking to each other. A few months earlier, they'd finally managed to rectify that situation. Even so, their relationship wasn't all smooth sailing. Dealing with Peg, Rose often felt like she was rocketing down the slope of a rather steep learning curve.

"Not even a cute foal?" Peg prodded. "Maybe an equine companion for Marmalade?"

Marmalade was Rose's kitten. What Peg thought Marmie might do with a baby horse, Rose had no idea. And certainly no desire to find out.

"Marmie gets plenty of companionship from me and Peter. Not to mention the women who come through the shelter," she said. "Now stop teasing and tell me why you're really here."

Two plastic lawn chairs had been placed side-by-side in the middle of the yard. Peg took one and gestured toward the other. "Put down your rake, and let's sit for a minute."

Rose looked down at the tool as if she'd forgotten she was holding it. She leaned it against the fence, then walked over to join Peg.

"What were you doing with that thing anyway?" Peg asked, as Rose swished her lightweight cotton skirt to one side, and sat down too.

"Raking leaves."

Peg frowned. She let her gaze travel slowly around the enclosed space. There were no leaves on the ground. It was much too early for that. "What leaves?"

"You know." Rose flapped a hand in the air. "In the yard. I'm tidying up."

"First of all, it's barely September. And second"—did Peg really have to point this out?—"you don't have a tree."

"Well, no. But our neighbor does."

Both women glanced at the large maple next door. Its spreading branches crossed over the wall between the two properties to shade a portion of the shelter's yard. Rose nodded as if she'd scored a major point.

Peg wasn't having it. "Yes, I see a tree. I can also see perfectly well that its leaves are still attached."

"You know me. I like to be proactive."

Peg stared. "I believe that's the dumbest thing you've

ever said. What's the real reason you're out here brandishing a garden tool?"

Rose sighed and rolled her shoulders. "Peter's holding a group counseling session in the living room this afternoon. This one's about managing stress and conflict resolution. As you might imagine, sometimes things get a little intense. To stay out of the way, I decided to come out here and make myself useful."

Useful. Peg eyed the rake again. She didn't think so.

"Also, I love my husband dearly, but sometimes I just need a little space," Rose admitted. "You know?"

A nod seemed called for, so Peg obliged. But she didn't know. Not really.

Her decades-long marriage to Rose's older brother, Max, had been an utterly blissful period in her life. She and Max were soulmates, content to share everything with each other. They'd lived, loved, and worked as a team. At least that was how Peg—who'd lost her husband to a heart attack ten years earlier—remembered that time now.

"Space," she said briskly. "I can help with that."

"How?"

"I have an upcoming judging assignment at the Bluegrass Cluster in Lexington, Kentucky. Four back-to-back dog shows over Labor Day weekend."

"Three days from now?"

"Indeed." Peg nodded. "I'll be judging the Non-Sporting Group on Saturday, then the Toy Group, plus several Herding breeds on Sunday."

Not long ago, that explanation would have sounded like gibberish to Rose. Now, sadly, she understood most of it. But that still didn't offer a clue where she fit in.

"And?" she prompted.

"Remember Lucky Luna?"

"Of course I remember Lucky Luna. We were just talking about her two minutes ago."

"The foal she produced last year is now a yearling."

"As if I couldn't do the math," Rose muttered.

Peg ignored that and kept talking. "There are plenty of people who breed racehorses, but have no interest in actually racing them. Those breeders sell their horses—usually when they're yearlings—to people who don't want to breed, but do want to race."

Rose peered over at her. "That sounds like the beginning of a riddle. Or maybe a joke. Is there a punchline coming?"

"No, but what *is* coming is the Keeneland September Yearling Sale. It's the biggest sale of its kind in the world. And Lucky Luna's yearling is entered."

"To sell?" Rose guessed. She hoped she had that right.

"That's the plan," Peg confirmed. "In the time I've owned her, Luna has had two previous offspring go through the sale. The farm where she boards arranged everything for me and I watched the proceedings from afar on the Keeneland website. This time, with a judging assignment taking me to Lexington just a few days earlier, I intend to be on hand to observe the process in person. I thought you might want to go with me."

Rose blinked slowly. "To Kentucky."

"Right."

"In three days," she added.

"Actually one day," Peg corrected. "I'm going to drive rather than fly, which means it will take us a day to get there. Plus, I'd like to arrive a day early so I can visit Six Oaks, the farm where Lucky Luna lives."

One day!

Rose gulped. "Let me think about it."

"Oh pish. As you just pointed out, there's no time for that. Just say yes, and pack your bags."

"No," Rose said firmly. "You can't just spring something on me like that and expect me to agree right away."

"Of course I can. I just did. Besides, you said yourself that you wouldn't mind getting away for a bit."

"I did not."

"You did." Peg sounded complacent, as if she was sure she'd already won. "I heard you. You said you needed some space."

"Yes, space—like thirty feet. Not a thousand miles."

"Actually, it's closer to seven hundred and fifty."

As if that was the point. Were Rose's teeth clamped together? It felt like they might be. Interacting with Peg often had that effect on her.

"What about your Poodles?" she asked, stalling for time. "Who will look after them?"

Peg blithely waved away that objection. "Hope will come with us, of course."

At the age of eleven, Hope was Peg's oldest Standard Poodle. She was also the one who was almost constantly at her side. At one time, Peg and Max's kennel had been filled with black Standard Poodles. Their Cedar Crest dogs had been known worldwide for their excellent quality and superb temperaments. They'd successfully exhibited their Poodles at numerous dog shows nearly every week of the year.

Now the kennel was gone and Peg was too busy with her judging career to breed more than the occasional litter. In addition to Hope, there were just two other Standard Poodles in her house. Coral and Joker were both young dogs. Coral had recently finished her championship; and Joker, who'd just turned a year old, was awaiting his turn to get back into the show ring.

"What about the other ones?" Rose asked.

Of course she remembered their names. Peg spoke about her Poodles often enough. She even made them sound like they were members of the family. Which irked Rose more than it should have—enough to make her want to annoy Peg by pretending ignorance.

"Coral and Joker," Peg supplied, rising to the jab as Rose had known she would. "They'll stay home with my dog sitter, Colleen. The Poodles adore her, which is a good thing considering how often I need to travel to shows. So everything's taken care of except you. I'm still waiting for an answer. Are you coming with me or not?"

Rose was running out of excuses, and they both knew it.

"I'll have to talk to Peter," she said. "And check my calendar. You know I often have other commitments . . ."

Trust Rose to want to arrange the fun out of everything, Peg thought. The woman was entirely too methodical. Maybe even a bit of a plodder. Peg, by comparison, was a free spirit, happy to be always on the go.

"What you really mean, is that you need time to think of another reason to say no."

"Don't put words in my mouth." Rose frowned. "That's not what I said."

"Said about what?" Peter asked. He closed the shelter's door behind him and started down the back stairs. A thoughtful and deliberate man who wore his years well, he was stepping carefully to avoid the ginger-and-white kitten that was bouncing around his feet. Peter's warm brown eyes twinkled behind tortoiseshell-framed glasses as he looked over at the two women. "Am I interrupting something?"

"Not at all," Peg said. "Please join us. I have a question for you."

Peter unfolded a third lawn chair that was leaning against the back of the building. He carried it over and put it beside theirs. As he sat down, Marmalade reared up to grab Peter's pant leg and use it as a scratching post. He gently disentangled the kitten's tiny claws, then turned to Peg. "I'm all ears."

Rose quickly jumped in before Peg had a chance to speak. "Peg's going on a road trip to Kentucky. It sounds as though she'll be gone for at least a week. She thinks I should go with her, but I told her I have responsibilities here."

"You do," Peter replied carefully. "But there's nothing that can't be set aside long enough for you to take a small trip. I think you should go."

"You do?" Rose was surprised.

A few weeks earlier, she'd been involved in a serious accident. A glancing blow from a speeding car had sent her careening onto the hard pavement outside the shelter. Rose's injuries were mostly healed now, but Peter still continued to hover over her as though she was made of glass. She knew he meant well, but his solicitousness was beginning to drive her a little crazy. Under the circumstances, she'd just assumed he'd take her side.

"When are you leaving?" he asked Peg.

"The day after tomorrow. Up and out at the crack of dawn. I've made the trip before and it can be done in a single day as long as we don't dawdle."

Rose snorted under her breath. Peg drove like a speed fiend. Dawdling wasn't an option when she was behind the wheel.

Peter turned back to his wife. "This sounds like a wonderful idea to me. A nice, relaxing vacation is just what you need."

"Relaxing?" Rose said skeptically. "With Peg?"

"I can be relaxing," Peg said.

Nobody even bothered to reply to that.

Instead Peter changed the subject. "What's the purpose of your trip?"

"Dogs and horses," Peg said. "I'll be judging at two dog shows, then attending a Thoroughbred sale."

"It turns out Peg owns several racehorses," Rose added.

Peter had seen a great number of things in his life. He'd first been a priest, then a college professor, a missionary, and now the proprietor of a women's shelter. Not much surprised him anymore. This did. It was also a topic he knew almost nothing about.

"Racehorses?" he echoed faintly. "How unusual."

"The first one came to me as an unexpected bequest," Peg told him. "As you might imagine, I could hardly refuse."

"No, of course not." He pondered that, then added, "Are you selling a horse at the sale?"

"I am. It's the first time I'll have the opportunity to attend in person, and I'm looking forward to observing the process. I think Rose might enjoy it too."

"Except that I'm too busy to go," Rose said.

"Doing what, exactly?" Peg inquired.

"Cooking, cleaning, keeping the books . . ."

"Maura can handle everything but the accounting," Peter said. Their live-in housekeeper, Maura Nettles, was a whiz at keeping things running smoothly. "And that can wait until you get back."

"What about painting the third-floor hallway and arranging to have the gutters cleaned?"

"I'm sure Jason is on top of both those things." Hiring Jason Abercrombie as the shelter's new handyman had been an excellent decision. Among other things, it meant that Peter now had more free time to devote to his counseling sessions.

Rose blew out a breath. "So what you're saying is that I'm superfluous?"

"No." Peter's tone was gentle. "What I'm saying is that everyone here cares about you. And that we're ready to support you in any way you need. Your body may be almost recovered, but mental trauma can linger too. It might be good for you to get away and enjoy a change of scenery."

"Now you're just ganging up on me," Rose said irritably.

Peter shook his head. "We just want what's best for you. That's all."

When he put it like that, there wasn't much else Rose could say. She looked at Peg and nodded.

"I'm glad that's settled." Peg quickly stood up before Rose could change her mind. "You'll see," she told her. "This trip is going to be epic."

Visit our website at
KensingtonBooks.com
to sign up for our newsletters, read
more from your favorite authors, see
books by series, view reading group
guides, and more!

BOOK CLUB
BETWEEN THE **CHAPTERS**

Become a Part of Our
Between the Chapters Book Club
Community and Join the Conversation

Betweenthechapters.net